I0719486

cursed
to
love

ANNA LORES

Blooming Cactus Publishing

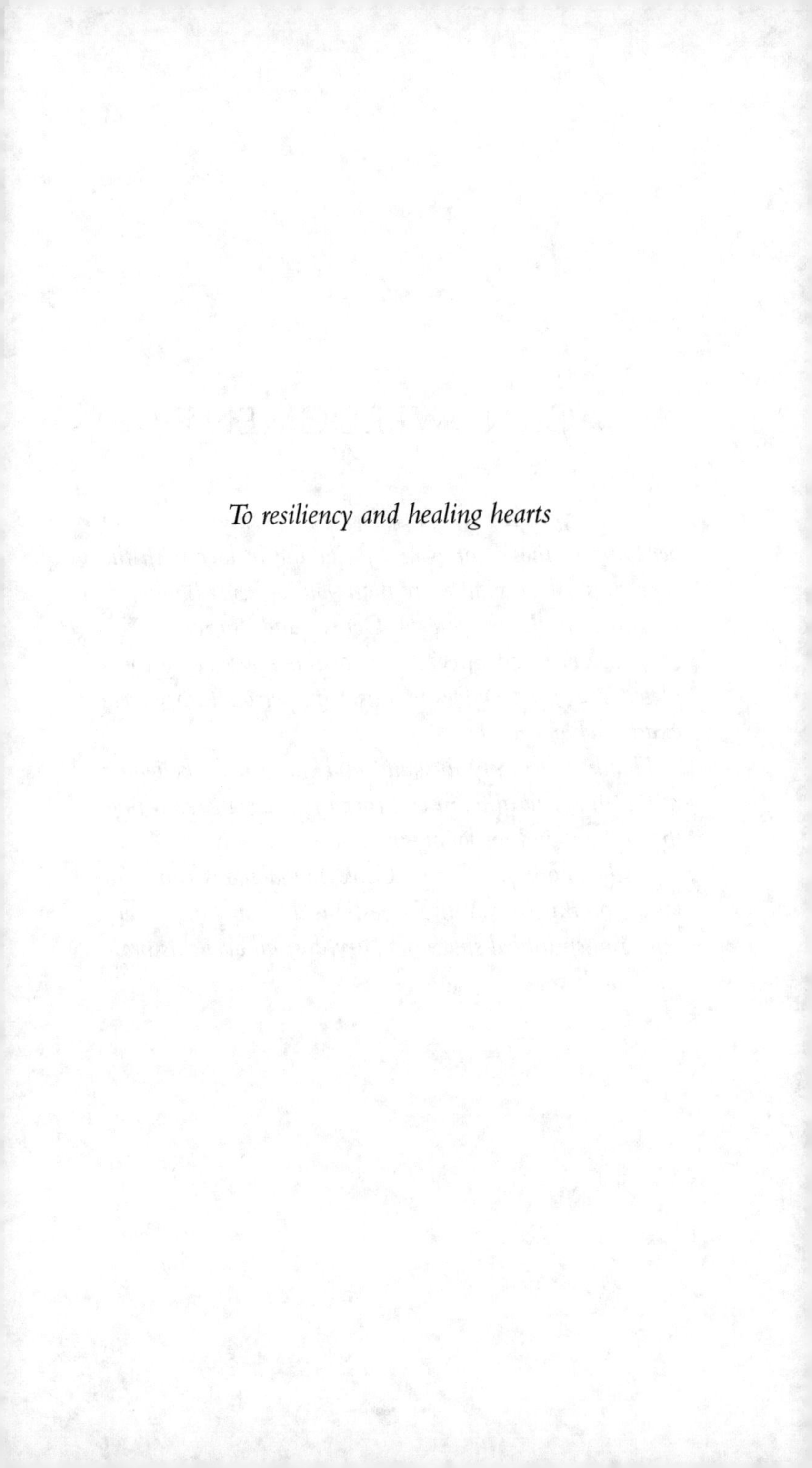

To resiliency and healing hearts

ACKNOWLEDGMENT

Thank you to my fans for reading my books, for believing in these stories and for falling in love with the characters. I love y'all more than you will ever know.

A special thank you to Denise and Suzanne. You two have been an integral part of this novel being completed. Your kind nudges to finish this personal story were exactly what I needed.

Thank you to my husband and children for believing in me, in my writing, in this crazy journey I keep bringing you on, and for loving me unconditionally.

Lastly, thank you, Kristi Cook, my fabulous editor for taking on this story. Your suggestions were spot on - every time. You sprinkled sparkling fairy dust all over this project. Thank you.

CHAPTER ONE

THE COLD WINDS OUT OF the north seemed to target Meredith Kilpatrick as she exited the warmth within the old stone church. Spots of pure white snowflakes dusted the cobblestone path leading to the newly cemented sidewalk.

She quickly buttoned up the white peacoat on which she'd splurged to protect her from the coming storm—predicted to be the worst winter storm in history to hit the Southeast. Hoping for more insulation from the cold, she removed the sparkling silver clip holding up her hair. Naturally thick, brown tresses fell in a rush of curling waves over her shoulders and down her back. *I need to leave and never look back.*

"I'm sorry," the priest said. He followed her outside and let go of the handle to the wooden door—a door that had somehow survived Sherman's March to the Sea while everything around it had been reduced to ash. "Give him more time."

I don't have more time. "I think he's had plenty. Thank you for staying and listening."

He opened his arms and she stepped into an

embrace she'd refused on every other occasion. "Don't lose faith. Jeremy filed the marriage license. He came to all the premarital counseling sessions. He loves you."

She nodded as her heart broke a little more. *He doesn't love me enough to marry me in church, in front of God.* Words repeated to her several thousand times over the years came right back as she held onto him for comfort…*Cursed to love but never be loved in return.*

"Meredith," he whispered, "I know you're scared to move. I know you wanted to have Jeremy with you as your husband at Sara's wedding, but he and Sara have years of resentment built up. She's the one who told him he was not welcome to attend the wedding. She's the one who has constructed an immoveable wall to block him from being a part of your life."

Mere nodded. She couldn't deny the truth. *But doesn't love conquer all obstacles?* "Love is supposed to be the great equalizer."

"You've given and sacrificed for Sara, denied a life you want with Jeremy because she refuses to accept him. She's moving on no matter what you do."

"She's a teen. She doesn't—"

"You were twelve when you took on the responsibility of raising her—a responsibility her grandparents should have assumed. You gave her shelter, food, education. You loved her and supported her and forgave her. What has she done in return?" He moved enough for her to see the frown on his face. "She's lied. Forced you to move every three months. She runs off and trouble finds her—or more likely, she finds it. You side with her. Where does that leave Jeremy?"

If she had it in her to cry, she would have, but the tears didn't come. She buried her face in the warmth of his thick, black robes and inhaled the aroma of sandalwood and ash…*Jeremy visited you today.* "Teens screw up."

"You didn't."

"It was my fault she was orphaned. It was my curse that caused all of this." Cursed to love a family who never loved her back. Cursed to be hunted by every feral wolf in the world. Cursed to be compatible to make babies with any being that procreated the same way, even zombies.

She pulled off the engagement and wedding bands Jeremy had given her for the ceremony that never happened and slipped them into the pocket of the priest's robe.

"You are blessed, not cursed," he whispered. He held her tighter. "You are blessed with a giving heart, with patience that knows no end, with kindness to those who do not deserve it, and with discernment of evil. You are a warrior and a protector of life. Without you and Jeremy, this city would have had a second burning, a destruction which will never happen because you fell in love with a being some consider wicked but is no such thing. Believe in him. Have faith in the future. There is a reason for everything."

"Why didn't he come?" She raised her chin and gazed at the tender-hearted old man with worried blue eyes and silver hair. "I know you saw him today." *I smelled him on you.*

"He went and talked with Sara. Asked her for

permission to marry you. Things got heated."

Meaning he did or said something awful and is waiting for my backlash. "He doesn't need permission from her."

"He extended an olive branch that she broke into tiny pieces and then stomped on. You are the only thing she has over him. He wants you to be happy and without her permission, her acceptance of him in your life, you won't be happy. You will run off to save her from every mistake she makes. She needs to deal with the consequences of her actions. The one she's about to make is going to come with a plethora of problems, and she doesn't care." He patted her back and released her. "After the wedding, come back home where you belong. You *can't* protect her from life or death."

She turned around and pulled the collar of her coat up. No matter what she did, she'd freeze by the time she got home. "I've got to go. I'll stop in for a visit next time I'm in town."

"Your blood-bond makes you married to him in his world."

"Not in mine." She hurried down the steps to the sidewalk and around the corner, out of the safety of the church's grounds.

She lifted the phone from inside her front pocket and flipped through the messages. *Sara.* She tapped the screen and called.

"Mom," Sara answered. "I didn't start the fight. I didn't do anything. I swear it's him, not me. He wants to kill you slowly like he did to that guy I went on a date…" She talked and talked as Mere walked down the old street in the heart of downtown Atlanta.

You need to take responsibility for your actions. I'll be there, but for once tell me the truth about your conversation with Jeremy. He tells me the good and bad. He doesn't hide his nastiness—why do you try and hide yours?

"…He's going to kill you, and me, and Ethan, and—"

"Hey, hey, hey. Slow down," Mere said. "Jeremy doesn't want to kill me." *He doesn't want to marry me either.* "He doesn't want to kill you or your fiancé or anyone else for that matter. Did he say why he came by without me there?"

The ominous chill in the air seemed to push her toward a change to move out West—a change she hadn't wanted until she stood at the altar for eight hours waiting on the man she loved.

"Why does he *ever* come by when you're not there? He held the regular inquisition. *Where's your mom? Are you really going to marry that kid? You're too young and marriage is a big commitment.* Blah, blah, blah. I'm so done with him. Have you kicked his ass to the curb for good?"

Mere took a shortcut and walked down an alley not far from Jeremy's Victorian mansion in which his best friend, Nicholas Carson, lived. *I'll never be done with him. Love doesn't just go away, at least not on my end.* "Are you packed or have you changed your mind?"

Sara huffed. "I'm packed and ready. The landlord came by and looked the place over. He gave me a check for our security deposit. Are you almost home? Ethan is waiting for me."

"I've got one stop to make. I'll be home soon."

"Hurry. I *need* Ethan."

"I hear you." Mere half-smiled. *You're in love for the first time. You have feelings you don't know what to do with. I wish you would wait and get to know him before jumping into marriage.* "You'll be with him in a couple days."

"Why can't we fly? Lainie said we could use her plane." Sara's impatience bordered on mental instability.

"My best friend has done enough for us. You can spare time for one last mother-daughter road trip, can't you?" She gazed up at the sky between the red brick apartment buildings. Her heartbeat slowed and sped up and slowed again. *Another cardiac episode without provocation. They're coming more and more often.* Her legs tingled and her knees weakened. She stumbled backward into the stone wall of a building with a loud bump.

"Are you okay? Are you being attacked again?" Sara asked.

"I'm fine. I wore heels and stupidly kicked a rock." Mere slumped and dropped onto her bottom as the heavy *thump, thump, thump* of her heart skipped into the slow drudge of a *tha-ump…tha-ump……tha…ump.* "I've got to go. See you in a bit." She ended the call as the darkness of the night closed in on her, questioning whether she would ever see the sun rise again.

Pure white flakes of snow drifted down from the gray clouds sheltering the earth from the sun's morning rays. *So fragile, so beautiful. Such a short existence.*

She opened her palm and watched as the unique crystals fell through her hand to the frozen ground. *Am I dead?*

She gazed at her limp body slumped over near the wall. She stood as a spirit at the crossroads between life and death.

A flicker of light caught her eye farther down the alley. The glimmer expanded into a tunnel of white light and beckoned her toward it. She walked alone toward the illuminated path to paradise like she had many times over the years. *Please, let me in.*

Golden figures of those she hadn't been able to save appeared and blocked the familiar portal to the afterlife.

Please. Let me in.

The golden figures shook their heads and melted into one as the lighted portal diminished and the alley appeared once again. Her spirit flew back and slammed into her body as her heart pumped the sludge of her blood through her veins.

She stayed in the alley and prayed for her curse to end.

Chapter Two

The handsome man with dark green eyes and black hair Meredith loved stood over her as the pink and blue lights of dawn found entry through every nook and cranny of the winter storm's weakness.

"Jeremy?" *You came for me.*

"My love," Jeremy Hunter, her fiancé, said. He brushed off the layer of snow that lay like a blanket over her and lifted her from the frozen earth.

The warmth of his coat melted some of the icicles clinging to the ends of her hair.

He carried her to the black limousine idling at the curb. "You look beautiful, but it's too cold for you to be sleeping outside."

"I fell on my way to see you." *I'm not cold anymore. I missed you.*

He wrapped her in heated blankets and held her as the car rolled forward. "Don't lie. I heard your heart falter. It's happening more frequently."

"I'm fine." She tried to wiggle her arm out of the blankets, but he'd swaddled her like a baby so well she couldn't move. "I need to go home."

"I want you home with me." He loosened the blankets around her. "Sara has made her choice. She doesn't need you, but I do. I need you. I want you."

"Do we have to do this again?" *I don't want to argue about Sara.*

"I'm sorry I was late." He buried his face against her neck. "You look beautiful in that dress."

The coals smoldering in her belly when he touched her became flames as his lips parted on her flesh. She tilted her head and offered him more than the life rushing through her veins. "Come with me to Arizona."

The sharp prick of his teeth and the long draw of her blood nourishing his body gave her more pleasure than she cared to admit.

"Mmm." He sucked and swallowed.

"We can get married and protect Sara." She closed her eyes and pulled his hand to her hip. "We can get married there. We can—"

He lifted his mouth from her flesh, breaking the free flow of her words. His tongue laved over the small incisions. "We get married and stay here, in Atlanta."

"She's my only family. Why don't you understand I want to be in her life and protect her?" *I've killed more feral werewolves this month than I have in a while. I need to get away from the violence.*

She thought of all the reasons he should jump at moving to Arizona. *It's warm. No werewolves. No zombies. No witches or beasts to fight off.* She shifted in his lap and straddled him.

He drew his sharp fang across his wrist and sliced the skin. Blood trickled from the wound as he held it to her mouth. "Drink."

"I don't need—"

"You do."

She licked the blood. Sandalwood and salt rushed over her taste buds. Fire burst through her veins, chasing away the last bits of cold from her extremities. Juices trickled onto her panties.

"That's it," he whispered. "It's been too long since we shared blood." He gathered up the skirt of her dress with his free hand as she closed her lips around the offering and sucked his magical blood. "Unzip my pants."

She fumbled over the zipper of his black slacks, but managed to open the prize. The harder she sucked the more her need for him loosened from the cage in which she locked away her desires. She grabbed his wrist and bit down as she swallowed more of his crimson gift – healing, youth, and strength. She lifted her hips. *I love you.*

He pulled her wet panties to the side.

He thrust, and she countered.

"My beautiful wife," he moaned. "I love you."

She couldn't stop the rising tide of bliss. Holding in her feelings became too much to bear. She rubbed her lips over the wound closing at his wrist. The vein in her neck throbbed for him to take more blood. "Jeremy, I love you."

He thrust, rolled his hips, and ground her clit in circles. One powerful thrust after another.

Electricity surged in quick jolts and caressed her flesh as his cock seemed to grow thicker and longer inside her. The special abilities that marked her as different her entire life rose to the surface and let out gold and crimson energy that swirled around them. Her thoughts scattered and a vision over-took her…

She lay on her side on white silk sheets in Jeremy's canopy bed. Her bare, tanned skin sparkled silver with a hint of gold at her neck. She gazed at her large pregnant belly and grunted. "She's pounding my pelvis."

Jeremy hopped on the bed. His pale hands void of glitter landed softly on her stomach. "You're so close…" His green eyes darkened to almost black like they always did when he was happy. He grabbed pillows and cushions and quickly arranged them behind her as she sat up.

"I'm ready to get labor going and see our girl," she said.

Moving in flashes of vampire speed, he gathered towels and medical supplies. He stopped and dipped his fingers into her pussy. "Get ready, my love." He swirled his fingers.

"Oh, my God. I'm going to throw up." The first contraction hit her hard. "She's coming."

"I can see her. Push."

Contraction after contraction, she pushed and breathed.

Their baby arrived with a head full of black hair like Jeremy's and a cry to wake the dead.

Jeremy kissed her lips and placed their daughter at her breast. "She's perfect like her mother."

She closed her eyes, and without a touch of pain, her body transformed to normal as if she'd never been pregnant or given birth. Heat filled her belly and chest. "Oh, God. Not again."

"I love you," Jeremy whispered over and over and over. "You can't control it, my love…"

The vision ended.

Jeremy thrust into her and grunted. "Yes. That is exactly what I want." He shuddered and spurted cum inside her.

She froze. They had sex without a condom. She had sex without any protection. She'd never been so careless. She gazed down at her pale hands. *No more glitter lotion for me. I'm not procreating with anyone, not even you. No way. No how. Never happening.* "We're not having kids, Jeremy. That was one fucked-up vision."

He cupped the back of her head and the panty-melting grin he often sported for her spread across his mouth. "Oh, it's happening. You're coming back after you marry Sara off to that boy. I can feel it."

"No, I'm not. I put a down payment on a house there. I signed a three-month contract with a spa. I'm committed to the move. I'm not coming back." Her stomach churned as fear crept along her senses, slithered into her pores, and entered her bloodstream. Every vision she'd ever had had come true. Every. One.

"Sara will not keep us apart forever. No matter how hard she tries, she will not end our relationship." He kissed her. "You may want a human existence in all your humanness denial, but you are going to be one of us. You are going to ask me to turn you into one of us. Your heart problems will be gone, and we'll live together for eternity."

She quickly pushed away from him and fell onto the floorboard. "No. I'm not going to be one of you. I'm going to die like I'm supposed to. One day soon, my heart will beat for the last time and…" *It will start beating again. Death refuses to take me into the afterlife.*

"I will not let you die," he said. "If I think for an

instant your heart has pumped for the last time or anywhere close to it, I'm going to turn you into a vampire. I will not give you a choice in that situation."

"Well, lucky for me, it's still pumping enough to get the job done." She pushed her back against the leather seat across from him. *You want me for sex and a blood exchange. Maybe to bear your children because my cursed body can.* "I'm moving to Arizona, and I'm setting down deep roots. I'm not coming back." *You don't love me enough to marry me in my world. The vision will never happen as long as I'm nowhere near you.* "Thank you for everything you've done for me and Sara, but it's time for both of us to move on."

"Is this about me being late for the wedding?"

She rolled her eyes. *Yes. No. Yes.* "I'm done, Jeremy. I've waited long enough for you to figure out whatever it is you need to figure out. Please stop the car."

Gazing at him, all the emotions and love that had grown throughout their relationship continued to hold her there. She needed his express permission to leave or she couldn't bring herself to make the breakup work. They'd always get together every now and again so she could feed him her blood and she could drink some of his. Even if she fell in love and married someone else, the blood-bond they shared linked their lives as one of necessity for eternity and beyond.

"We'll get married. I'll turn you into a vampire, and we'll have a family of our own exactly like in your vision."

"When will we get married?" she asked. *Children*

are not in my future. I'm not passing along the curse, and I'm never becoming a vampire. No amount of glitter oil or mind-blowing sex will take me there.

"As soon as you choose me over Sara."

She clenched her jaw. "Why do you hate her?"

"That girl is a chatterbox of destruction. You can't trust her, yet you stand by her. She's fucked you over at every turn. If I had let her into my home, I would have had every damn feral shifter, witch, and zombie knocking on my door trying to kill us. Now, they only do that to you and her, and damn it, I'm ready to kill her myself." His voice rose slightly, but the green in his irises morphed to a light neon chartreuse, revealing his increasing fury.

"Let's not go down this road. She's my responsibility and so are her grandpar—"

"She's not even your daughter. She's your niece, Mere. And you're not the one who is protecting her grandparents." His fangs extended and his dark bangs drifted down, concealing half of his handsome face. "It's almost time for another visit to the preacher and his wife. They don't want to see their flesh-and-blood grandchild, but they want to watch the non-related *cursed* human and the *evil* vampire having sex."

"They do not." She huffed. "They want to make sure we're not having sex out-of-wedlock. They haven't spied on us since that—"

"They have spied every time we visit. Every. Time. They are fucked up."

"Then let's not sleep in the same bed. They won't have a chance to see anything because there will be *nothing* to see."

He glanced away. "I'm not changing my life for them."

"Right." *You don't change anything you don't expressly want to. A marriage ceremony in church is out of the question unless I'm one of you. Not happening, sugar. Love doesn't have requirements or conditions. You don't love me.* "I need to get going."

He ground his teeth. "I warned Sara not to go. I warned her that marrying that boy is a bad idea. Remember *that*, when trouble comes, Meredith. Remember that I backed you up at every opportunity, when it came to disciplining her. She's heading into a life she is not prepared for, and she's bringing you along for the fucking rollercoaster ride. She'll be lucky if she survives three days with that family. Remember this conversation when the shit storm hits and your choice is me or her."

The car slowed to a stop.

"Duly noted." Mere opened the door.

"We are blood-bonded, Meredith. We are married in my world, no matter what kind of lover you take on to hurt me. You are mine, and you will come home to me."

She climbed out of the vehicle and stepped onto the sidewalk in front of her shitty apartment. She looked over her shoulder into the dark interior of the car. "I love you. I wanted you by my side at her wedding. I wanted you to choose me, even with obstacles thrown in your way. *You chose you,* like always."

"You're young, my love. I'm hurdling obstacles left and right—in the air and underground—to be with you, to protect you, to shelter you. You can't see them now, but you will. You will."

The door closed and the limousine drove away, leaving her heart aching and her mind made up. *Whatever life throws at me, I'm staying in Ulvene, Arizona until the day I'm welcomed into the afterlife.*

CHAPTER THREE

SITTING AT THE DESK HE made as a teen with World Alpha Dietrich Wolfgang, Jeremy flipped through the consent forms for their blood donors who would live within the confines of the Coven for most of their contracted time. The background checks cleared. The rooms where they would stay were opened and inspected for comfort.

He ran his finger down the list of names and then picked up a pen and signed his name, giving approval of the new humans they referred to as bleeders.

His best friend, Nicholas Carson, stood patiently across from him, waiting for the paperwork.

Jeremy tapped the spot where Dietrich branded the wood with Jeremy's family crest. "I left a message with Dietrich about the growing number of feral beasts in the area. Let me know if he contacts you."

"Yes, sir, but he'll call you, eventually." Nicholas gazed at him with the neon green eyes of an angry vampire.

"What has you upset?" He leaned back and

waited to hand over the paperwork.

"Sara."

"She'll be back here with her mom in less than three months. You have nothing to worry about." *I won't last three months without Mere. I won't last three days without knowing where she is and what she's doing.*

"I think Sara is going to be dead in a couple days. I had one of my men go check out their hotel in Tempe. Only they aren't there. They arrived in Ulvene, Arizona this afternoon. Mere is so geographically challenged that she thought Ulvene was a suburb. My guy listened to Mere's miserable conversation with the Tempe spa owner. Our Meredith was forced to pay the termination fee in Tempe and then sign a contract with the only spa in Ulvene because Sara lied to her. I don't know how she doesn't rip into Sara for all the bullshit. She lets Sara walk all over her."

"Ulvene?" If Jeremy had a working heart, it would have stopped.

Nicholas nodded. "Yeah. Ulvene. As in, the place where the Warrior Army of Mr. Dietrich Ulvene Wolfgang, the World Alpha, lives and trains. Sara is marrying Jack Ulvene's boy, Ethan."

Logic took over Jeremy's thoughts. "Sara won't survive the transition. She's too weak. Mere is going to have a stroke when she finds out Sara has married into the deadliest werewolf pack in the world. She will be home in days, not months, whether Sara lives or dies." He stood up and his chair fell over with a thud. "Sara will have finally stepped over the line."

He picked up his chair and pushed it against the desk. "And the one place the World Alpha goes for any special occasion will be void of his presence. He won't show up for one of his warriors who will not survive the mating ceremony. Sara is going to kill off one of the strongest wolves in the world." He laughed. "Dietrich will stay in his beloved castle in Germany and stew over the weakest of humans taking down one of his wolves. He hates humans almost as much as Mere hates werewolves."

"He might go. He came here for your birthday fifty years ago and stayed in the bleeder room with everyone," Nicholas said.

"It was a special birthday and he did raise me after my parents died, but he's not going anywhere for a human and werewolf union. If Sara survives, Ethan will be at the bottom of the pack."

Nicholas picked up the stack of papers and walked to the hallway's entrance. He handed the documents off to his assistant. "Pick five and prepare them to travel for a few days."

"Yes, sir," Nicholas's assistant said, and left.

"May I call Dietrich for assistance with Sara? I want to make a case for my side," Nicholas said. "If she becomes a werewolf, she's lost to me. I could save Ethan's life. He might respond to a call for that."

Jeremy hugged his friend. "I have called about the feral situation many times over the years. He only shows up when the signs indicate a problem, and I guess the numbers aren't high enough to make it an issue for him. If he cared that much about Ethan, he would have called me to see if there was anything I could do. He doesn't ask for favors. He doesn't want to return them. He will not interfere in this situation. I should probably tell him about Mere's paw print birthmark, but she's human. What's he going to do?"

"There's no point in telling him about it. Mere would rather die than meet with a werewolf to show him the one part of her body she doesn't like anyone seeing. If anything, she'd start a fight with him," Nicholas said. "With Dietrich's disdain for humans, he'd pass by the house and go home after one sniff with his super nose, or worse, he'd walk in and ignore her. Can you imagine how Mere would react?"

Jeremy rubbed Nicholas's back and released him. "Yes, I can. She'd most likely break his nose or attempt to take him down and show him who was boss." Jeremy smiled. "My wife is going to be the best Queen barring none in our history. Let's go. You talk to Ethan and Sara about the situation you can resolve for them, although if you do, Sara will be in and out of the torture room for the first year or two of her new life." *I'll ride in like a knight in shining armor and save my girl. Mere will thank me. We'll make love, and I'll turn her. She'll be my Queen and the Coven will shower her with all the love she ever wanted or needed. I'll have the life I've always wanted with the woman who Soulburned me.*

Nicholas ran his hand over his bald head. "I want Sara not as my special lover—I want her as my wife."

"Do you really want to deal with—" Jeremy stopped. If anyone besides him could change the wild child bitch of a chatterbox into a rule-following vampire who silenced her tongue in matters of the Coven, it was Nicholas.

"Sara agreed to turn and be my wife when she

graduated high school," Nicholas said. "She hasn't graduated. She forged her transcripts and her high school diploma. She lied and lied and lied about everything she's done since that concert she went to this summer. Her actions went to the extreme, even for her."

The muscles in his face and neck twitched like they did when he lost control, something that rarely happened. "Now I know why she wanted to suck my cock. It was for *him. That boy.*" He squeezed his hands into tight fists. "It was the mating call. She used me, but she wants me. She *wants* me. She's *stuck* with *him.*"

"Something isn't right. Mates stay with mates. She shouldn't have even considered touching your cock, let alone sucking it."

Nicholas moaned and squeezed his groin. "She did more than suck my cock. Mere would kill me if she knew what I did with Sara. How I snuck into their room while they were on tour and fucked Sara every damn night while Mere was working. Sara promised me her virginity and she willingly gave it." He shuddered.

"You snuck into their room? Ethan didn't catch you? Mates don't leave or separate for more than a couple days. Maybe two weeks. That concert was three or four months ago."

"She's human, not a werewolf," Nicholas hissed. "Humans are ours, not theirs. She's never going to survive the transformation. And I will lose the woman I love because I did the right thing and waited for her to mature."

"You can't go into Ulvene County and start a war." *Not over Sara. On the other hand, Mere is worth waging every kind of war against every earthly or angelic being—*

"They're exchanging vows as we speak. The mating is happening tomorrow night. I have one chance to—"

"They haven't mated yet? That's not possible. No one can stop the mating call. It's scent driven. They're werewolves—they go crazy over their mates."

"I need your help. There is something changing the natural course of things. I don't believe it's the mating call. I think Sara must have a diluted scent." Nicholas rubbed his face and neck. "Feral werewolves sniff her and go toward her, but they go nuts over Mere. They lose their minds with Mere. Could Sara have the mating scent on her, but it might really be someone else?"

"I've never heard of that happening. You're grasping at straws for something to hold onto." Jeremy put his hand on Nicholas's back and guided him into the bleeders' chambers. *You need a distraction. Potential vampires whose fertility levels are off the charts should get your mind off Sara.*

The rich reds of the bedding caught Jeremy's eye first. The colors of the coven highlighted the job the bleeders were tasked with—cuddling for warmth, sex, and blood. The beige walls and white trim seemed to be a hit with the bleeders and the neutral color allowed for a quick change in décor for holidays and themed parties.

Five lovely ladies stood in a circle near the largest of the six beds. A pretty pink flush on their pale skin showed their excitement.

Nicholas took off his clothes and laid them on

the bench near the door to the Domination Room.

The ladies pivoted and stood waiting patiently for them to approach. The red flush from newly waxed pussies marked them as open and willing to turn with the right vampire.

"You should think about taking on one of them," Jeremy whispered to Nicholas. "Maybe you should take two or all five. Increase the population of vampire warriors. It's been a long time since you've added a child of your bloodline."

Nicholas's cock beaded with cum. "Sara can't have children. We talked about her being a stepmother to my children. Mere's latest vision showed me that I would have many children over the years."

Jeremy guided him to the ladies. *I do not want you taking Sara into our Coven without testing your loyalty to the vampires you vowed to protect. You have to help grow the populations of warriors within the Coven.*

"You know all of Mere's visions come true. And these females are strong. They'll turn quickly. They're ovulating so they could conceive immediately after the turning. Your mother will take care of the women for you, and we'll leave for Arizona. We'll get there in time for you to postpone the Mating, maybe even stop it. But your commitment to the Coven comes first. Always."

"Always the Coven first." Nicholas took the hand of the leader of the group of women. "You will not be my wife. Are you willing to join my line and do your best to bear my children until one day the man you Soulburn takes you into his home after asking and receiving my permission?"

"What would happen to my children, if we conceive together?" she asked.

"They would be trained by me, but you would be welcome to visit my home or stay in my home with or without your husband anytime, day or night," Nicholas stated. "There is no jealousy or stigma attached to your choice to join my blood-line. Your husband would be honored to know you birthed my children."

"Would we be blood-bonded?"

"No. Blood-bonds are eternal. I have never blood-bonded with anyone. I have four children with women who have since been Soulburned and married. Unfortunately, those women have not had success with carrying more children, but our lives are long and they are strong."

"Are my chances for children best with the man who turns me?"

Nicholas smiled. "No. Your chances for children are best with the man who you want to dominate you in and out of bed. That isn't always the one who turns you or who you will fall so madly in love with that your soul will be burned by his blood."

"What if the man who turns me is the one I want to dominate me?" She gazed at Nicholas's cock and licked her lips. "Are my chances best to have a big family with him?"

"Do it, Nicholas," Jeremy whispered. "Sara doesn't have a uterus. She wants you to have more children, is that correct?"

"Yes. She wants me to have more children. She knows I choose lovers that have the best chance at conception." Nicholas's cock squirted cum at the woman.

"Your cock only does that when the woman will conceive your child," Jeremy whispered into his ear. "A Carson family trait. It's never steered you or your ancestors wrong."

"I want to test the one on the right," Nicholas replied.

"What's your name?" Jeremy held his hand to the woman to the right.

"Claymora." She stepped in front of the other woman. "My father was a blacksmith."

Cum shot from Nicholas's cock onto the woman's pussy.

She shuddered.

"Do you want to join my bloodline as my lover, Claymora?"

"Yes, sir," she whispered. "I would be honored. I'm ready to be turned immediately. I've signed all the papers. I'm in no rush for true love or marriage, but I do want children. My only request is that if you blood-bond to a woman, you hold off on marriage until either my body rejects a conception or I've given birth to five of your children. Marriage is sacred, and I want our sexual relationship to end the minute you take vows in church under God."

Nicholas moaned and clenched his balls to stop his cock from marking her again. "Claymora, follow me." He nodded to the other woman. "You too."

Claymora hurried to his right side and the other stopped behind them.

"I'll be the most fertile in thirty minutes," Claymora whispered. "Will the turning affect my ovulation?"

"The turning will enhance your ovulation during the first two years," Nicholas whispered. "It will increase the amount of eggs available for fertilization."

"I probably shouldn't have taken the fertility pills this month," she whispered.

Nicholas gripped his balls tighter. "You signed the papers yesterday, but you started the fertility program already?"

"I started the fertility treatments three months ago. I wanted to know what my body was capable of first."

He glanced over his shoulder. "Did you prepare for today with treatments?"

"This was my first month in the fertility program. Claymora encouraged me. We're best friends. I'm Spatha. My mother was a blacksmith. Our parents died in the fire that swept through the manufacturing district five years ago. We chose to come here together and hoped to be chosen to turn around the same time. Thank you."

"She talks more than me," Claymora whispered. She lifted onto her tiptoes and kissed Nicholas's lips. "I was one of ten siblings, until the fire. I was the only one who wasn't at work when the fire broke out."

"I'm sorry for your losses." Nicholas walked them to the door to the turning chambers, and opened it. "Jeremy, could you send my mom here? Let her know I've got two."

"Yes," Jeremy said. *Maybe you won't want Sara after turning them.*

Nicholas opened the door to the crimson room. "Thank you, my King."

Jeremy walked over and hugged him. "Good luck."

"You have never taken a vampire as a lover to increase your bloodline. Consider one of the others and join me," Nicholas said.

Jeremy smiled. "I'm waiting for Meredith. I'm Soulburned. I want her and only her."

"Sara Soulburned me, but I still want children from lovers I choose."

"Your bloodline is known for having harems of women. Your father had many lovers in his home and was Soulburned by your mother. You are the same as your father."

"I am," Nicholas replied. He kissed Jeremy's cheek. "I will increase our population and our army as I have vowed to do just as all the male ancestors in my bloodline had vowed before me." He let go of Jeremy, walked into the turning room, and closed the door.

The process would be over and the women would either be pregnant or they wouldn't within a half-hour. If they didn't conceive with Nicholas, they likely wouldn't conceive in their lifetime. If they did and the pregnancy and turning of the children went well, they had a better chance of more children with Nicholas, or with the man who would steal their souls and burn them with blood and love forever.

Jeremy sat on the edge of the bed and the three bleeders in the room gathered around him. "I'm here to feed, that is all."

"May I offer you a female who isn't ovulating, my King?" the older brunette asked.

He nodded. "That would be lovely."

She sauntered to an adjoining chamber. "Sloane, the King needs a snack."

A redhead he recognized skipped into the room. "My name is Sloane, and I'm available for a feeding but"—she pointed to the light dusting of red hair on her pussy—"she's not ready to take the sex plunge quite yet." She laughed. "I'm getting rid of the hair as soon as I can."

"You should wait for love," he said. *A virgin should not be in this chamber.*

"I'm thirty. Love hasn't happened. My human biological clock is ticking." She climbed onto his lap. "I want a chance at a family for hundreds of years instead of a few more."

He lifted her wrist to his mouth and kissed the delicate flesh. "Having a family is wonderful, but making love for the first time should be magical and that only happens when you love the other person. You've waited this long—wait a little longer. You've gone on dates with humans? Vampires? Anyone you think you might love?"

He searched her face for anything he could find to put her on the right path. This place was for women and men who lost families, spouses, or wanted to belong to someone and to have children if things worked out. Very few were accepted into this program. The ovulation bleeder chambers went centuries without any suitable humans. They had a tightknit group at the moment and a few being added within the next two weeks.

He slipped his teeth into her veins and sipped.

"I've been on dates." She leaned her warm body against his and kissed his shoulder. "I'm hoping Nicholas Carson's son, Roman, will come for me, but he's so handsome and strong and I'm small compared to the women he seems to like."

"Mmm," he mumbled.

She straddled his lap and rubbed against his bulge, but nothing the girl could do would get his cock excited. His powerhouse moped as much at Meredith's loss as he did.

I can change the course of this girl's life. He gripped her bottom and pulled her closer to him, then removed his phone from his pocket.

"Oh, King," she moaned.

He tapped Roman's pic and started typing a text.

Roman, get your ass into the ovulation room in the bleeder chambers. The little redhead, Sloane, you've been talking to me about is here. Her blood tastes like yours. You Soulburned her, and you haven't done anything about it. Do something.

-VKJ

He licked the small incisions and kissed her wrist. Juices from her pussy wet his slacks.

She gasped. "Oh, my God. They told me I would have one hell of a start to my ovulation cycle. But damn. I'm so sorry." Her cheeks flamed as red as her hair. "I am so, so sorry."

The vampire in charge of the room ran to the waxing cart. She raced as she rolled it to the bed.

Sloane spread her legs and held her breath. "I'm ready."

"No, you're not ready," Jeremy said. "Go to your room and wait. I will not allow you to do this. Not until the man you love comes for you."

"What if he doesn't?" Sloane gazed at him with the saddest blue eyes he'd ever seen. "I'm supposed to go into the turning room."

He kissed her lips and helped her off his lap. "Not today." He strode to the turning room. If Claymora and Spatha turned quickly and without any complications, they would be trained as warriors in his army when they completed the two-year vampire maturation process inside these walls.

Sloane followed close behind. "Please, my King."

Nicholas lifted his head and grinned. He thrust into Spatha as Claymora rubbed his back and glanced over her shoulder.

Emerald eyes met Jeremy's. A big smile spread over Claymora's face. She adjusted on the bed and faced Jeremy. She slipped two digits into Nicholas's dark passage as she caressed her hand over her belly. "Create life inside my friend."

Nicholas hissed as he thrust. He shuddered and rolled over onto his back.

Spatha sat up, her naturally green eyes darkened to a happy black. Claymora caressed Spatha's belly. "Feel anything?"

The sharp fangs of a new vampire extended down, scraping against Spatha's ruby lips. "It was intense, exactly like the doctor said. I felt it in my heart. But that can't be possible."

"You feel the Heart of our Coven, not your own heart." Nicholas spread his legs and his cock rose. "Inside the inner chambers of our Coven is where the Heart of the Coven resides until the Queen has risen and accepted the Heart into her body. When we're all gathered together in her presence…mmm…The heat and sound of couples caressing, rubbing, making love is hypnotic. There is nothing like it. When The Heart of the Coven glows within our Queen, our population increases exponentially."

Claymora climbed over Nicholas and held her folds open as she lowered onto his cock. "Sloane, is the King turning you?"

Sloane shook her head. "Meredith's vision isn't for today and most definitely not with the King who waits patiently for his Queen."

Jeremy stopped and tilted his head to the side to listen more closely.

"Meredith Kilpatrick gave you a vision?" Nicholas asked.

"Yes, she saved my life," Sloane said. "She pushed me out of the way of a car that would have hit me head on. In that brief moment, I saw the future I could have here. I started going to her church and joined it."

"Mere was one of the massage therapists who arrived to help soothe families and first responders after the warehouse fires. She and three others set up tables and chairs." Claymora told a story Jeremy hadn't heard. There were so many stories of Mere's kindness. She always gave without expecting anything in return.

"When Mere touched my hand, I saw five handsome boys with green eyes and dark hair. They'll have my father's smile and Nicholas's nose. They will become strong warriors like their father."

Sloane stepped forward. The sound of her pussy contracting and squishing with juices for sex rose in volume. She stopped short from entering the room.

Jeremy checked his phone. *Roman, where are you? Come and get your girl.*

I'm stuck at an airport in London. It's going to be a

while before I can get a flight. Put her away. Do not let anyone have her. She shouldn't be in that fucking room. Heads are going to roll when I get back.

-Roman Carson

"It's time to go to your room." Jeremy guided Sloane from the open doorway to the turning room.

"Visit me when you can," Sloane said to the girls. "One day, I hope I'll join you." She ran her fingers through the light dusting of red at her mons. "I don't see how the vision can come true now." She walked slowly across the room where she'd been waiting for her chance at a new life as Jeremy strode from the room into the passageway.

"Have faith, Sloane," Spatha said loudly. "I was heading toward death when Mere showed me the family I could have, if I came to this church and went into this program. I witnessed Mere's future too. She had changed. She had long, almost-white blond hair with pale blue eyes and was taller. We called her Queen and something else. I can't remember what though."

Jeremy dismissed Spatha's vision. Only toxicity would cause such a deviation of Mere's natural look. That had only happened…*Had that happened? Did I read about the possibility of it happening in our history?*

He strode forward into the tunnels. *I'll check the records when I get back. Mere's visions always come true. But none of her visions with me showed a problematic transformation.* His mind raced as he made his way to his chambers.

If Mere's turning goes bad, I might need World Alpha's help to protect the Coven until she recovers. First, I need to get her home where she belongs.

CHAPTER FOUR

THE OPPRESSIVE ACHE IN MEREDITH'S heart weighed her down in the wooden pew as the child she raised made vows to love, honor, and cherish a young man she'd met twice.

"The Ulvenes updated the church for this wedding," Lainie Ivanovski Wolfson, Mere's best friend, said. "So stop frowning."

Mere curled the corners of her lips up. "Yes, they told me. It's a beautiful church."

The newly renovated church kept the same rows of ancient wooden benches that had stood the test of time and probably would survive long after their deaths, but of all the things to leave the same…*the miserably hard-on-everyone's-ass seating, really?*

Changing the originally cave-like entrances made more for animals than humans to the enormous arched entrances with beautifully crafted wooden doors made sense for the taller population. Adding the latest technology available to cool the building from the oppressive desert heat seemed like it should have been done decades ago. *Why wait so long?*

Raising the low ceilings to more than thirty feet high gave the room an element of freedom and space. The new energy-efficient windows helped reduce the afternoon sun's rays from overworking the air conditioner. Modernizing, yet keeping the same architectural designs of the original doors, arches, and stained beams in the sanctuary, added to the beauty of the church built centuries ago by the Ulvenes who settled the land. The Ulvenes who would be part of Mere's family within minutes. The Ulvenes who saw nothing wrong with their son proposing to a girl the same day he'd met her at a concert. The Ulvenes who rushed Sara into finishing high school early in order to move to Arizona to get married. The Ulvenes who welcomed them into the family immediately without ever questioning their son's choice in a wife he spent a total of five hours with until today.

Mere's plans to move from Atlanta, Georgia to Tempe, Arizona for one year so Sara could go to the celebrity massage school after graduation changed as soon as Ethan proposed. Now, Mere was out from under Jeremy's protection, a virtual sitting target for feral werewolves to hunt her down in a small town owned and run mostly by the Ulvene family who had no idea the beasts even existed.

"I present to you Mr. and Mrs. Ethan Ulvene. Ethan, you may kiss your bride," the minister said.

Lainie whispered, "Ethan is a good man. He comes from a great family. He's a distant relation of Luke's."

Mere glanced toward Lainie's husband Luke. *Because of your encouragement my barely eighteen-year-old daughter is married. You helped plan this after I told you I was against it. You stepped out in support. You… God, you smell so damn good I want to rub all over you. What is wrong with me? I must miss Jeremy more than I thought I would.*

Luke leaned toward her and his alluring ocean breeze scent fell over her like a sprinkling of precious nectar from the gods. "I guarantee they will be happy for the rest of their lives. Trust me."

She nodded. *Get it together. He's Lainie's husband.* She cleared her throat and exhaled more of the sexy fragrance she couldn't get away from. *God help me.* She scooted closer to the married man she wanted in more ways than one.

A smile crossed Lainie's lips. "What's going on with you?"

"Tell Luke to stop wearing that ocean breeze cologne. It's making me crazy," Mere whispered. "I can't think when he's near. I'm sorry, but your Mr. Sex is putting out so much energy that the entire city will have a baby boom nine months from today."

"Oh, my God." Lainie rolled her eyes. "You must be smelling something else because my man does not smell like…" Her blue eyes widened. "Oh." She elbowed her husband in the side. "Did you hear that?"

Luke stood up and clapped.

The sanctuary erupted in cheers and applause.

Mere bolted up and whooped and hollered. *Nothing I can do now, except support and protect her.*

The applause died down and Luke stepped behind Mere. "What do you smell on me?" His hand slid around her waist and her body heated uncomfortably.

She wasn't one hundred percent certain, but she could have sworn he sniffed her hair. Without meaning to, she breathed him in, pulling in the fragrance of the ocean she desperately needed to be on anyone but him.

"Your ocean body spray. It's got an undercurrent of mountain snow and desert sand. Stop wearing it." She inhaled deeply and savored more of the sensual scent.

He turned her in his arms as the happy couple floated down the aisle toward the narthex. They should have followed the bride and groom, but Luke held her back. "Where exactly do you smell that scent on me?"

"Ugh…this is embarrassing," she whispered. *I do not want to get closer to you. There is something different about you. I can't put my finger on it, but it's not only your incredible sexuality. I might as well be the damn sex police patrolling for the right partner, but only finding married men or liars or sociopathic werewolves or the most powerful vampire in the world who will never love me like I love him.*

"Tell me," Luke said, as though he commanded her to answer him.

She gazed at Lainie. *This is a bad idea. There is no telling what I'll see. I like your husband, and I don't want to not like him.* "Just stop wearing it, Luke."

"He didn't put on cologne this morning," Lainie insisted. She placed her hand on Mere's back over the expensive lace. "You're picking up someone else, and Luke is as sensitive as you are to scents and energy. We've talked about this. There are things you and I can do in our massage practices that can't be explained by traditional means. You have my permission to find what is making your girlie parts wake up. I guarantee you, it's not my Luke."

"Girlie parts wake up?" Mere groaned. "Really?"

Lainie's gaze meandered around the room. "There are kids nearby. Do you really want me to say what I'm thinking?"

"No, I don't. Let this go." *Your dirty mouth is worse than mine.*

"Open up your…" Lainie frowned and glanced around again. "You know that thing you do."

"Not now." *Jeremy isn't here to ground me in reality.*

"Yes, now. Everyone is hurrying to the reception. It will take a minute at the most," Luke said. "Lainie will keep an eye out."

Mere clasped Luke's hands. "I don't have a good feeling—"

"Do it," Lainie demanded.

"Fine. But I'm against this." Mere closed her eyes and opened her other senses as she breathed in the air of life around her. Darkness pushed away all distractions.

A tingling at her lids forced her to open them. A burst of vibrant colors and a rush of buzzing sounds met her as she took in the man's aura, life force, and peacefulness of his soul.

Power surged around her. The barriers of protection she normally held firmly in place to keep the visions and other people's problems and bad energy out of her daily life fell like the walls of Jericho. She glided one hand up his arm, over his shoulder, and down the center of his chest. She stopped at the buttons on his starched white shirt over his heart. Images of Luke participating in emotionless sex before he saw Lainie bombarded her.

Holding his hand with a steel grip, she leaned her forehead against his chest. She panted as her heartbeat sped erratically. The stress involved in opening up the boundaries between the physical and metaphysical strained her already damaged heart. "Lainie is your true love." *Praise God. You're as true to her as I hoped. You love her as much as her late husband had.*

She breathed through the worry of walking into a glimpse of the person's future that occasionally came after a vision of the past. Cold shivers rattled her bones before sweat beaded on the skin of her chest. Hot flames licked the perspiration from her flesh as she melted into the foreign scene unraveling around her.

Snow from the mountains melted, forming a river that flowed down steep cliffs to the valley below and continued along the worn edges of an unstable bay along curves of sandy beach leading to the magnificent blue ocean waters.

Luke stood on fine grains of white sand along a private beach with Lainie by his side, holding their infant boy in her arms.

Mere waded waist-deep in the gentle currents of the crystal-clear sea. Her long brown hair morphed to thick, platinum-blond tresses. The sun glinted off the beautiful white crests of the waters blinding her. She lifted her hand, shielding the light. The brown and gold in her eyes shifted to an almost-white light blue, changing the future within the vision.

A man about her age swam as if he were born from the gods of the ocean, possibly part-fish and part-man. He dove under and arose from beneath the waves before her with a smile that warmed every inch of her platinum sparkling, sun-kissed skin.

His blond hair shined like golden threads spun together from the sun gods. His serene ice-blue eyes opened up a secret portal reserved exclusively for her to enter into his old soul. His tanned flesh shimmered with an angelic silver glitter that called for her touch.

"As devastating as the ocean's wrath, as old as the earth's mountains, as hot as the desert sands…" She *breathed the mystery man's aroma in and—*

The connection to the impossible future of her vision severed. Like a toddler learning to walk, she lost her balance and tumbled into the center aisle. Luke caught her head before she cracked it on the edge of the pew.

Sprawled on the white satin carpet rolled out for the ceremony, Mere lifted her unsteady head from Luke's solid hands. *No. Impossible.*

"It's not me," Luke said. His face moved so close to hers as he shifted to her right side and gazed at his wife. "She not only sees the future, Lainie, she can show it to others. She showed me. She's going to—"

"Hey, we need to talk." Lainie knelt at Mere's left side. She cupped Mere's cheeks and demanded her attention. "You're not going to the reception. I'm sorry."

"You're crazy," Mere said. *I am coming apart at the seams. You smell good too—like the merman from the vision. I'm not into girls. I need a stiff drink.* "I'm going to Sara's reception. I shouldn't have touched Luke like that. I'm adjusting to the move." *I'm going to keep it together. I have to. I'm not running back to Jeremy after only a couple days.*

She turned over and rose to her feet. She ran her hands over the curve-hugging, cocktail-length lavender dress Lainie had loaned her. She shuddered once as she glanced at gorgeous, brown-haired Luke Wolfson. *It wasn't you at all. Some nonexistent blond merman rising from the ocean wearing nothing but a sexy—*

"We're taking you back to the hotel," Luke ordered.

"The heck you are." Mere dropped her chin, pursed her lips, and glared at him. She added a shoulder and head roll to emphasize her solid position. "I'm all back together." *I'm not getting involved with a mythical creature.* She waved her hands to make clear that she was one hundred percent going to the reception. "My wacky spiritual side is closed for the rest of the day." *I'm not opening up to anyone like that again. Definitely not willingly.*

She dropped her hands. "I'm dancing with my son-in-law at the reception like I promised." She might not be happy about Sara and Ethan rushing into a wedding so young, but it was their decision, and she was supporting them in every way she knew how. Being a part of their lives and helping them work through hard times would give her the purpose she needed to keep living, keep protecting the only family she had left, and keep her from pining away for Jeremy.

"Mere." Luke held out his hand. "We all know Sara is your niece, not your daughter. You would have been eleven when you had her. We understand why you lied and skirted the system. We get it. But you don't need to go to the reception when you're struggling with your *abilities*. Sara will understand and so will Ethan."

"What on earth are you talking about?" Mere

lowered her voice and glanced around the empty sanctuary. *They sure did clear out quickly. At least they didn't hear big mouth Luke.* "I'm a little off-balance because I agreed to do something I had a bad feeling about, kind of like the marriage ceremony I just witnessed." She exhaled and straightened her spine.

With her voice back to normal she added, "Sara and I told y'all about her guardianship in confidence today. I raised Sara. My half-sister might have given birth to her, but from the minute I…" The horrible memories of the day her family was slaughtered overwhelmed her. The weight of the world crushed down on her.

Images of the dark-skinned man, Sara's grandfather, who found her in the woods bleeding to death from werewolf bites and Sara swaddled and strapped to her chest broke free from the compartment in her brain where she kept the memories locked up. The recovery. The visions. Learning how to dull her senses to keep from going crazy. Then the day that same man who acted like a real grandfather to her, the man who healed her, the only man who seemed to care about her future, had sent her away.

"Mere?" Lainie said. "You okay?"

A quick shake of her head and the memories returned to the private cell inside Mere's mind where they belonged. "Yeah. Anyway, I want to be there." Sara had given her a reason to live when she'd wanted to give up and die along with her half-sister, brother-in-law, and her parents all those years ago. "Y'all helped pay for the reception. Don't you want to be there, too?"

Luke's hand stayed outstretched. "Mere, you're trembling."

She rolled her eyes. "It's the aftereffects. I'm good. I need some fresh air and to par-tay." *I am falling apart. I can't keep going back to Jeremy for help. I made my choice, and he made his.*

She winked at them to hide the depths of distress she lived in since she left Jeremy. "Maybe I'll have a drink and get a smidgen wild with one of the single guys."

"That is not a good idea," Luke said.

Mere shook out her arms in hopes the excess energy she absorbed would release back into the universe. *Drinking and sex is exactly what I need. I need to find a man without any serious excess baggage to get crazy under the sheets for one night only. Then, maybe I can get all my spiritual guards back into place and forget about Jeremy…at least until he needs a taste of my blood.* "Thanks for offering your hand, but I am going to decline your help." *Touching you opens up places I don't need to go.*

Lainie stepped in and wrapped her arm around Mere's shoulders. "How about a compromise?"

At least you know how to close down your spiritual shields in order to touch me. With her shoulders sagging in a battle she couldn't win, Mere nodded. "Since you're driving me home, I have no choice."

Luke chuckled. "My wife is brilliant."

Lainie guided Mere toward the nave of the church. "If I see you struggling to keep it together at the reception, I'll make an excuse for us to leave early."

"I have to leave early anyway. First day on the job is tomorrow." The luscious scent of Luke seemed to swirl around Mere like a lazy tornado, tearing down her emotional boundaries layer by layer and opening up more and more of the spiritual gifts she kept locked up like gold in Fort Knox.

CHAPTER FIVE

ETHAN HELD SARA IN HIS arms as the photographer snapped a photo of them near the double archway leading to the narthex.

The desire to join them, to touch the couple and delve into their future hoping to see a love like Lainie has experienced made her wish for control over the ability she'd had since childhood. The spiritual gift seemed to control her more and more these days. Crossing the border into Arizona sent her body and mind into a tailspin. The minute they'd arrived at the hotel, visions had surfaced. Visions that made no sense. *White-blond hair. Light-blue eyes. Red lips more crimson than Jeremy's. Sparkling skin. Nothing would make my coloring change like that.*

With barely a brush of Ethan's father's hand against hers when he'd picked up her suitcase, Mere's assumptions of Ethan's parents' skepticism vanished and were replaced with visions of the determination of the Ulvene family to bring Sara to their town and marry Ethan. Since the concert, where Ethan and Sara had met, the Ulvene's strategy remained flawless. They made sure nothing, financial or otherwise, stood in the newlyweds' way from building a life together. Only Mere.

She reached outward, through the vibrant pinks and yellows of her daughter's aura, to cling to the one person on earth she couldn't live without. *I need to make sure you're happy. I need to believe they didn't force you to do this.* "Sara, take my hand."

"Personal space." Sara backed away. "You've got that look in your eyes."

"Shit." *Right. Never enter her personal space.*

"I do not want you seeing me and Ethan doing…" Sara flattened her expression to the one she usually held for lies. "Ethan and I want our first time to be experienced, not seen through your creepy shade of spectacles."

Wow. "I'm not interested in seeing that," Mere said. Witnessing Sara and Ethan having sex remained off Mere's agenda. Forever. "Sara, all I want is for you to be happy and healthy."

Ethan cringed. "Thanks, Mere. I'm going to do my best to make Sara happier than she's ever been. We'll see you at the reception." He straightened his posture and, for the first time, Mere saw a man, not a kid. "I'm ready to dance whenever you are. I'm good with a little cuddle too. I keep my feelings bottled up. Not in a weird, I-need-therapy way, but more to keep my feelings secured for the ones I love." He ended with a knockout smile and a wink.

People weren't usually that friendly when they found out about her abilities. "Yeah, okay, Ethan." Mere bolted for the door. *Fresh, cleansing air. They are a strange people. Not so strange as…different. Maybe I'm the freak, always looking for problems that might not be there. I'm overanalyzing. Jeremy always tells me to slow down. Not everyone wants to hurt Sara and me.*

She raced down the steps and stopped on a dime behind Jack and Paulina Ulvene, Ethan's parents.

Paulina's long brown hair floated outward over her bare shoulders as if she had a fan blowing at the perfect moment in the exact direction to make her look like she was turning around in a hair commercial, not outside in the sweltering heat of the desert. "I thought that was you. Hi."

"Hey, Paulina. Uh…Jack, hey there. Wow. The kids are married. I can't believe it…" Mere babbled. Her body heated to a boil as the warm desert breeze lifting Paulina's caramel and dark cocoa locks gently blew from the west and carried the scent driving Mere mad straight into her lungs. "I need a drink."

Jack laughed. "I could go for a protein smoothie too."

"Yeah, a protein smoothie sounds great." *Not. I'll be drinking at the adult bar.* She took a step to go around them.

"Mere, walk with us." Jack blocked her way. "We'll start planning how we're going to manipulate the kids' lives so they do what we want them to."

Like you've already done? Only, I bet you didn't count on me staying in this little town. Well, here I am, and I'm staying for the rest of my short life whether anyone wants me here or not. Mere swept away the beads of sweat forming small streams trickling downward from her neck and chest. She joined them walking at their leisurely pace in the sauna they called Arizona.

"Are you okay?" Paulina asked. The woman glistened as they walked, seemingly unaffected by the desert heat.

No. I'm not okay. Not at all.

The aroma of her merman circled her like a cloud of gnats that wouldn't go away.

I need to borrow a single guy about my age for a wild night of kinky sex to get rid of this…this…I don't know what the hell is going on with me. Sex. Heat. Smell. Touch. Sight. All I need is a taste and my senses will be on overload.

"Oh, I didn't expect such high temperatures this time of year. I might actually be melting from the heat." *Melting from the scent of a sex god. I need a fully stocked bar. A heavy shot of whiskey covers damn near everything even that wonderful cologne.*

The couple tilted their heads and scrunched their noses. Together, they sniffed as if they were recovering from a head cold. Their eyelids rose to their brows and the brown in their eyes showed larger specks of green she hadn't noticed before. They turned and stared at each other as if they were in some kind of silent conversation.

"We've grown up here, so we're acclimated to the warmer temperatures." Jack held his wife's hand and blinked. He nodded his head.

Paulina glanced at Mere and motioned for her to follow as they began the short trek to the reception half a football field away from the old church. "I was born and raised here. I love it."

"Have you ever visited Germany?" Jack asked. "I was born there, but moved here when I was pretty young. Germany is beautiful and has four seasons, unlike our two seasons—summer and summer." He chuckled.

Germany? Are you trying to get rid of me so soon? She cracked a smile and faked a laugh. "I like it here." *Not.* "By this time next year I'll be wearing a heavy sweater and coat instead of turning into a puddle of sea water. I mean water. Not salty man. I mean." *Shit. Get the merman off my damn brain.* "Uh, visiting Germany isn't on my bucket list. I'm not fond of traveling or snow or being away from Sara. So, let's make sure these kids set down all their roots right here."

Paulina grinned with a happiness that sent twinkles of joy oozing from her cozy-brown eyes.

Strange. You're not vampires or your eyes would be a dark shade of brown or green and changing hues in that spectrum with your mood. You're not werewolves or you'd be drooling and your fangs would be lengthening and cutting into your lower lips. You'd have already attacked me by now. You're not a witch or a zombie or a—

"We are going to be best friends. Jack and Ethan…and now Sara too are my entire life." Paulina slid her hand between Mere's waist and arm, giving her a quick side hug before letting go. "We want Sara to work at our fitness and training facility. What do you think? Does she show signs of enjoying sports massage as a future career?"

"I'm not sure what modality will interest her most. She wanted to be like Lainie and work with musicians and tour with them, but now…" *Stop thinking about the negatives of Sara's choices.* Mere strode forward with a higher purpose. "Sara will be an asset anywhere she chooses to work." *She probably won't go to massage school like she'd planned. She will probably—*

"She told us she wants to work with us as a membership coordinator while she's getting used to married life. She wasn't sure you'd be comfortable with her working for us." Paulina stepped behind her as they reached the entrance to the Ulvene Country Club.

Luke appeared at the door and held it.

Jack and Paulina stood and stared at her.

Mere stared back, frozen in place. *You're taking over Sara's life. Go for it. You have no idea what a handful she is.* "Y'all go first."

"It's through the main banquet hall and into the garden," Paulina said. She kept a comfortable distance from Mere. "We can go in together."

Lainie's confident hand touched Mere's back. "Step forward. Find that extrovert hidden deep inside you, and let it out."

I don't have an extrovert bone in my body.

One step at a time, Mere entered the building. Wait staff systematically moved from what had to be the kitchen inside the back left-side entrance to the lovely, wood-and-glass doors half-open lining the back of the room.

She crossed the sunburnt tiles, passed over the glossy planks of the ballroom's dance floor and the tiles leading to the outdoor fairytale reception made for royalty. Her throat constricted from a lump of emotion and her feet stopped moving as if an invisible barrier prevented her from entering. *I will never be able to repay you, Lainie.*

"Go on," Luke whispered to Jack and Paulina. "I need to talk to Mere."

Jack and Paulina nodded and stepped forward into the garden entrance.

"The mother and father of the groom…" a deejay called out, announcing their arrival.

A roar of applause erupted from outside.

Lainie and Luke forced Mere toward the open doors to the reception.

Mere trembled as she stared into the magical garden. *Too many people. One, two, three, four… twenty, forty…* Nerves, adrenaline, and the potential for chaos captured Mere in a choke hold. *What if we're attacked? I need Jeremy. I can't protect everyone by myself. People will die…Sara.*

Jack and Paulina stood in the center of the dance floor on the right side of the garden as the enormous crowd closed in on them as if they were a small, close-knit family.

"Welcome the mother of the bride, Meredith Kilpatrick," the deejay said.

"I have to do this for Sara," Mere mumbled.

"Hey," Lainie whispered. "One foot in front of the other. You got this."

The ocean breeze haunting her rushed in. Her panties moistened. The heated desire for sex that she'd managed to get a handle on during the walk with the Ulvenes raged out of control.

"I'm a fucking mess," Mere whispered and began to tremble. *One hundred ninety-seven. Too. Many. People.*

"I've got your back," Luke said. "It's an intimidating crowd, but you have nothing to fear."

"Our special guests, Luke and Lainie Wolfson," the deejay said, but words made little sense as Meredith reached the count of two hundred. Memories swarmed her mind of the enormous wolf beasts with blood dripping from their extended fangs that had attacked her.

Luke wrapped his arm around Mere's back and hugged her. He pulled her under his wing and led her forward with Lainie.

As they neared the dance floor, Mere pulled away. "Where are you going?" Luke asked.

"Over there." Mere didn't wait for a response. She hurried to the one place the scent, the people, and the memories would leave her alone—the bar.

On the other side of the room, far away from where the Ulvenes gathered to drink their protein smoothies, Mere stood alone at the alcohol oasis constructed specifically for her. Surviving the miserable event remained top priority. Drinking dulled the fears of being attacked, dulled her abilities when she touched anyone skin-to-skin, and dulled the senses that sent her running to Jeremy.

She reached into her purse for her wallet. *Drunk and relaxed is better than anxious and ready to fight.*

"Everything is paid for, even the tips," the bartender said.

I love you, Lainie. "Then I'll start with a double shot of whiskey to drink and one to hold."

"Are you old enough to drink?" the bartender asked.

"I may look barely legal, but I assure you, I'm thirty." Her hands shook so hard, she almost dropped her driver's license before he could take it. "Don't let me get sloppy drunk. I don't want to embarrass the bride." *No one else matters. The place could burn down and Sara would be the only one I'd walk through fire and certain death to save.*

CHAPTER SIX

THE LUSCIOUS MATING AROMA GREW stronger with each step Dietrich Ulvene Wolfgang took toward the wedding reception of one of his favorite and most powerful warrior werewolves to a human who likely wouldn't survive the mating ceremony. Months of suppressing Ethan's desire to mate the girl had come to an end. Fate would decide whether the couple would live or die.

I have my own mating issues. Ethan got the short end of the stick with his human mate —short, mousey, weak. But mine will be strong and tall, a warrior of unparalleled skill. Her beauty will rival those of the ancient angels.

He quickened his pace as he envisioned the perfectly formed female who had unfortunately been born human. *One look at me, and she'll beg me to change her into a wolf. One sniff, and she'll obey every one of my commands.*

He journeyed through the flower garden he and Jack had planted, along the private path of natural stone pavers he had hand-picked and placed, to the Ulvene Country Club he had designed where all the celebrations for the Arizona Werewolf Pack were held.

The fragrance of magnolia blooms releasing from the human who would soon know she was his mate made his heart race and the ready-to-bust-through-his-slacks bulge enlarge to painful proportions.

He sniffed, searching for her exact location at the reception. *Found you. Get ready for your life to change.*

He adjusted his fake glasses as he sauntered toward the makeshift bar near the southern exit, farthest away from the dance floor.

Her petite body leaned too far over the bar counter. *Small, weak, but lovely curves. You're not going to last a day in my world. I've waited thousands of years for this moment, and you're what I get? I'll have to protect you from the weakest of us.*

The human compatible with his specific werewolf genes emitting a mating scent created only for him held a shot glass filled with whiskey to her nose. Her hands trembled. Her gaze focused on the newlyweds exchanging pieces of cake near the large cypress tree strung with white ribbons and lights. The woman didn't even glance his way.

Stupid. Oblivious to the world. Worthless…but gorgeous. He sidled up to the bar beside her. "I'll have whatever she's having."

"Yes, sir," the bartender said. "Can I see some ID?"

Human trash. "Of course." He reached inside his jacket pocket and showed him a German passport.

"Is this real?" The bartender glanced at him and quickly returned his gaze to the picture on the passport. "You don't look twenty-seven."

The woman beside him glanced over while

keeping the drink to her nostrils. "Let me see that. I'm not letting some kid get drunk." She raised her eyebrow and snapped her fingers. "Hand over the ID."

"I'm not a *kid*, and you're the lush, not me." *Stupid. Drunk. Bitch.*

She tried to snatch the papers from the bartender, but missed his hand and almost knocked over the wine bottles displayed near the corner.

I am not mating with you. I should go back to my room and fuck Zoe again to ease the mating call. If only sex with her had worked, but your scent makes me… The most alluring brown eyes with specks of lustrous gold stared at him.

"Fine," she hissed. "Give the kid a light beer." Her voice softened and a sexy smile graced her lips. "I'll take another two refills." She raised the empty shot glass in her left hand and winked at the bartender.

"You haven't finished the one in your right hand. You know, the one at your nose," Dietrich said. *I'm mated to a bona fide alcoholic with no manners. I should let the challenges proceed before I ever touch you. You'll lose, and I'll wait for destiny to send me another mate.* "I am not fucking you."

She downed the whiskey and slammed the glass down on the cheap counter that never should have been there in the first place. Werewolves didn't bother consuming alcohol. Their metabolism countered the sedative effect.

She straightened up to her full height, which wasn't much. The high heels she wore added five inches, but even then she barely reached his chest.

He narrowed his gaze on her muscular legs and

the shakes she'd had since the minute he spied her suddenly disappeared.

She picked up the new shot glasses filled with amber liquid and held one under her nose.

"Get the heck out of my daughter's wedding reception. You don't have anything I want. In fact, your accent is a joke along with your bullshit for-eign"—she tilted her head, seemed to think for a minute, and then lifted her head straight again—"that probably fake ID you're sporting."

Loud gasps bombarded his mental pack links as the private conversation became very public to delicate werewolf ears.

He reached forward to grab her arm, but she twisted to the left.

He missed. He never missed *Are you faking your drunkenness?*

With one hand on her hip, she downed the shot and raised her glass. "Another, please. Mr. I'm-Not-Fucking-You is leaving, even if it comes to me hauling his sorry butt out myself." She had the nerve to reach past him and replace her empty glass with a full one.

"I'm not leaving," Dietrich said. *Sassy girl. I like sassy.* "Unless *your* drunk ass can haul *my* sorry butt out of here." He reached for her glass. *What is with you and the drink at your nose?*

"You touch me and I'm calling the cops," she said. "I will charge you with every damn thing I can…asssssaulllltttt…Ummmm…" She wobbled in her heels but seemed to find her balance and stepped back on solid legs. She gulped her drink. "Fuck. I'm drunk which means your ass is getting chunked, and I don't give a damn what anyone says. Ha."

You're wasted, yet you can still walk and dodge me? Have we started the mating ceremony's challenge of dominance? Do you actually think you'll win?

The straightest white teeth appeared from a show-stopping celestial smile. She giggled as she swayed from side to side.

"I'd like to see you try," he dared her. *Yes. We have started the challenge.*

She turned her back to him. "Children don't"— she seemed to try to contain her laughter, but failed miserably as snippets of chuckles rose into the air—"get to play at the adult table."

"Disrespectful girls get punished." *I'll enjoy correcting your behavior, my disobedient mate.*

She glanced over her shoulder and her defiant eyes lit up the room. "Oooooh, I'm soooo scared." Her gaze drifted up over his head. She twisted her torso and bit her lower lip. "Make this one a double, please." She leaned toward Dietrich and almost fell into his arms, but again righted herself as she pivoted on her heels and avoided contact. "The bartender is kind of cute. He's the one I want to go home with."

She sashayed past him and leaned over the bar. Her perky breasts swelled with the same flush of pink all over her chest and face. The back of her dress rode up almost to her ass cheeks, showing off the strong, muscular legs of a runner.

"Hey. I know I said to cut me off, but I'm dealing with an asshole." She circled her hand in Dietrich's direction as she spoke. "And I really do think I'm going to have to show him who's the real boss in the room."

Not one person—alternative being, animal or spirit—besides his father ever questioned his authority, ever challenged it the way the woman before him did. No human ever pushed back when tested. His mate needed to be put in her place. He couldn't let her undermine his authority. Not in front of his favorite pack. Not in front of his Beta Luke Wolfson.

He unleashed a portion of his Alpha power to make her submit to him – that which he'd cultivated over thousands of years as World Alpha – and pressed his front against her back. The energy in the room thickened and the air became dense as his dominance blanketed them.

He wrapped his arms around her and pulled her out of the flirting posture. *You are mine, not his.* "You've had enough to drink. I'm cutting you off."

She wiggled in his arms. "Asshole."

He lifted her up and spun her around to face him. The scent of fresh magnolia blooms threatened to drown him with desire. *I need you. Mine. Mate.* "It's Mr. Asshole to you." He slid his hands down her back and bent his knees as he squeezed her tight ass.

"Get your hands off me or I'm"—her voice lowered into a sexy southern drawl—"going to give you the best night of your life and never allow you near me again."

"I've changed my mind," he whispered. "I do want to fuck you, but it won't be one night. It will be the first of many." He stared into her eyes and released more Alpha werewolf energy to make her follow him. *You should be dropping to your knees with the weight of my power.*

The woman refused to bow down.

He rubbed his cheek against her soft brown tresses on the top of her head. *I'm going to rub my scent all over you. I'm going to claim you as mine.* He squeezed her ass again. *Surrender to me. I'm your Alpha.*

With a quickness uncommon among humans, she pushed away from him and slapped his face.

His glasses flew off.

He blinked. "Did you just hit me?"

"I warned you," she said.

What the fuck? "You said you were going to give me the best night of my life," he huffed. *I believed you.*

"Dude, she isn't interested," the human bartender whispered. "Apologize, and she might not press charges."

He gazed deep into her eyes. *You're giving off sexual energy like you're in a werewolf heat. You love this. You want me to work for you, dominate you.*

"What's your name?" he ordered.

"Weldon Wright," the bartender shouted.

Her mouth opened, and she stepped into his arms. "Meredith Teresa Kilpatrick. Since you know mine, what is yours?" Her lips twitched. Her eyes widened. She lifted her hand and gently caressed the cheek she slapped. "I shouldn't have done that so hard."

"You shouldn't have done it at all," he whispered. "We should be on our way back to my hotel room so we can get to know each other, intimately." *Will you follow me now? Or are you going to be difficult?*

Her mouth dropped to a frown. "I told you to stop, but you pushed. You deserved it."

"You need to be put in your place," he cooed. "You'll like it." He slid his hand to the edge of the curve of her bottom and gently tapped it. *I'm going to mark you here.*

"Mr. I'm-Not-Fucking-You, you're not capable of *putting* me anywhere. You have three seconds to take your hands off me or that slap will be nothing compared to the night in jail you're going to have when I—" She panted for air. Sweat beaded on her forehead as the haze of the mating trance spread over her eyes. She leaned against his chest while the wheels in her head seemed to spin out of control. She tensed and relaxed and trembled and froze.

"I've got this," Luke said as another human approached.

Why are there more than two humans here? Dietrich peered through his wolf's white eyes, which gave him the sudden appearance of blindness to those around him.

"Ma'am," a man said. "I'm an Ulvene Sheriff Deputy. Is this guy bothering you?"

She pushed out of Dietrich's light embrace. "Arrest this man. He groped me… and I-I wanted him…No. He warned him. No. I…"

Her head wobbled as if it would fall from her body. "Mr. Merman from the Blue Sea thinks because he's seeexxxy, and I neeeeddd seeexx…" The fog of the mating trance slipped away and the glassy eyes of a drunk filled her mesmerizing bronze stare. "I'm older than him and single. Well, I'm not that much older. I'm not thinking right. He touched me, and I licked…No. Liked…No. Arrest his ass." She snapped her fingers and pointed at Dietrich's chest.

Luke handed him the glasses Mere knocked off.

Mere is a handful, Luke said to him through their mental werewolf bond. *She actually might press charges. What is the merman reference?*

Thanks, Dietrich answered. He placed his glasses on. *I have no idea what the hell is going on with her. She's probably got some kind of ocean fetish. She's sniffing drinks and avoiding me while the mating trance is fighting for control. The trance isn't affecting me, but she's a fucking mess of restrained desire.*

"Thank you, Officer," Mere cooed. She curled her arm around the Native American almost as big as him as she held another shot glass filled with whiskey under her nose. "I don't know his name. I think I have bruises on my ass from his fingers, and it's not from any sex scenes we were debating on playing out. Not that I'm kinky or anything." She giggled. "With you, maybe I'd be kinky. I'd let you take a picture for evidence, but not with him here." She pointed directly at Dietrich again.

Dietrich sniffed as the woman created specifically to be his mate snuggled closer to the other man. *Why aren't you at my feet begging for sex like a normal mate?* He breathed in and called his wolf to rise closer to the surface.

"Officer," Mere whispered in a sexy southern drawl. "Thanks for rescuing me."

"That's why I'm here," the officer said.

She licked her lips and glanced at Dietrich. A glimmer of the mating trance held strong inside her defiant eyes.

How did you stop the trance from taking over? Why are you hanging on to him when you want to be all over me? I want you to be all over me.

The drink sloshed over the sides of the glass Mere held under her nose. Her entire body trembled.

Your fingers will be curled around my cock as soon as I get you alone.

Dietrich's wolf held back from fighting for control, but softly growled with displeasure at not being released. He gazed at Mere's nose.

She sniffed and sniffed and sniffed at the liquid.

The drink… You're trying to block my scent with the aroma of the amber liquid so you don't fall into the trance. Sly, sneaky mate, you're playing a game I will win.

"Officer," Dietrich said. "Let's not ruin the happy couple's special day. I got delayed and missed the ceremony along with most of the reception. It's late, and Meredith and I can work this out."

Pack, gather around, Dietrich ordered through his mental pack link. *Close in on Meredith Kilpatrick and me.*

The officer blinked several times as the guests gathered around.

"Momma," Sara said. "I'm so happy you've met Mr. Wolfgang. He flew all the way from Germany to be here today." She lowered her head and whispered, "Don't screw this up for me."

You have a lot to learn, little girl. If Ethan doesn't straighten you out, I will. No one speaks to my mate like that.

Meredith gritted her teeth, but smiled and continued to hold the glass of alcohol to her nose. "Yes. That's wonderful, sweetie. We chatted at the bar. He and the officer are going to talk for a bit outside." She shooed Dietrich away with her hands like he was a child. "They were just leaving."

Sara clasped her hands together and inched closer to Mere. "He's kind of cute…and single." She glanced at Dietrich and opened her mouth. "Mr. Wolfgang, my mom wants to dance with you."

Mere gasped. "*Sara*, I do—"

"I'd love to." Dietrich took Mere's hand. "Miss Kilpatrick, we've experienced the bar together. Let's see if the dance floor will be more productive."

If fire could have flamed from every pore in Mere's body, it would have by the amount of crimson that overtook every visible inch of her.

Swiftly, he led her to the dance floor before her mouth started working again. He pivoted and twirled her out and then in, wrapping her up in his arms.

The woman somehow kept the drink under her nose from spilling.

Unbelievable. How are you standing on your own?

She inhaled and swallowed hard.

"No throwing up on me, darling," he whispered. "Do you think you can hold it together?"

She squeezed his hand like a vise and let go, dropping her hand from his. "Keep your mangy hands off my ass and stop acting like your lack of sight gives you the right to touch women inappropriately. I may be drunk, but do not fuck with me."

Dietrich focused on the feisty brunette sweating in her pretty purple dress, talking trash, and sniffing her alcoholic beverage.

She swayed on her feet, but somehow gathered enough balance to remain inches from him without a single, delicate touch of her flesh.

"You can't hold that drink and dance with me,"

he whispered.

She held up her empty hand with her index finger up. "Hush." She drank the shot and extended her hand, holding the glass toward Lainie. "Tell the bartender to have another drink ready for me."

Lainie sighed and took the glass. "I'm cutting you off."

Mere stuck out her tongue. "You're no fun."

Lainie laughed. "Sara and Ethan are leaving in a few minutes. Don't make a scene. You and alcohol don't mix."

Mere slouched. "Killjoy."

Dietrich grinned. *I think I actually love you. You're not at all what you seem.*

Lainie shook her head and walked off the dance floor with Luke beside her.

Mere tilted her head to the side and the raw fury in her eyes lessened. "Are you legally blind? Can you drive? Did you know you were grabbing my ass?"

The softer side of her voice called to his beast.

"I can drive, although I don't. It's safer that way." He held back from explaining his sight was fine, but when his wolf's power surfaced his eyes changed to more of a snow white, making him look blind, but they allowed him to see spiritual and energy variances others lived their entire lives unaware of. "I'm sorry I got touchy with you, even though you were talking dirty to me."

She shuddered. "Don't do it again." The bold red in her face drained to a lighter shade of pink. "Do you need me to lead, so you don't bump into anyone?"

My sight is better than yours. He offered his hand to

her. "Following isn't really my thing. I'll keep you safe from everyone else's unwanted touch."

She placed her small hand in his. A jolt of electricity like none he'd ever felt before struck the center of his heart at her tender touch.

The gentle strumming of a guitar resounded from the speakers. A sorrowful female voice filled the room.

"One moment you were with me. One moment you were gone…" the woman sang. "One chance to be your lover. One dream vanished before dawn…"

He tugged at her hand, and she stepped into his personal space.

She curled her hands around the back collar of his white shirt. "Do not make me regret this."

He slid his hands to the small of her back and nudged her closer. "No regrets, beautiful."

She inhaled and softened against him.

"Your voice. Your lips. Your kiss. I'll cherish…" the woman sang.

Meredith raised her chin and the haze of the mating trance covered her gorgeous eyes. "You're not part fish, are you?"

"No," he chuckled. *Are you fascinated by the men of the sea?*

"You smell so dang good," she mumbled. "I want to touch you."

"Do it," he whispered. *You want me. I want you. Yet, you resist. Why?*

Her hands glided down his arms at her back and lingered at the cuffs.

Almost there. Slide your wrists into my hand behind your back. Surrender. I will reward you with a—

Electricity sizzled down to the tips of his toes and dove into the depths of his beast's spirit as her fingers grazed the inside of his wrists along the heels of his palms.

Vibrant colors exploded around him in layers of turbulent waves. Thousands of intricate ripples of intense energy unlike any he'd experienced flowed into him. A vision from *her* moved through his mind.

Her fingers played with the top button of a man's white dress shirt.

"Stop teasing," the man ordered. "Kiss me again."

"Stop ordering." One by one she unbuttoned his shirt, revealing pale skin that had never seen the light of day. "You don't have to be in control all the time."

"I do." He clasped her hands. "It's important I'm the one always in absolute control."

She pressed her black T-shirt covered chest against his and gazed into the black soulless eyes of a feral werewolf. "No matter how good you smell. No matter how sexy or how much I want you…I will never surrender to you."

"I love a challenge."

"I love to win." She slipped her hand behind her and pulled out a knife. She stabbed the man over and over and over but the wounds healed within seconds of each of her attacks.

She lost strength in her arms and her heart stopped beating.

He pushed her away and laughed. "It takes more than a little pin prick to hurt me, honey."

Her body jerked with the return of her heartbeat. The pain of survival hunkered down and held her in its tight grip. Bruised but determined, she stood up on unsteady legs and nodded. "I know." She inhaled and blew out the air in her lungs. "See, the thing is, I'm cursed—"

"You're not cursed. You're my mate."

She lifted her finger and shook her head. "Don't interrupt me." Her lips trembled and her chin crinkled as her heart fluttered in and out of an erratic rhythm. "I'm cursed with the compatibility gene with your kind, really all kinds—werewolves, vampires, witches, et cetera—but I'm mated to only one. He happens to be a werewolf. You ain't that one. I warned you last time to stop hunting me, but you didn't listen."

He strode toward her, his body cracking and popping with the slow metamorphosis of an infected werewolf. "You will either die or become my mate."

"There is the rub, I've already died today. I'd prefer not to do it again." She leaped at him, and with her rapid burst of movement wide ribbons of red and black energy waves exploded outward from her small body.

Unlike any other human, she landed with incredible precision. One blow to the head and he went down. Blood splattered everywhere…The heart removed… The head separated…Body dragged and thrown in the sunken fireplace.

Blue flames wicked up the sides of the stone hearth, incinerating the remains of the diseased werewolf. "You were the last one…The last one."

"Not the last one," a man's voice said. "You're marked, sweet girl. You've got the blood curse on you—mate to one, compatible with all. You will fall in love, but never know real love in return. They'll continue to come one by one, two by two. You have to keep moving."

A dark-skinned elderly man with white hair walked barefoot into the room. He carried a pair of crisp jeans and a camo T-shirt matching his clothes. "The larger the city the more places to hide. You're no longer welcome *here. Take your kin and go."*

The ache in her bones hit her harder physically, but the emotional devastation resulting from his words was the pain that brought her to her knees. "Please, at least keep Sara. She's your kin too. Protect her."

"Ain't no keeping that child safe as long as you're alive. They'll come for her to get to you. They'll smell your blood running through her veins. They'll end up killing her, me, and her granny. I love her, but you should have let her die with her momma and my son. I shouldn't have given her a transfusion of your blood to save her from that nasty bite. If you stay, our deaths would be on you." His dark gaze dropped from hers. "You don't deserve that extra burden. You have to go. Now."

The vision ended.

She froze in his arms. Rigid fingers held the cotton fabric of his shirt open, baring his chest. He glanced around the room as he mentally checked his wolves for any indication they saw the vision too.

Nothing…until he heard Ethan's voice.

Mere's dangerous, Ethan said to Jack through their pack link as Dietrich eavesdropped on them. *Something is wrong. Sara won't talk to me. She's staring at Mere and mumbling, "Please don't kill him. Please don't kill everyone. I finally got you away from Jeremy. Please don't bring him back into our lives. Not now. Not here."*

"It can't be you," Mere mumbled. She pressed her cheek to his chest as her hands left a web of desire on his flesh as they traversed the hard muscles of his abs. She unbuckled his belt and slid her hand over the front of his slacks and outlined his bulge. "You're not one of them. None of you are." Her hot lips kissed the center of his chest. "I bet you could wear me out in bed."

He slid his fingers into the back of her hair and made a fist. He gave her no indication he saw the vision. "Please tell me you like sex gentle *and* rough."

Shudders surged through his body as her tongue licked along the right side of his collarbone. "Be careful what you wish for."

He jerked her head back and gazed into half-trance and half-calculating eyes. "What are you planning?"

"You want me?"

"Hell, yeah."

"You're never going to have me." She kicked him in the nuts.

"Fuck!" His vision darkened, and he let go of her.

The tapping of her heels on the wooden platform along with the light vibration of the floor signaled her rushed exit.

"Sara, we have to leave. We can't—"

"Sara is my wife," Ethan said. "*You* aren't responsible for her anymore. I am."

Sara stepped in front of Ethan. She held her hands out in front of her and waved them from side to side, pleading. "He didn't mean it that way, Momma. I swear he didn't."

The officer joined them. "What's going on?"

"Arrest the man on the dance floor. He shoved my head against his nasty chest and pulled my hair. I have whiplash from his manhandling." Mere turned toward Dietrich and pointed. "I'm pressing charges. I don't care who he thinks he is. No one is above the law."

Chapter Seven

Facing the wall inside a one-cell jail, Meredith stared at a portion of a desert mural encompassing the entire room. A lone white wolf howled at the rising full moon in the distance. Levels of medium and dark grays draped down from the ceiling and blended into gloomy blue hues around the shadow-filled moon. Bright silver stars peeked through the darkness as if they waited to show their brilliance until the last warm colors of the sun faded. Burnt orange shimmered in a thin layer above the golden sand of the Arizona desert.

I should be in bed, but no. I'm stuck in tight quarters with Mr. Sexy Merman, and I have to apologize to the jerk in order to get out.

"You can't ignore me forever," Dietrich announced.

"You lied to them." She focused on the sparkling silver stars painted above the moon instead of the alluring scent making every damn inch of her boil and perspire.

"You did too." His deep voice made her want to drop her panties and get him naked on the cot in the corner.

"I'm not your fiancée. We were not role playing some kind of kinky fantasy. That was my daughter's reception." *If you hadn't shown up, I would have stayed drunk and alone at the bar until it was over. You ruined it. I am never apologizing to you.*

She crossed her arms over her chest and squeezed her legs together to quell the need for a naked Dietrich riding the curves of her body…hard.

"You mean your niece's reception," he corrected her. "The secret is no longer a secret, darling."

The soft sound of his bare feet padding on the cement floor forced her gaze to wander downward as he drew near.

"Don't come any closer." She quickly pivoted away from the man who short-circuited her brain. *I'm either going to hurt you in a very bad way or get all sexy crazy with you under the watchful eyes of whoever mans the cameras.*

"Mere," he whispered in her ear without actually touching her. "Let's start over now that you're semi-sober."

More like stone-cold sober, horny, and angry. "I'm not kissing you. I mean, I'm not apologizing."

"Then we're never getting out of here." He exhaled along her neck. Her hair drifted over her shoulder, uncovering the area she wanted him to caress, to lick, to kiss. "I'll accept one heartfelt apology and then maybe you'll accept mine. We'll be able to leave without anything going on a report. We're lucky we're in Ulvene county limits, or we'd be waiting for bail to be set and facing contempt charges…among other things."

I have to be at work in three hours. I can't miss my

first day. I'll lose my job, and there is no other place in town hiring a massage therapist with fabulous recommendations from clients but horrible ones from bosses. Heck, there's no other spas in this one-horse town. I'm screwed.

She rolled her eyes, and the most unapologetic tone came out of her mouth. "Sorry."

He chuckled. "I don't see a guard letting us out for that lame attempt. You're going to have to do better. I'd consider a kiss since words seem to be a sticking point with you. If not, I could take a nap. I sleep in the nude."

She spun around and poked his bare chest. "You're not taking off any more clothes." She gazed up at his smiling lips. *You goad and I fall for it every damn time. I'm never this gullible.*

"Keep assaulting me, sweetheart." He opened his arms. "I see freedom in my future. Not so sure you'll be seeing the outside of this cell anytime soon."

The door to the room opened, and she scrambled around him to the bars locking her inside. "Hey, can I leave?"

Lainie strode in wearing jeans and a red T-shirt with "I Love Georgia" written in black on the front. "Apologize, Mere." She leaned in and whispered. "Find a way to make up. The guard watching you was one of the guests at the reception. He's upset Dietrich has apologized and you haven't. The man saw you"— she cleared her throat—"on the dance floor, getting close and dang near giving Dietrich a hand job. End this however you can. We all heard him apologize to you. Stop being pigheaded."

The door swung open.

Luke stood at the threshold wearing jeans and

an army green shirt with "I Love Nevada" in black. "This needs to stop. Everyone's upset. I've got all the Ulvenes carrying on about some sexual scene play shit going down at the wedding reception."

"There was no scene play." Mere slammed her hands against the bars. "I was stressed and drunk. None of this is my fault." *All of this is my fault. He touched, and I wanted. God, I want him.* She pulled at the bars. *I never should have left Georgia.* "I need. Out. Of. Here."

His hands covered hers around the metal rods. "I was rude. I'm sorry I was a jerk when we first met. I had a difficult day and took it out on you."

Her heart stopped beating, and the pain that always accompanied the rhythmic shift weakened her. She slumped, but he caught her and lifted her into his arms.

"What happened?" he whispered.

She inhaled and her heart erratically started beating out of control. In the past, she'd recovered quickly and her heart started pumping at a steady, normal beat. In the last twenty-four hours, nothing seemed or acted normal. "I have heart issues." *Understatement.*

He sat down on the bed bolted to the cement floor. "What kind of heart issues?"

Without the strength or the will to get up, she stayed in the comfort of his arms. "My heart stops beating for seconds, sometimes minutes, before it starts back up again. I'm not a candidate for a pacemaker, and I'm allergic to anesthesia."

"I accept your lack of apology," Dietrich said. "I'm going to kiss you so they think you apologized and we've made up. Don't punch me."

"Not…" She struggled to breathe. "…done… recovering."

His lips met hers and a vision bloomed.

She lay naked under him on a private beach at night. Her legs tangled with his.

The chilly low tide splashed their warm feet. His mouth covered hers. The tip of his tongue slid along the edges of her teeth.

She opened her mouth and joined him in an intimate kiss. Heat flared inside her…

His lips left hers. "That was us. Our future. I'm going to make sure we have it."

"You saw that?" she asked, panting. *I want a future like that, but it's a dream. I will never fall in love again. Not with a human. And you will never love me in return. No one does.*

"Us, making love on the beach. Yes." He mumbled something in another language. He pressed his mouth to hers, and the vision continued.

She curled her legs around his thighs as he thrust. His cock tunneled deep inside her.

Ocean waves rushed over their legs as if tuned into the rhythm of their bodies joining as one.

"I love you," he whispered. "Only you. Forever." He rolled over and carried her along until she lay atop him.

She pushed up against his chest and gazed down where they remained joined. Her paw print birthmark on her belly sparkled a beautiful silver, matching his glittery skin…

She gasped for air as if she'd been drowning in the very ocean she'd envisioned.

His fingers held the sides of her thong. She sat straddling him on the bed and rolled her pussy over his huge bulge. "I don't know what that—"

"That is our future," he said as if he believed it.

She shook her head. *No. Something is wrong. I want you in a way that's different. Different than Jeremy. Only werewolves fall in love in seconds. You can't be one of them. You can't.*

She climbed off him. "Apology accepted. It's time to go." She adjusted her dress and grabbed her heels.

"We'll take this back to my room." He grabbed his shirt and slipped into his shoes.

A man she recognized from the reception unlocked the door to their cell and held it. "Glad you two worked things out. Have a great morning."

She hurried out of the cell and strode through the small squad room with Dietrich by her side.

The desert breeze that had evaded her before nearly knocked her over. Dietrich caught her once again before she tumbled to the ground. "You're coming home with me."

"I have a life and things to do. I'm not playing house with you."

Luke sat in the driver's seat of his white SUV idling in the parking lot. He rolled down the window. "Mere, climb in."

Dietrich walked her to the car and opened the back door. "We're staying at the same hotel. We'll ride together." He helped her in, joined her, and closed the door.

"Luke, do you know where my cell phone is? My purse?" Mere settled on the other side of the backseat as far away as possible from the sexy man she wasn't going to fuck. "How angry is Sara?"

"Lainie has your purse," Luke answered. "Your

cellphone is being charged. Sara isn't really thinking about you right now. She left for her honeymoon thirty minutes ago."

All the air exited Mere's lungs. *I didn't talk birth control with her. I should have bought her condoms or something. She's not even gotten her period yet. She'll probably get it now.* She leaned back against the tan leather seat. "She's going to get pregnant."

"You say that like it's a bad thing." Luke pulled onto the main road leading to The Ulvene Howl at the Moon Hotel.

"What is with you and his family?" Mere said. "She's eighteen. She's a kid. She doesn't need to be a mom so young."

"She'll be a great mother," Luke huffed.

"She will. She…" *She thinks she can do anything and everything she wants. Babies are vulnerable and need constant care.*

Mere turned and gazed into Dietrich's eyes. "Do you understand what I mean? It's not that she can't do it. I don't understand the rush." *Sara is too impulsive. She has so little control normally, and she's been crazy since she met Ethan. Waiting for a couple years might mature her enough that a baby would be a wonderful addition to their family. But now? No. She doesn't need the pressure of caring for a child. She's a child herself.*

"She and Ethan would have help," Dietrich said. "Our family is large, and we're very close. When one of us needs something, a team of people come to the rescue and stay as long as needed. Sara will never be alone. She and Ethan can decide what is best for their future. There's nothing to worry about." He cradled the back of her head with one hand and took off his glasses.

She blinked, and she somehow ended up in the stairwell of the hotel with her legs cinched around his waist. He strode up the stairs to the top floor.

With her arms curled around him and her lips pressed against his neck, she squeezed her pussy muscles to stop some of the sensual hunger rumbling inside.

"I want a baby with you," he whispered. He stopped outside an unmarked room. "Let's go inside and make one."

She inhaled, and her logical mind screamed at her to get the heck out of his arms and run as far away as she could go, but hope for a future of unconditional love instead of curses grew inside her soul.

He opened the door and strode through a golden foyer, passed by a formal living room, down a hallway and into a grand master bedroom with a king-sized sleigh bed.

Photos of him with Luke, and more pictures of him, Luke, and Lainie's friend Michael Flanagan from Atlanta were displayed on built-in shelves on the right side of the room. Leather-bound books, sketch pads, and intricately woven baskets filled out the expensive décor.

"What is this place?" *How often do you come here?*

"Luke and I own this hotel. This is where I live when I visit. Do you like it?" He supported her as he climbed onto the bed.

"Do you visit the Ulvenes often?" *If sex with you is awful, will I have to see you all the time?*

The small town of Ulvene remained the wealthiest county in all of Arizona for three hundred years, and the population remained pretty much the same, too. When people moved in, they stayed forever or left within two months—at least that's what her new boss told her when the woman insisted on a three-month contract. But, since it was such a small, close-knit community, Mere'd probably run into the same people all the time.

"I visit regularly." He unbuttoned the top few buttons on his dress shirt and pulled it over his head.

She drew her bottom lip into her mouth to stop from moaning over his ripped abs. *Maybe running into you here and there might not be so bad. A sexy look from you might send me into orgasmic bliss. We'd never even have to touch.*

"We'll live and raise our children in Germany, but I promise we'll visit here often," he said.

"Yeah," she mumbled. Her thoughts seemed slow on the uptake. His lips moved, but she couldn't for the life of her remember anything he said. *I want that mouth between my legs.*

"Have you had much sex?" He unzipped his black slacks. "I don't want to hold back."

"I…" *What? Hold back?*

He pushed down his slacks and let go. The black material seemed to caress his legs on the way down and pooled at his feet.

She blinked and swallowed hard. "You must live in a gym." *I sound like an idiot.*

He chuckled. "I live a healthy lifestyle."

"I can see that." *Jeremy lives a healthy lifestyle full of schedules and rules to follow. You're like Jeremy, but you're human. You're fragile. I can't have forever with you.*

The man lived in another country and *vis-*

ited Ulvene. He would expect hookups when he dropped in. She didn't do regular hookups. If Jeremy found out about Dietrich, Jeremy would make a *visit* to Germany to see Dietrich, and the Ulvenes would lose their beloved family member. "We're moving too fast. I…"

He fisted his cock and the length seemed to grow.

Damn. Not even sexy Luke Wolfson has a body as powerful and god-like as you. I want you. I want—

"Take off your dress," he ordered.

She held the zipper at the back of her neck with her fingers. *I can't bring him into my life. I can't be responsible for what might happen if Jeremy shows up unexpectedly or a pack of feral werewolves comes through town hunting me.*

"This is a mistake. Sorry. I—I can't." She rolled off the bed and ran out of the room, away from her feelings and a man she couldn't control.

CHAPTER EIGHT

THE SECLUDED CABIN IN THE desert Jeremy and Dietrich had constructed together hundreds of years ago had been the house all the area settlers wished they had. Through the years, Dietrich called Jeremy to help make additions and update the place where Dietrich planned to plant the private army of werewolf warriors. Being the adopted son of the World Alpha had its perks, but dealing with Dietrich on a home designed for the Ulvene bloodline of the Alpha's beloved sister…the man wanted what he wanted, the way he wanted it. Everything in it had to be made by hand, from the cutting of the logs, to the making of the pipes, to the mixing of the mortar. The man mixed and poured his own concrete.

Jeremy watched Sara stand in front of the window of the bedroom upstairs. *They should be fucking like rabbits. This is not a normal mating. Not at all.*

Nicholas moaned into his cellphone. "Baby, I can make all your fantasies come true." The man slid his hand under his slacks and cupped his cock. "Yeah?" His eyes tracked Sara's movements. "I've got work to do, but I'll be back in the morning." He ended the call and stared at his phone. He swiped through the texts. "No one likes Sara. They don't see what I see in her."

"You've taken the most insolent vampires and turned them into some of the best warriors, doctors, and educators. I don't see Sara like you do, but I trust you. As much as I hate the girl, you and Mere love her. Youth isn't an excuse anymore. She—" Jeremy's phone buzzed. *Sara.* He tapped the speaker and answered. "Hey, Sara. I heard you married a werewolf. How's that working out?"

"It's going to be great as soon as we get to fucking," Sara said. "And you know what?"

"What?" Jeremy watched as Ethan, Jack, and Luke cocked their heads and looked up at the room Sara stood in above them. *They can hear you, little girl.*

"Mom is over you. So over you she's getting it on in a hotel room with a hot guy as we speak." She fake laughed. "Get it? He's hot. You're cold."

"Ha, ha." Jeremy replied. *I hate you. I fucking hate you.* "When are you going to mate with your big bad Ethan Ulvene?" He looked over at his best friend.

Chartreuse glowed in Nicholas's eyes. The man was not going to take her mating or death well. But both their lives would be better with Sara out of it. Let the Ulvenes deal with the bitch. With any luck, she wouldn't make it through the transition.

Please don't make it through. Meredith will have no reason to stay and no reason to avoid turning. Jeremy grabbed his dick and squeezed. *Whatever happens to you, whether Nicholas turns you or you become one of them or you choose the afterlife, Mere will be mine. She will finally be mine.*

"In a few hours we'll be at the cabin where all the Mating Ceremonies are done in this Pack. Mom will never know what I've become. She'll never know what Ethan is. Best of all, you will never see her again."

"Really?" *I see you in the window, liar. You will learn not to lie to Nicholas, if you end up one of us.*

"Yes, *really*. Mom believes everything I tell her. She will never step foot in Atlanta again."

"Mere will be back home and living with me where she belongs, and your betrayal will send her there. I really should thank you for being such a conniving bitch. You're in for an awakening you can't even imagine. What are you going to do when Nicholas shows up at your love fest? Have you told Ethan you're no longer a virgin? That you can't have children? Have you told your husband you've been—"

"Nicholas is not coming and you know it." She lifted the window and stuck her head out. She peered from side to side. The pulse in her neck throbbed.

You're caught. Vampires and warrior werewolves punish liars, cheats, and the unfaithful. "Nicholas is watching you now," Jeremy hissed. He ended the call.

"When I get through with her, she will never deceive anyone again." Nicholas held his hand on the car door handle.

"I'm counting on it," Jeremy said.

Sara ran downstairs and stood with her back to the window. She pulled Ethan into a kiss and the mating process Jeremy understood well began.

"How long do we have until she is made into

one of them?" Nicholas hissed. "I can't turn her if she's a werewolf."

"Her spirit will shift and try to form into beast. She's too weak to take on a beast," Jeremy said.

With Sara on a course to self-destruct, Nicholas on a mission to save her, and Mere left in the dark about it all, Jeremy needed permission from the only man who could stop him from turning Sara into a vampire. He bit the bullet and took a different approach with the World Alpha. He texted.

World Alpha,

I'm in Ulvene County. I could use your help in a delicate situation. My Army General is in love with Sara Kilpatrick – Ethan Ulvene's wife – and neither of us believes she will make it through the mating ceremony. If things go bad, I need your permission to turn her. I'll assume no response to the contrary, within one minute from you, means we have your approval to intervene.

-Jeremy, Vampire King

He hated texting Dietrich. Hated even more using the old wolf's tactics—lack of communication gives permission. He'd never done it before, but as much as he hated it, Mere loved Sara, and his General was Soulburned by the girl. He had no other choice but to push the boundaries.

"She's downstairs," Nicholas hissed.

"Sixty seconds for an answer," Jeremy said. He stared at his phone. *Don't answer. Don't answer. Don't answer.*

The light flashed with a text.

Do what you have to do.

-WA

"Holy shit," Jeremy mumbled. *He hates her too.* "It's a go. It's a go."

Nicholas ran like the planets were about to collide and the world would end unless he got to her in time.

Ethan bit into Sara's flesh, starting the part of the sacred ceremony no one was allowed to stop.

Jeremy halted him at the door.

"It's started," Jeremy said. "We can't interrupt."

"Please, my King. Please?" Nicholas pleaded in a whisper barely audible to their exceptional hearing.

Jeremy shook his head. He drew his best friend into an embrace. "Close your eyes and connect to her soul. If you two are truly Soulburned, she will shed her aura layers until a golden light absorbs her. She'll ascend. I'll ask if she wants to return, and if she loves you the way you love her, she will come back to you."

"She will," he mumbled.

"You'll take a quick taste and test her for wolf toxicity, but I believe no wolf spirit will enter her. She's with an Ulvene and they would infuse a warrior wolf into her spirit. She doesn't possess any of Mere's strength, not even with the transfusion Mere gave her a long time ago..."

Shit. Ethan isn't mated to Sara. He smells Mere inside her. The faintest drop of Mere's blood from close to eighteen years ago would send a mating call to a wolf that is highly compatible with her. Sara and Ethan's attraction is a false mating. Dietrich must know it. The World Alpha must know something isn't right with the couple. The blood will tell. The bite will send her to the other side.

"She's so fragile," Nicholas whispered. "I need her."

"You'll have her," Jeremy whispered. *She will love*

you more. So much more than anyone in this world or afterlife.

The shadow of death covered the cabin until the gray spirit exited the building and stopped beside them.

"I'm sorry. I love you, Nicholas, but I have to see my mom. I have to make her promise to protect Ethan. She has to save him…" The spirit floated along the path. *"I wished for forever with you, Nicholas."*

"You can have forever," Jeremy said. "I'll call your spirit back."

"Yes," the spirit answered. *"Call me back. I love—"*

Jeremy opened the door and walked into a rush of confusion.

Sara's body lay in Luke Wolfson's arms. Jack stood beside Luke. Lainie stood on the other side of Luke comforting the young werewolf.

Luke's head jerked toward Jeremy, recognition appearing in his eyes. "Jack, we've got a major problem."

"We're taking over from here," Jeremy said. He nodded at Luke and swept his hand to Nicholas to move in and start turning her. "The World Alpha gave me permission to save her life. Nicholas will take Sara now."

In a flash of black, Nicholas held her with his mouth on her neck and his teeth in her jugular. In another flash, he and Sara vanished.

Jeremy nodded once more at Luke. "There will be some problems with Ethan for a short period of time, if he is strong enough to live through her turning. It is up to him whether he will join us in my Coven while he attempts recovery from an incomplete mating ceremony. It might help him to be near her. It might make the pain worse. He might die anyway. Depends upon which bonds linked to her soul and which didn't."

The three of them stared at him without saying a word.

Jeremy tapped his foot. *I have places to be and Meredith to tell. Finally, she'll come home and accept the inevitability of becoming a vampire. We'll have a family. The Coven will rejoice. We'll have many children. My life will be exactly the way I want it.*

"Where's Sara?" Ethan glanced around. His nostrils flared wide. He tilted his head right and left. One of his ears sprouted fur and grew into a wolf's while the rest of him stayed human. "I hear her. She smells different."

Jeremy threw up his hands. *You're stupid, Ethan. Haven't you ever—no, I suppose you haven't. I bet none of you have. Only Dietrich has been around long enough to know how a turning works or to have witnessed one.* "She's been changed into a vampire. She now smells more like Nicholas than anything or anyone else. Are you coming or not?"

"She's a vampire?" Ethan gasped. "That's not possible. It takes days to transform into one. Wait, she's poisonous to you. She's part werewolf."

"The turning of a human can be very quick with a vampire who is *mature*. She remained human and rejected the mating and the wolf, *your wolf*." *Not everyone wants to be one of you people.* Jeremy texted the leader of Nicholas's security unit to come get them and bring an extra car.

"I'm coming," Ethan said. "She's my wife. You…" The youth went on about his responsibilities as her mate and husband. Neither of her statuses in their world mattered. The girl was Nicholas's to do with what he pleased. Lucky for Sara, Nicholas wanted her for his wife, not for his army.

Taking a play from Sara's book, Jeremy rolled his eyes. "Whatever. I'm only extending the offer because World Alpha cares about you. So, are you coming to Atlanta with Nicholas and his soon-to-be wife or not?"

The kid wobbled as he took a step, but he continued on. Whatever bonds he'd completed with Sara would be a bitch to remove, even after Sara fully recovered from the trauma of both ceremonies. Keeping Ethan alive would keep Dietrich happy, and keeping Dietrich happy made Jeremy's life less complicated.

"Coming," Ethan mumbled.

"Okay, pup." Jeremy picked the big kid up and tossed him over his shoulder in a fireman's hold. "He'll check in with someone."

"I'm coming with him," Jack said.

"We'll set up a room for you and your wife. This is going to be miserable for your boy. He'll need lots of support in the next few weeks." Jeremy walked slower than he preferred while Jack gathered Ethan's bags.

"I can walk," Ethan said. The slight wiggle the kid attempted didn't even loosen Jeremy's hold.

"Yeah, whatever makes you feel good, pup." Jeremy patted him on the legs. "You will hurt like you've never hurt before. You will cry like you've never cried before. You will have to connect to another wolf, one you trust and admire. You will have to latch onto that wolf and trust that lone wolf to save you as if he or she were your mate,

your soul connection, and your lifeline forever –
because that wolf will be those things for eternity."

"Are you going to try to turn my son?" Jack
asked.

"No, Jack. We don't accept *wolves* into our
Coven." *The World Alpha would have to sanction it
and the wolf would have to be like Mere, an anomaly,
compatible with all alternate beings who conceive like
humans. My Mere would never become one of them. She
hates them. She'll hate them even more when she finds
out the truth.*

CHAPTER NINE

THE HOT PINK ROOM WITH neon green trim did nothing to set the mood for relaxation. The thunderstorm music set to burst-your-eardrum volume by the gray-and-purple-haired owner made tears form in Mere's eyes. The ocean fragrance following her around like a special oxygen source only she could breathe had her new hypersensitive emotions pushing against her calm exterior.

One last stroke and I'm done for the day.

Mere inhaled and visions of Dietrich standing above her naked with those intense eyes staring at her like he wanted to rock her world appeared everywhere she looked. Wet panties rubbed uncomfortably against her pussy as she adjusted her shoulder-width stance even wider. She closed her eyes, forced her naughty thoughts of Dietrich into the background, and focused on the task at hand.

The long line of muscles of her client's back softened like butter under her touch. She added a slow, gentle circle above his hips to loosen more of the tight muscle as a treat for putting up with the extreme sounds and colors of the room. A gentle caress along the defined trail leading up to his neck connected his body to his mind once again, and produced a deep cleansing breath for both of them. She silently prayed for health and healing as she held her hands at the base of his skull, then she released contact.

The loud music abruptly ended.

"Damn," her client sighed. "I heard you were good, but they lied. You're great. I don't think I can move."

She chuckled. *And this is one of the reasons I love my job.* "Take a minute and breathe a few cycles before you move from the massage table." She pumped hand sanitizer into her hands and rubbed. "I'll see you in the reception area."

"Thanks, Mere."

She exited the room into the neon orange hallway and walked past the other massage room and into the living room of the three-room cinderblock house her boss called a spa. She'd done massages in tight spaces, with and without music, but this took the cake for the most difficult atmosphere to work in.

The owner peered behind the high counter. "Turn that music back on."

"No," a man who sounded like Dietrich said.

Her heartbeat tripled and electricity seemed to crackle in the room. *He can't be here.*

The gorgeous man she spent most of the night in jail with appeared from behind the purple laminate counter wearing black basketball shorts, a matching dri-fit athletic shirt, and a black baseball cap.

He adjusted his black rectangular glasses and met her gaze.

"There she is." Dietrich strode around the fluffy owner and across the room. "Ready for a bite to eat?" He offered his hands to her.

She swallowed down the desire to curl around his luscious body and satisfy the craving to finish what they'd started in his hotel room. "Uh, no?" She placed her hands in his. "What are you doing here?"

He guided her forward against his front. "We have dinner reservations." He brought her hands behind her back and held her. "I see you're more old-fashioned when it comes to sex. How many dates before we start making babies?"

"I don't even know what to say to that." *Why am I listening to you?*

"Dietrich Wolfgang? That can't be you," her client said. "I had no idea you were still in town."

Saved by the client whose name she couldn't remember, Mere moved away from Dietrich and strode toward the thirty-year-old man. "Hey, how are you feeling?"

"I'm here for a little while." Dietrich joined them. "Are you still coming in from Tucson once a week and working out with Jack?"

"You know it," the man said. "He nearly killed me this morning, but after Mere's massage, I feel like I could take on the world."

"My Mere does that to people," Dietrich said. "But she's not going to be working here much longer. She is moving to Germany with me."

"Congratulations," her client said. He ignored her and man-hugged Dietrich. "Jack mentioned you'd met someone. He told me all about the night in jail you orchestrated for a kiss." He slapped Dietrich on the back. "That was thinking outside the box. But he never mentioned marriage. I'm losing my wingman."

The man pivoted to her and grinned. "You are marrying the best guy I've ever known. When and where is the wedding?"

Mere's mouth dropped open.

"You're moving?" Mere's boss gasped. "You signed a three-month contract."

"Uh." She stood flabbergasted and frozen. The only man she ever wanted to marry was Jeremy Hunter, and she would have, if he had shown up at the church.

"I'm suing you for breach of contract," her boss said.

Mere shook her head. "I'm not moving or getting married. I'm here. I'm staying. I'm buying a house near my daughter."

The client winced. "Gun shy over a divorce?"

"No. I've never been married." Mere's voice rose from sheer frustration. "You're not losing your wingman or whatever it is y'all do together."

"You're done here," her boss said. "Don't come back tomorrow."

Mere walked to the crazy middle-aged lady who got her to sign a decent contract but had lied about the location and the shape of the spa. "Don't go threatening me."

"You were late." The woman backed up and swung her hip out as her hand landed on it.

Mere cracked her knuckles and clenched her hands into fists. *You want to get real with me? I'll show you real.* "Your clocks are fifteen minutes fast. I was not late. I. Was. Early."

The woman gasped. "They are not."

"They sure are, and I know you do it to charge the clients a late fee. It's outrageous. And you didn't renovate or do anything to this place except upgrade the sound system to make my ears bleed," Mere screamed.

"You're fired," the woman shouted as she cornered herself behind the reception desk. "F-I-R-E-D. Fired."

Mere grabbed her purse from the cubby under the counter and strode to the door, past the guys who stared but didn't say a word. She glanced back at her ex-boss as she opened the door to leave. "I'm reporting you to the Massage Board. Fuck. You."

She walked outside into the darkness, the moon and stars the only light because the stupid streetlamp outside the "spa" was broken. *And this is why I can't seem to keep a damn job for more than three months. I can't bring myself to apologize when I'm in the right or keep my dang mouth shut.*

She turned the corner and continued walking down the empty street two blocks off the main strip. If Sara hadn't met Ethan, she could have lived in Tempe while Sara went to the massage school there. Mere could have worked at a nice spa and Jeremy might have moved with her to live with her for a year. But no. Sara had to fall in love with the son of one of the richest men in the entire country. And, they had to own a county in the middle of nowhere with one stinking spa and one fitness center where they had a room for a massage therapist, but none worked. The Ulvene Training

Facility had a worse reputation for retaining massage therapists than Mere did in keeping jobs.

A dark sedan drove past her and made a U-turn. She walked closer to the inside of the sidewalk along the line of empty lots slated for construction.

The passenger window rolled down.

Mere picked up her pace and tried to ignore the car hovering in her peripheral vision.

"Meredith?" Paulina Ulvene leaned over the passenger seat. "Is that you?"

Mere turned her head toward the car barely moving beside her. "Hey, Paulina. How are you?"

"I'm fine. Why aren't you with Dietrich?" She stopped the car.

Mere exhaled. *You people are everywhere.*

She walked over and stood by the passenger window. "Things didn't work out with my job or with Dietrich. Have you heard from Ethan? I tried calling Sara earlier, but she's not answering her phone. Where are they?" *If something happens, I need to get to her. I need to know that her first time with a man was a good one. That Ethan was gentle…*

Paulina's warm smile settled some of Mere's nervousness about her daughter's well-being. "They're at the cabin in the desert where Jack and I had our honeymoon forever ago. He sent word that they arrived safe and sound, and not to worry if they didn't contact anyone for a few days."

"That's all well and good, but I need to talk to Sara," Mere said. *I need to hear her voice.* "I want a phone number and address where she can be—"

Her phone vibrated in her back pocket. She grabbed it and stared at the screen. *Jeremy.* "I've got to take this. I'll talk to you later." She swiped her finger across the screen and held the phone to her ear. "Hey."

"How are things in Ulvene?" Jeremy asked.

"Yeah, well, about that…" *I should have told you I wasn't in Tempe, but everything was so…* She turned from Paulina's car and stepped away from the curb. "Moving has been one clusterfuck after another. Sara is gone. Something weird is going on with me. I miss…" *I miss you so much.*

"Meredith," Jeremy whispered softly. "This isn't the best place to settle down, my love."

"Mere, let me drive you home," Paulina said.

"Hang on a sec." Mere placed her phone against her thigh and turned around to face the car. "Paulina, I'll have to chat later. Can you tell Ethan to have Sara send me a text or something with her location? It's important."

"Sure," Paulina said. "Give her until tomorrow."

"Tonight, or I'm going out looking for that cabin you don't want to talk about," Mere demanded. *Sara must have them all keeping her hideaway a secret so I don't show up. I won't show up. I just…Ugh. That girl is going to be the death of me.*

"Okay," Paulina said.

A beige SUV pulled up beside her as Paulina drove away.

Mere turned around and walked down the street. She quickly brought the phone to her ear. "Hey. Sorry."

"I didn't realize Sara was marrying Jack Ulvene's son. She didn't tell you about them, did she?"

"Meredith," Dietrich shouted.

"Who's that?" Jeremy asked.

"Some pain in my ass," Mere mumbled. She

glanced over her shoulder at the man she couldn't shake. She pressed her lips together and stopped. A shudder of sensual longing filtered through her. *One night with you would never be enough.*

"I've got a friend picking us up." Dietrich waved on the SUV. The client she'd last worked on waved at her as he drove by.

Automatically, Mere waved. *A day's work and nothing to show for it but an empty wallet and a happy client. Back to the job drawing board.* "I'm going to walk to the hotel. I'll see you another time."

Dietrich casually jogged toward her. "Mere, we need to talk."

She turned away from him and quickened her pace. She whispered into the phone, "Hey, I've got to go."

"I need you," Jeremy said. "I'll pick you up at the hotel in five minutes."

"What? You're here?" *When? How? Shit.*

Dietrich slid his arm around Mere's waist and he brought her phone from her ear down to her side. "Darling, we need to talk privately. The hotel is the best place to do it."

Mere's hands warmed. Her breathing became shallow. Her skin tingled and that feeling she couldn't control rushed over her like a buffalo stampede and nearly knocked her down. With her knees weak and her heart pumping at increasing speeds, Mere didn't know quite what to do.

"We have to finish what we started," he said.

"Me and you alone is not a good idea." *The longer I'm with you the more I want you and that is not good.*

She glanced around. Nothing but lonely streets in a deserted district of the county. She raised her phone back to her ear. *Where are you, Jeremy? How do you know where to find me?* "I'm back. Sorry."

"I'm not far from Howl at the Moon Hotel Ulvene. We're going to celebrate." Jeremy ended the call.

"Who was that?" Dietrich said.

"No one." She gazed at the screen. *Jeremy, you will never know about my feelings for Dietrich, and he will never know about you.* She tapped her phone and called Jeremy back.

"Yes, my love?" Jeremy answered.

"I'll meet you…" She turned around and stared at Dietrich. *You might be strong, but you're human and no match for a normal vampire let alone the King of Vampires.* "I'll meet you…uh, at…I'll call you when I'm in my car."

"Mmm. Now that Sara is taken care of, we can be together." Jeremy's voice softened.

Mere stopped on a dime. "What do you mean?"

The aroma of peaches surrounded Meredith. A soft whisper of her daughter's voice accompanied a gentle kiss of a warm breeze on her cheek. *"Protect Ethan. It's not his fault. Don't blame him. He loved me in a way I didn't love him."*

She grabbed Dietrich's arm as her world shattered and a vision appeared.

Ethan clung to Sara's lifeless body. "No. Don't go. Don't go. I'll do anything to save you."

Lainie gently pulled Ethan from Sara. "Hang on, Ethan. Keep praying for a miracle."

Jack and Luke lifted Sara's body from the bed where she lay.

"Her spirit left so"—*Luke choked and cleared his throat*—*"quickly. Ethan's fading too."*

Jack's hands trembled. "I don't understand what happened. Everything was going so well."

"I don't know. It doesn't make sense," Luke whispered. "Mere is going to come unglued. Lainie is barely holding it together." His head jerked and his eyes widened. "Jack, we've got a major problem."

Dietrich's firm squeeze pulled Mere into the present. "Are you okay?"

Mere blinked at the black phone clenched in her hand and then up at a broken street lamp.

In the near distance a white light the size of a pin prick appeared in the evening sky and expanded in a downward spiral gaining mass like a portal to another world. The light headed toward a shadow of a young woman standing across the street. The woman's gray figure shifted as the light approached. Spindles of gold energy crawled out from inside the petite figure, unraveling the layers of darkness and revealing the shining spirit of the young lady Mere had raised as her own. Long, lovely, caramel strands of hair Mere had untangled and brushed until Sara could do it herself turned to golden rays of sunshine.

The white light shimmered like snowy glitter as the golden beauty ascended. One spirit morphed into a family of three.

"I'm going home," Sara's faint voice whispered into her ear.

The family frame stretched and grew as more of her ancestors joined Sara and Sara's parents' reunion. The white and gold energy shimmered, mixed, and as it reached the heavens, burst and rocketed through the sky like a cluster of shooting stars.

Mere closed her eyes, avoiding the finality of her spirit vanishing from the world.

The phone vibrated. She glanced at the screen as her chest clenched in misery.

We need to talk. I'm coming to get you.

-Lainie

"Talk to me," Dietrich said, but something about his tone seemed off, as if he knew Sara had died. "Tell me what you're feeling."

An engine revved.

She glanced over her shoulder as a black limousine raced down the street. A screech of tires and the vehicle abruptly stopped across the street from where she stood.

Shit.

The muscles in Dietrich's jaw tensed and his nostrils flared.

The back door to the vehicle opened.

"Meredith, get in the car," Jeremy's voice echoed from inside the ebony interior.

Dietrich's grip tightened.

"Fuck." She slid her hand over his. "I've got to go."

"No." Dietrich hunched over her. "We need to get to know each other better."

No matter how much she wanted to be swept up into his world, she couldn't. She guided his hands from her body. "No, we don't."

She gazed into his eyes and pushed the center of his black-framed glasses up farther on the bridge of his nose. "Take care of yourself." She pulled the bill of his black baseball cap down, concealing his identity as much as possible. *Jeremy won't be able to distinguish you from any other human in town. You're all tall, fit, and health nuts. Ulvene seems to be the training epicenter for world-class athletes.*

"Where do you think you're going?" He had the cutest confused look on his face that made her want to stay.

Ignoring her instincts, she ran to the car waiting for her. *Please, Jeremy, don't get out of the car.*

She slid into the darkness of the backseat and the door closed automatically. "I'm here."

The pulse in her neck throbbed faster with the adrenaline rush of his presence and the crackling of energy surrounding him.

The car rolled forward and gained speed.

The light green eyes of the most powerful man she'd ever met stared back at her.

"I see you've met someone," he said. "A play-thing?"

"Since when have I been interested in someone younger than me?" She crawled into his lap and pressed her cheek against his. Nothing and no one kept her from the afterlife anymore. Death would welcome her. The vow she gave ended when Sara passed into the afterlife. Ethan wasn't in danger. The promise to protect him, futile. Jeremy could give her what she wanted. She only had to con-vince him letting her go would be the best thing to do. "Want a drink of me?"

His warm tongue slid along the curve of her neck and stopped at the vein where he made their blood bond. "You let that boy touch you."

"I told him to go home to his mommy. He's no one, Jeremy." *I'm not over you.*

He grazed his fang across the throbbing vessel. "You gave him good advice."

"Are you going to tell me what you mean about Sara being taken care of?" She tilted her head and offered her neck to him. *You're going to be the one to send me into the afterlife where I belong. I am tired of trying to make you love me. I'm tired of all the violence chasing me. The death surrounding me.*

"I warned her it was a terrible idea to come here. I told her she wasn't strong enough to handle the transition, but she kept pushing and pushing—"

"What transition? Becoming a wife is not a "transition" for humans. It's a part of growing up and falling in love." *Is this another one of your prejudicial comments against humans?*

His teeth traced along the vein in her neck. "I offered her my world because I love you, Mere, and she accepted. Nicholas turned her after she breathed her last human breaths."

"Nicholas. Turned. Her? She's a vampire now?" *You hate Sara. She hates vampires.*

"Nicholas has always been in love with her." He licked over her pulse. "They'd secretly planned to be together when she graduated, but Ethan happened. Only Ethan wasn't who any of us thought he was. The upside to the situation is that Nicholas won't have to kill any more of her boyfriends because he finally has her blood-bonded to him for eternity."

"No. Please no." *Death would have been kinder to her than becoming one of you.*

The energy surrounding her thickened as he gently wrapped her up in an embrace. "Oh, Mere, Sara has been on a path leading to the other world since the moment I met her. I thought you'd be happy about her new life."

"You thought I'd be happy about this?" She pushed against his chest, but the strongest man in existence held her in place. "That's bullshit, Jeremy."

"It isn't bullshit," he said like he believed it. "I saved her. She will live by *my rules now*. She will be stronger, smarter, and she will be honest or she will be *punished*."

"So you saved her life so you could enhance it through torture?" Same arguments. Same fears. Same reasons she never agreed to live with him. Everything revolved around their humanity. How Sara didn't have Mere's strength, or intelligence, integrity, or loyalty. Ultimately the truth always boiled down to Sara's full-fledged lack of trustworthiness. The girl lied all the time, whether she needed to or not.

He dropped his chin and smiled as if he'd taught her some amazing secret to life. "Yes. She will *never* disobey me again."

"Are you going to turn me against *my will* like you did Sara?"

In a flash, she landed flat on her back on the leather seat, his face millimeters from hers and his body pressed flush against hers, pinning her down.

"I spoke with her spirit and asked her soul what she wanted," he hissed. "She asked for it. Sara didn't give a shit what happened to you or what you thought about it. When that girl confesses everything to you, remember I warned you of what a vile creature she was. I. Warned. You."

Mere jerked her hips up and threw him off her. "Stop the car."

His neon gaze cut right through her. "You want to get out?"

"Stop the damn car, Jeremy," she shouted.

"Sara is on her way to Atlanta with Nicholas and Ethan. If you want to see her, you know where to reach me."

The wheels screeched to a stop.

She opened the door. "We're through. It's over between us for good. I'm done. Tell Nicholas I'm coming for Sara." She climbed out of the car and slammed the door. The ache in her chest expanded down her arms as her heart pounded to a frenetic beat.

The blacked-out window rolled down. "We are far from through, Meredith. You're going to beg to be a vampire once you realize I saved her for you. I saved her *for you*."

"You saved her for *you*, not me."

"You better be packed up and on your way home within twenty-four hours or I will—"

"What, Jeremy? You'll do what? Kill me? Right now, I wish someone fucking would." She turned and walked to the other side of the road. *Please don't turn Ethan. Paulina and Jack will lose their son… Oh, God. I've ruined their lives too.*

Ready to walk home, but needing answers to why Jack, Lainie, and Luke were at the honeymoon cabin with Ethan and Sara, Mere sucked down her emotions and called Lainie.

"Hey," Lainie said.

"Hey, I need a ride. Please, just you, not Luke."

"On my way. Text me where you are."

Mere texted her the closest mile marker and slid her phone into her pocket. Part of her loved Jeremy for saving Sara, but more of her hated him for changing her into a violent predator. Nicholas wouldn't keep Ethan around for long. Only an equal or stronger man would survive in Nicholas's world. Ethan was a weak human. Ethan would die. They all died within the Coven…or turned.

CHAPTER TEN

"DRINKING ISN'T THE ANSWER," LAINIE said.

Mere walked straight into the Full Moon Bar and Boutique and sat down on a leather barstool.

Lainie sat down next to her. "What is going on with you?"

"Thanks for the ride. I really don't want to talk anymore. Sara asking you and Luke *and Jack* to drive them to the cabin and stay for dinner while I'm getting fired is too much for me to deal with right now."

"You'll bounce back from that firing. Paulina and Jack want to hire you, but they are afraid you'll take it the wrong way. They don't want to run your life. They love Sara. They—"

"Lainie, I don't want to talk about anything right now."

"Sara and Ethan went to Atlanta to look at houses, okay. She was worried you wouldn't understand considering she all but forced you to move here."

"Lainie, I'm begging you to stop talking." Mere looked around the room for some kind of subject to talk about so Lainie would stop trying to make the betrayal seem less horrible, and the lies told to Lainie less…painful.

A blonde with purple highlights, silver hoops through her nipples, and wearing nothing but a purple tulle skirt that stopped at her hips slipped kinky lingerie over a mannequin. The woman's pussy and ass were on full display for any onlookers.

"What the hell?" Mere mumbled. A piercing and kink store inside an upscale bar didn't make any sense.

"That's Violet. She's nice."

"Living in Vegas has changed you a bit. I don't mind nudity, but it's still a shocker." *I bet Violet knows where the bartender is. I bet she's fucking him.* Mere slid off her stool and walked over to her. "I'm looking for the bartender."

Violet looked her up and down. "You're over-dressed. He's not coming out for any frumpy overclothed chicks." She cringed to the point the woman looked as though she was going to throw up. "Follow me."

"I'm looking for a drink, not a wardrobe change." For some unknown reason, Mere followed the woman to the back of the boutique and behind a purple curtain. *Maybe I need a new look, a new lease on life or more like vengeance for changing the course of it.*

Body jewelry marked *sanitized* in plastic envelopes lay inside an open display case. The most enchanting diamond jewelry on the top shelf caught her eye. A massage table prepped for a new client seemed to call to her.

*Jeremy hates piercings. He hates tattoos. He hates…
hmm. He'd lose his crap over the tiniest of this kind of
disobedience.*

"I want some piercings," Mere blurted. "What
do you suggest?"

"Mere." Lainie joined her behind the curtain.
"You've never been into piercings. We should talk
before you consider this."

"Nope. No talking. I'm getting some piercings."
Jeremy is going to shit a brick when he sees me. "I'm
getting my ears pierced, my navel pierced, and—"

"Nipples and clitoris hood double pierced," Violet said. "You deserve the entire package."

Mere gazed at Lainie's worried eyes. "What do
you have? Does Luke like it? Do you think most
guys are into piercings? Should I go for the whole
shootin' match?"

Lainie swallowed hard.

*You're acting really strange. You know Sara is alive and
with Ethan. You are in Jeremy's mind fog from whatever
he did to make you forget Sara's death. So, girl, why
aren't you telling me to live it up, like you usually do?*

"I have a few more extreme piercings. Luke likes
them. He asked me to…uh…get them."

"Good enough for me." Mere took out her
credit card and handed it to the woman. "I'd like
it all. Nothing sparkly. I'm on a budget, but something simple and pretty. And as soon as you're done,
I want a fruity drink with triple the alcohol." *Sara
should have called me. She should have had Ethan call
me. But, no. She hides and lies as if I'll never know. As if
Jeremy wouldn't tell me.* "Damn it. I know."

Violet raised her pierced brow. "Did I miss something? Did I offend you somehow?"

"No," Mere said. "You didn't do anything. I was thinking out loud."

"Are you sure you want a bar beverage instead of a nice protein smoothie? Sometimes talking is the answer. Lainie is a good listener," Violet said.

"I've done enough talking. Thanks. I'd really like a drink without protein." *I'll do anything to let go for an evening. Meet a nice human who is crazy good in bed and a control freak so I don't have any visions. No more weirdness. I can't take much more.*

"One fruity drink coming up." Violet moved the purple fabric aside and stepped out into the boutique. "Undress, and I'll be back in a few minutes."

Mere took off her shirt in front of Lainie. Mere was pretty sure Lainie had seen the birthmark during the jail visit. She'd never guess what it meant. "I know you think I've lost my mind, and maybe I have. I'm jobless, Sara is married, and… Jeremy was here. I'm so done with everything in my life. I don't care if misery follows me. I can't afford the house I put a down payment on without that fucking job I lost. All I wanted was a little normalcy, Lainie. Was that too much to ask?" She unhooked her bra.

"There was an accident," Lainie said. "Sara almost died."

"I know. I know. I know. I saw it. She didn't have anyone call me. She wanted Ethan. She wanted you. She wanted Luke and Jack. I would have been fine if she had just wanted me there with her, to help her. All that shit my family burned into my brain is true. I can't run from any of it. I am cursed to love but never be loved in return." *I'm cursed to be hunted for the rest of my life by diseased werewolves, by diseased witches and those sick-ass zombies. Well, fuck that shit. I'm doing whatever I want tonight. Fuck Jeremy. Fuck all of Sara's lies. Fuck it all. They wouldn't give a shit whether I lived or died. Nobody would. I'm disposable like I've always been.*

"I've changed my mind," Lainie said. "You do need a drink. Hell, I'll help you get drunk tonight."

Mere laughed and unlaced her shoes. She dropped her trainers to the floor. "There's my partner in crime. I'm getting drunk. I'm taking some hot guy up to my hotel room for one night and rocking his whole damn world."

Mere shimmied out of her jeans and panties.

"Do you need me to hold your hand?" Lainie stared at Mere's belly.

"It's not cancer. It's just a strangely placed, enormous birthmark."

"It's pretty."

"No. It's not and I know it." Mere sighed.

"I think it is. It's unique, like you." Lainie smiled. "Beautiful like you."

I wish. "I'll be fine with the piercings. You don't need to hold my hand. Just pick out something sexy for me to wear. I might as well do it up right tonight."

"One night of love got me knocked up, Mere."

"I don't have a problem putting a condom on a cock. You seem to be opposed to that."

Lainie rolled her eyes like she always did. "Fine. I'll pick out your sexy attire. You focus on breathing and relaxing. The pain of the needle isn't that bad." She left the room.

Buck naked on the table, Mere looked between her legs. *Can she pierce me there while I'm so wet?*

What if her fingers slip? This might be a stupid idea. Jeremy said the only piercings he wanted on her were the ones from his fangs…Screw Jeremy. He held information from me for the last time. I'm done with him. He's broken that blood-bond. Sara never would have agreed to be one of them. She was untouchable, and he had her turned.

The rustle of the curtain as Violet entered reminded Mere of the falling of autumn leaves in the deep woods of north Georgia. *Those miserable days are gone.*

Violet approached with a red smoothie-looking drink in a tumbler. "It's the house special filled with herbs and fruit and a splash of yummy goodness." She handed it to Mere. "I left your card with the bartender."

Mere took a sip. Refreshing raspberries with a splash of sweet lemonade filled her mouth. "Mmm. This is delicious. I'll definitely have another."

"We believe in safe, sane, and consensual play in the bar and wherever else it leads." Violet walked over to the display. "We make everyone sign agreements to our rules."

"That's fine. No one can do anything to me I don't want them to."

"Hard limits?" Violet asked. She picked up a tablet and several packets of jewelry.

"What are you talking about?" Mere asked. *Is this a swingers' club night?*

"We try and match lovers," Violet said. "I have two in mind for you."

"I'm straight and not into multiple partners. I don't screw with married men."

Violet handed her the tablet. "Sign and mark any

actions you are not willing to do."

Mere signed and clicked almost everything on the list. She thought she was pretty knowledgeable about sex, but apparently she was very wrong.

"Interesting," Violet said and placed the tablet back on the top of the display case. "I'll check your clitoris and see the types of piercings that will work for you."

Mere gulped down the drink as Violet examined her.

"Trust me," Violet whispered.

"Okay." Mere clenched her jaw as Violet placed a tray of sanitized needles of different sizes and shapes on it along with half a dozen different sets of jewelry.

Mere blinked and her drink was filled to the top again and her earlobes burned with the sudden rush of blood. She gasped as a needle pricked. She gazed between her legs as Violet wove the needle in and out. Two bars with diamonds sparkled between her legs.

"They'll rub and peek out between your folds as you walk. Sex will never be the same again." Violet took off a set of medical gloves and put on new ones.

As Mere stared at the expensive diamonds between her legs, Violet swiftly shocked her with the pinch of nipple rings.

"All done," Violet said.

"That was quick," Mere mumbled. *Shit. No sex tonight.*

The scent of the ocean rolled over her in gentle waves. Her hot pussy and nipples throbbed against the jewels.

"Normally, I'd tell you to wait to have sex, but the way your body is reacting…" Violet grinned like a woman with special secrets to tell. "Be gentle. Start with doggy style and see how it all feels."

"Yes, ma'am," Mere whispered.

"Stand up. Time to get dressed." Violet helped Mere off the table and handed her another tumbler filled with the delicious smoothie cocktail. "Lift up your arms."

Mere raised her arms and Violet helped her into a gold, see-through silk tank top. Mere inhaled the aroma of the ocean and licked her lips. *Dietrich.*

Violet slipped a teeny-tiny wrap-skirt made of the same golden silk fabric around Mere's waist. "You look as enchanting as you smell."

Mere chugged the smoothie. *I shouldn't go out there like this. What if Jeremy followed me back? What if he's waiting in the bar for me? Maybe after seeing how pretty the gems look, he'll love them.*

Mere peeked out from behind the curtain, hoping. Her heart sank to her stomach. No one was in the boutique or bar besides Violet. *He didn't show up at the altar when he promised he'd be there. He would never follow me, chase me, want me more than…*

She ducked back behind the curtain before Lainie or Violet could see her. *I'm stupid for even hoping.*

Violet opened the curtain.

An invisible wall of energetic power slammed into Mere. Her knees wobbled with weakness unlike anything she'd experienced before. Another layer of power crashed over her head and slid under legs like a riptide, weighing her down and dragging her forward out of the dressing room and into the boutique. Her feet seemed to have a mind of their own and moved farther into the room toward the bar. Again and again, layers of energy grabbed and pulled and moved her far-too-willing body until she stood at the edge of the bar.

The bald man behind the bar counter wore a gray, fitted tee that showed off the incredible muscles underneath.

Mere boldly glanced over the charcoal-and-gold granite counter and checked him out. *I would take you home in a second, big boy.*

The man's tight jeans held nothing to the imagination.

Yes. I would definitely take you to bed.

He cleared his throat. "Another Full Moon Roar?"

"Yes, sir. Thank you." *I would roar for you all night long.* She handed him the empty tumbler. She blinked and the man held out a fresh glass filled with the wonderful concoction. "It's slow tonight?"

He nodded. "Violet and I are the only staff on this side of the hotel for the rest of the evening."

Mere took a sip. "Do you know Lainie Wolfson?"

"Yes, ma'am. She took your purse and card up to her room. Whatever you want is on the house." He raised his bushy black eyebrows. "I'm supposed to call her if you get out of hand."

"I'm always in the utmost control. No worries there, sir." Mere edged her butt onto the bar chair, being careful not to put pressure on her new piercings. "I'm Mere."

"I know who you are," he said.

"Bad know who I am? Or good know who I am?" Mere leaned against the bar, pushing her breasts onto the counter.

"Good." He grinned. "Mind if I adjust your top?"

Something she couldn't quite put her finger on compelled her to keep flirting. "You seem to me like you're a control freak. Are you?" *Please let me be right. I want you to touch me without any visions taking control.*

He nodded. "Are you a Domme?"

"I'm not a Domme, but it's hard to find someone who can handle me." *I'm going to give you something I don't hand over easily.* "You can adjust my top." *Order me to get on the bar counter and I will.*

He ripped the silk at her shoulders and drew it down over her breasts. "You're not the usual kind of girl that comes in here."

She watched as his gaze stayed on her nipples. "Really?"

"Mmm," he mumbled. "Big breasts and curvy hips on a petite thing. You're the girl next door with a dirty side…my favorite kind."

"Yeah?" She tilted her head, ready to offer her neck like she always did for Jeremy. *I can pretend you're my Jeremy.*

Warmth rose within her belly. Juices slipped from her pussy onto the leather seat, and she didn't care. She had nothing to lose. No one to protect. One night of selfishness is all she'd need. One night to let everything go the way she longed to. One night with a man who would know how to give her what she needed. Only one night.

"Oh, yeah," he said with a low rumble in his throat. "Stand up and take off the rest of your clothes."

It didn't take much of an order to get her to let

go of any inhibitions. She slipped from the stool onto her feet. She wobbled as she unwrapped her skirt.

The drink seemed to be working as her self-consciousness slipped farther and farther away into a lovely haze. She held the skirt up over her head and let the soft fabric slip from the tips of her fingers to the floor. "What are you going to do?"

The lights in the room dimmed. The strumming of a guitar broke the silence.

She picked up her drink, guzzled it, and placed the tumbler on the bar. *I think I'm drunk.* She giggled. *Drunk without a werewolf within a thousand miles. No vampires. No witches. No other freaky beings. Only humans and more humans like me. And no one knows what's happened to Sara yet. Not really. Jeremy wouldn't allow it.*

"My life unraveled when you came into town…" a woman sang.

A familiar hand enclosed hers. "Dance with me."

She pivoted on trembling legs to see the one man from whom she had to stay away. The one man who she wanted as much, maybe more, than Jeremy. "I—"

"Darling, no excuses." Dietrich stepped back and guided her into the center of the room as the voice of the singer faded far into the background.

His gaze dipped between her legs. "You are my ultimate fantasy."

She couldn't be sure because the night seemed so…so surreal, but she could have sworn he squatted down and licked her clit, then suddenly stood as if he'd done nothing at all. Yet, she'd felt the slide of his tongue lapping the juices, caressing her as if to tell her more was coming, so much more. Her body tingled and thrummed with the tease. It happened so fast that he couldn't have done it. She had to be hallucinating, but she wanted more. She couldn't stop this time. She wouldn't stop for anyone, not even Sara.

"Am I really your ultimate fantasy?" She breathed him in. *You've got on too many clothes.*

As if he heard her, he unbuttoned his white dress shirt. "You are."

She slid her hand over the soft leather of his belt. *Would you know how to use this for pleasure? What am I thinking? I don't do that.*

He pulled his shirt from his pants. "Do you like the feel of leather?"

"Uhh," she mumbled. *I don't know. I can't believe I'm thinking about…* The tips of her fingers traced the thin line of silver holding down the leather. *God, you are probably a master at all kinds of sex games. Games that I've never heard of from that list of Violet's. Games that I bet I'd beg for you to teach me. I would beg. I would do much more than beg.*

He brushed her fingers away. "Not yet."

"Please," she said in a voice altogether different than anything she'd ever heard before. *Need your mouth on me. Everywhere.*

He groaned and her body temperature rose higher. She needed to hear him moan again.

"I'll do anything, Dietrich," she whispered.

He slipped the leather from the buckle and unzipped his pants. "Kneel."

She immediately dropped to her knees. Juices flowed from her pussy as it contracted and pleaded to be licked, to be filled with his cock, to be pleasured.

Flawless skin over a long, thick, and hard rod jutted from his slacks and pointed at her.

"May I, sir?" She parted her lips. *Please.*

"Lick my balls and work your way up to the top. Do not take me into your mouth."

Shivers of pleasure rocked her so hard, she grabbed onto his hips for balance. She leaned forward and offered him the one piece of herself she'd only given Jeremy—her vulnerability.

He firmly cupped the back of her head and guided her closer. "I want you just as much. Actually, I want you so much more. Lick, darling."

She glided her tongue along the smooth skin clenched tightly over beautifully proportioned, large balls below a cock that looked like it was a gift to all womankind. Each long lick from the bottom of his sac to the tip of his cock turned into wet caresses, gentle kisses of worship.

"Yes," he whispered. "More."

His cock seemed to grow with each stroke of her tongue. Up and down. Up and down. She closed her eyes and rested her head into his hand, offering him her submission. Slight pressure from his fingers guided her along his cock. She inhaled the ocean aroma and bathed in the salty air.

"You're going to obey me." He pulled her head from his cock.

Like a dog waiting for her master's next command, she gazed up at him with her mouth open, her body relaxed. "I will do everything you ask." *Tonight, I'm yours.*

"I've waited a very long time for us to be together."

"We just met a couple days ago."

"Yes." He grinned. "But those visions…your beauty…your scent." His glasses slid halfway down his nose. "You've made me wait much longer than you should have."

"I'm yours tonight." *I'll be gone tomorrow.*

"Yes, you are mine." He inhaled deeply. "You will never be the same once I take what is rightfully *mine.*"

Words that would have sent her into attack mode from anyone else soothed her mind, body, and soul.

"Hands on the floor, Meredith. Hold the position. Do not move."

She leaned forward on trembling hands and legs.

"Yes, sir," exited her lips too quickly.

He let out a rumble that awakened a new sensation inside her, a raw, savage side.

"Like what you see?" She gasped as his warm, wet tongue caressed her pussy lips, dipped between them, and sent shock waves over her flesh and into her bones. "Please. Please. Please. Please," she pleaded. Any other man, she would have pushed back, broke position, but for him, she stayed.

His tongue dove in, deeper than she thought possible. In and out. Around her folds, over her piercings that slid along her swollen clit.

Her pussy throbbed and ached. Her body flamed with new desires, new needs.

Sharp teeth slid into her flesh below the piercings. The coldness living within her heart burst into the fire of unconditional love she offered too easily.

The muscles of her heart strengthened. Blood pumped into her veins in a new steady rhythm.

Her arms stopped shaking. Her legs held strong. "What are you doing?"

The heat of his body pressed against her back. His wet lips met her ear. "I'm making you mine."

"I want to be yours." And she did. She wanted a normal life, a normal man, a man who rocked her world and didn't hold back. A man who would show up at the altar. A man who would stand by her. A man who believed love conquered all obstacles.

The tip of his cock slid into her wet pussy. He thrust.

Invisible sheets of electrical energy thrummed and sizzled as layer upon layer slammed into her, pummeled her, shot through her, and strengthened her.

He pulled out.

"No, please don't stop," she pleaded.

"Oh, my Meredith," he whispered as he brushed his lips along the edge of her shoulder. "I'm not stopping until my mouth, my teeth, my tongue, my fingers, and my cock have touched every inch of your scrumptious body." He thrust hard.

His cock tunneled like a miner searching for mystical treasures inside the depths of her channel and wouldn't stop until he found every fragment of his prize.

She squeezed her walls surrounding his hard rod. Her insides twisted and turned and seemed to latch onto him…and pulled him deeper into a place of pleasure.

She shuddered and screamed and lost her mind, until time seemed to cease, and she floated into a beautiful space of peace and pleasure.

CHAPTER ELEVEN

THE PRIMAL ROAR THAT LEFT his mouth sent an energetic shock wave that expanded outward like a nuclear explosion, letting the world know he claimed his Mate. Cum released from his shaft and swam up to fertilize her eggs.

With his cock tucked securely into her mating niche, Dietrich straightened his back and gazed down at the woman who held her position even though her muscles were ready to give out, and she was immersed in a trance of bliss. He gripped her hips and pushed her forward and watched her pussy drip with juices.

"Alpha," Luke whispered. "Are you ready to move to a room?"

Dietrich pulled Mere's hips toward him and watched her pussy expand to take the rest of his cock. He reached under and pressed his balls against her jeweled clit. He shuddered with her orgasm. "You want more of my cock?"

"Yes, sir," she whimpered.

He pushed her hips away and his cock stretched from the intense hold she had in her mating niche.

He gritted his teeth and pounded his cock into her.

"More," she cried out.

In and out, inch by inch, he thrust until he couldn't give any more.

Her arms buckled from the strain of keeping still, but he held her so she didn't fall. He would never let her fall as long as he walked the earth.

"Alpha, you need to take her to a room," Luke said. "Please. She's human. She won't understand the blood everywhere."

She released his cock from the mating niche within her pussy walls.

He lifted her leg and carefully turned her over until she was on her back and he hovered over her. A small heart sparkled silver on her cheek. He dropped his gaze, finding sparkles of silver covering every inch of her body from her neck down to the tips of her toes.

"Damn, I don't remember doing that," Dietrich mumbled.

"I closed down the hotel for a week while you were *doing* that," Luke said. "I don't know how much longer you two are going to fuck, but it can't be in the open anymore. She's pregnant and probably going to kill you when she finds out about all of this. In fact, I know she's going to try and kill you when she comes to her senses. Mere attacks instead of searches for peaceful resolutions."

"A week?" Dietrich stared at Mere's pretty pink nipples with his family heirloom diamonds. *I love you.* He thrust his pelvis and moaned as his cock found the place in her pussy reserved only for him. A jolt of electricity shot through him as she pulled him inside the niche, accepting and loving him as if it was his first time there.

"Twelve days to be exact," Luke huffed. "I need help."

"This is where Meredith chose to mate with me. This is where…" He glanced around the room. Dried blood splattered the floor and walls. He rose with her wrapped around him. "Good idea, Luke. I'll try not to bite her anymore."

"Yeah, that would be great." Luke walked beside Dietrich out of the bar and down the hallway to the Howling Honeymoon Suite. "Try to get her to stop biting you too." He growled. "She needs to eat, and so do you."

"We'll eat when the mating ceremony is complete." He carried her into the bedroom and climbed into bed. Her shiny dark hair spread across the pure white pillow. Sexy brown eyes sparkling with gold gazed up at him, her body poised and ready to obey every one of his commands. She took his breath away while making the need to fuck her even more intense.

She rolled her curvy hips and moaned.

He gazed into her eyes and heard her sweet voice for the first time in his mind.

I love you, Dietrich.

He held back from speaking to her through their mating link.

"Alpha." Luke stood beside the bed.

Dietrich rolled on his back, ignoring Luke. "Mere, suck my cock."

Mere crawled between his legs and closed her mouth over the top of his long length.

"Alpha," Luke said. "Feral wolves are showing

up here. The Alphas all over the world are dealing with diseased wolves arriving in packs at airports, seaports, and train stations. They're heading here. They're all heading here."

Dietrich blinked. Red walls blinded him for a second. *Where am I?* He glanced around the room.

"You changed rooms last week to the Red Wolf Lovers room," Luke said.

"What are you doing here?" Mere moaned.

My mate needs me to make love to her. "You're interfering with *my* mating ritual."

"I need help," Luke pleaded. He lowered his gaze. "Something strange is happening. As long as I've been alive, the feral plague has not been widespread. We've gone in and cleaned it out. But, suddenly, it's all over and indications confirm this is where they are all converging."

Mere lifted her head and smiled. She squeezed her breasts together against the sides of his cock. "Fuck my breasts again." She rubbed her nipples with the tips of her fingers. "I want to taste your cum."

"She's still in the trance," Luke gasped. "How can that be?"

Mere lowered her chin to her chest and opened her mouth.

Dietrich thrust for her.

"Oh, my God," she moaned. "I'm going to come. I'm going to come."

"Darling, open those beautiful lips, and I'll give you what you want."

She shuddered and writhed as she opened and closed her mouth.

He thrust between her breasts as she rubbed them against his cock. Pleasure bubbled up from his balls into his cock. He reached behind his back to her wet pussy and shoved his fingers inside.

"Yeeesss," she screamed. Her pussy clenched around his fingers like a vise.

Cum spurted from his cock. He shuddered and growled as her tongue, lips, chin and neck dripped wet with his cum. He slid over her belly and more seeped from the tip onto her breasts. *Mine.*

"Straddle my cock," he whispered.

Mere crawled up his body and held his cock to her entrance. "Please?" she whispered in the sultry southern drawl that made his belly tingle and his dick want her even more.

"Yes, darling. You won't break me." *Love of my life, I will make love to you anytime, anywhere, always.*

Her eyes rolled and her lids closed as she sank down onto him. She arched her back and lifted her breasts. "Do you really like my body?"

"I love every dip and curve. I love your smooth, pale skin. I love your beautiful chocolate and golden eyes. I love your big breasts. I love your piercings. I love the warmth of your pussy and the way it hugs my cock. I love the way your body moves. I love everything about your sweet body."

She stretched on top of him and rubbed her sticky flesh over his. "You've got the biggest cock I've ever seen and you know exactly how to use it." She closed her eyes and sighed.

He curled his arms around her and held her. "I love you."

"I love you," she whispered. The pattern of her breathing slowed and soft sighs of sleep drifted over his chest.

He sniffed. *Magnolias and ocean. My Mate. Ocean and sand…our baby. Dirt, compost, ashes? Vampire?* He sniffed again. *Vampire blood-bond.*

His heart pumped faster and faster. *No.* He turned her over gently and inspected her wrists. The evidence of faint, fang scars under his silver markings ran from the base of her wrists to her armpits. *Vampires used you as a child bleeder.* He traced the bites. So many years of abuse. *The King of Vampires wouldn't allow this. Jeremy would kill everyone involved, if he found out.*

Dietrich examined the left side of her neck. Nothing. He ran his fingers over her collarbone to the other side of her shoulder and up the right.

No. No. No. His fingers slid over raised skin in the form of a familiar vampire crest.

Jeremy Hunter. You blood-bonded with the King of Vampires. You're married? No. He can't marry you in his church without turning you, but he can give you the title of wife in his Coven. He can have children with you. Shit. He loves you and never told me. He saw your birthmark and never inquired about it.

He gazed down at his mate, focused on her heart, and placed his hand on the center of her chest. Silver threads of energy expanded from his soul, came together forming thick braids, and shot down his arm into his hand and into the intricate gold and silver web connecting her blessed spiritual energy to her newly formed werewolf chi created from the transformation.

Her mouth opened and the teeth of a wolf extended down. She inhaled. New silver threads formed a tragic mosaic of her life that played like a movie before his eyes. He closed his lids, but the vision continued.

Dirt, storms. Always outside, always hungry, always thirsty, always working. Working and working. Fighting. Dying. Reviving. Protecting her family from feral beasts and alternate beings. Hiding her fears of weakness and wishes for death turned into everyday life struggles. Loving and never being loved. Heartbreak found her over and over and over again. Jeremy arrived. He fought beside her, protected her, loved her.

The most intimate moments of her life revealed her profound love for Jeremy and Sara. The constant arguments with Jeremy over Sara along with Mere's refusal to turn for Jeremy continued for years. Mere's attempts to make Jeremy jealous failed and Sara's efforts to tear them apart remained futile until Sara became a vampire.

Dietrich spread the silver web of love and life he created and filled each strand with unconditional love until her entire body glowed silver with only golden shimmers remaining in a thin layer over the blood-bond she had made with Jeremy.

He held back from opening his entire past to her. He put psychological locks in places and invisible keys for her to find and open them after she'd processed each step in her emotional transition. He held too much history for a new wolf, let alone a human, to be able to take in at once without going mad.

Time would allow her to absorb all the information as she and her wolf matured. He suppressed the voice of the growing wolf within her, allowing her to adjust to her new life. She would need years to process the land changes, the rise and fall of the animals, and the war between the fallen angels he'd witnessed and played a part in.

With the links and locks complete, he kissed her lips. *One day, you're going to love being a wolf. You're going to love me more than Jeremy. You're going to forgive me for what I'm going to do. You have to.*

"I love you," she mumbled.

"Alpha," Luke whispered. "Did you hear me? What do I do? Is our army susceptible to the plague?"

He closed his eyes. *No, Luke. The army is immune as are all of the Alphas that come to the International Alpha Conferences at my home. Prepare the army to move at a moment's notice. Wherever Meredith goes, the army goes. Meredith is the key to ending the spread of the disease. Contact Jeremy Hunter, the King of the Vampires. Tell him I'll be visiting with my army to talk about the plague.*

CHAPTER TWELVE

MERE AWOKE PLASTERED TO THE man all the Ulvenes wanted her to date. She carefully scooted from Dietrich's snuggle and crawled off the red sheets.

She inhaled. *Salt and sex.* Her pussy buzzed like they'd just finished making love and mini-orgasm aftershocks moved through her. She slid her hand down her belly to her pussy and moaned. Glancing at him, her heart melted. He sparkled with silver glitter from his neck to his toes. *You are the sexiest man alive.*

She gazed at her hand and belly. *Damn. We must have bathed in it or painted it on or…I wish I knew what we'd done. I'm sure I'd be replaying it in my head and masturbating.*

He sighed and nuzzled against the pillow.

She tiptoed around the room looking for clothes and condom wrappers. No condom box. No wrappers. *Shit. I bet I'm fucking ovulating.* She opened drawers in the walk-in closet. *What kind of hotel has walk-in closets?*

Two luxurious red robes to match the red-themed room lay folded in the bottom drawer.

"Mere?" he said.

"I'm going to run up to my room and grab some clothes." Her stomach grumbled. "I'll bring back food." She quickly slipped on the robe and cinched the belt around her waist. She ran her hand over her belly. *Please don't let me be pregnant.*

"I'll order room service. Don't be long."

"Yeah, sure." She squeezed her thighs together. *Pussy needs to shut the doors. Fun time is over.* She exited the room and hurried down the hallway.

Luke walked toward her from the lobby. "Is Dietrich awake?"

"Yes, sir." She pulled the collar of the robe close together. "This is a bit embarrassing."

"Why?" Luke turned around and walked with her to the lobby receptionist.

Right, sex god Luke wouldn't think me walking out of someone else's hotel room in a robe is weird. "I left my room key somewhere. Could I—"

The woman behind the counter handed her a new key without any request for identification or room number. "Here you are, Ms. Kilpatrick. We can have your belongings moved to Mr. Wolfgang's room at your request."

"Oh, thank you, but that's not necessary." Mere's cheeks heated. "We're just friends." She grabbed the key and scurried across the lobby to the elevator with Luke fast on her heels.

"Are you okay?" Luke asked.

She nodded. "Fine. Is Lainie up?"

Luke reached into his jeans front pocket and shoved the huge bulge to the side.

Big cocks must run in the family.

He withdrew a phone from his pocket. "Here. Call her. She has your purse and phone."

The doors to the elevator opened.

He placed his hand on her back and guided her inside. "Dietrich gets intense. If you need to talk, I'm here."

"Uh, thanks. There is nothing to talk about."

Luke's brow rose and the parental expression of disbelief and disappointment she'd used almost daily on Sara appeared on his face. "I highly doubt that."

"I know you're talking about the sparkles. It was nothing." *Lainie is going to have to tell me how to get it off my skin.*

He frowned and looked down at her with the same look she gave Sara when her little girl said that Ethan was the love of her life. "It *wasn't* nothing. Dietrich is—"

"Dietrich is the least of my concerns," she said. "So, you can save that look for someone else."

The doors closed and she was stuck with the interrogator. He pressed the button for the third floor. "The way I look at it, he is your only concern."

"Luke, I know he's your family. It was one night. There is no love match." *Jeremy can never find out about him. I need to forget he exists.* She gazed at the screen of Luke's phone and tapped on Lainie's picture. Immediately it dialed.

"Hey," Lainie said.

"Hey, it's Mere. Can you meet me at my room?" Mere glanced up at gorgeous Luke. *You followed Lainie across the country to be with her. Will Dietrich follow me?*

"Yes, ma'am. I'm walking over now." Lainie ended the call.

The elevator stopped and the doors opened.

"We need to talk about Dietrich," Luke insisted.

She walked out of the elevator and took a right. "Your uncle or cousin—or whatever relation he is to you—is a good guy. I feel sort of but not super bad for the jail incident, and hitting him, but at the time, he deserved it."

She shook her head. *Focus on the problem at hand. Not the man with whom I did things I can't remember.* "Anyway, I have other issues to deal with right now. I need a job. I need to see if I can get my house deposit back."

"I got that back for you. I answered your phone and handled it. The funds are in your account. You have a job at Jack and Paulina's fitness facility. Lainie negotiated the contract. You start whenever you're ready."

She stopped on a dime. "You got my full deposit back? Lainie did that for me?" *Shit. When the Ulvenes start asking questions…they won't figure anything out. Jeremy will make sure they never find out.* She hugged him. "Thank you."

Luke patted her on the back. "You're welcome."

"Hey, what are you doing with my man?" Lainie asked.

"Get in here," Mere said. "I want to hug you too."

"Miss I-Don't-Hug is very affectionate today." Lainie laughed and joined the group embrace. "So, are we moving you into Dietrich's home on the fourth floor?"

"Uh, no." Mere wiggled out of the hug Lainie and Luke seemed to want to continue indefinitely.

She grabbed Lainie's hand and walked toward her room. "One night with a man does not constitute a moving-in-together scenario."

"Believe me, what we saw at the bar, and on the way to the first room…" She coughed. "You've never been afraid to show some skin when you're going adulting without Sara, but that was extreme, even for you."

"You saw?" She glanced back at Luke who walked too closely behind them.

"We saw, all right," Luke mumbled. "Learned a few things."

"Luke. Not the time," Lainie growled. She squeezed Mere's hand. "Sometimes chemistry gets the better of us. It wasn't a big deal. No one else was around."

"Liar," Luke coughed into his hand

Mere would have died inside at that moment if the look Lainie gave Luke hadn't made her laugh.

"I'll check on my uncle. We'll catch up for lunch in the restaurant?" Luke asked.

"That sounds perfect," Lainie said. "See you then."

Luke retreated down the hall.

Mere tapped her keycard on the lock and opened the door. "Teach me how to do that look that shuts him up and makes him do what you want."

"You have better stern looks than I do. Expand your usage of them to others besides Sara." Lainie strode into the room and sat down on the couch. "So, you're nervous because you really like him?"

"Seriously, Dietrich is really great, but I don't remember anything. Nothing. I must have blacked out or something, but he's not the kind of guy who would keep going if he thought I didn't know what I was doing. I don't think he realized those house specials knocked me on my ass."

"There's no alcohol in those. They pack a wallop of adrenaline, but it's filled with all these performance enhancing vitamins and protein. You know how serious Luke is about his health and mine and everyone who has any contact with him. You were not drunk."

"There was alcohol in it. I felt all weird and really, really good. Like I was in a super *high* state of mind." Mere laughed and then groaned. "I don't remember anything except dancing and the sexiest moment of my life when he brushed his lips against mine and stole a kiss. The worst part is I bet the sex was phenomenally great because my entire body is still buzzing like I've won the damn lottery."

Lainie lowered her chin and squinted at her. "You really don't remember that moment on the floor getting it on in that downward dog yoga pose? Luke's mouth dropped open. Like. Dropped. To. The. Floor. Open. I would have fallen over the way Dietrich thrust. I keep telling Luke that I'm not going to do that, not even after I pop this little person out."

Mere's pussy clenched as if it remembered the event, but damn if she did. "I don't remember anything but the kiss and waking up to his incredible body snuggled up around me. As much as I'd like to experience what we did, I'm not getting that close to him again. Bad things happen when I spend more than a night with a guy." *Jeremy finds them and suddenly they've moved or landed on the front page of the obituaries.*

"Well, what are you going to do? Dietrich is like Luke, and they don't give up so easily when they are in love. Dietrich is in love with you."

Mere sighed. "All I know is I need to get my ass on a plane back to Atlanta and find out what the hell is really going on with Sara. I know she and Ethan are with Jeremy and…" *I'm going to probably kill Nicholas and Jeremy and then ground Sara for the rest of her life. How do you hide being a vampire from your husband? Only the old vampires can go out during the day, and Ethan and I will be long dead before that happens.*

"Hey, she's okay. They're enjoying an extended honeymoon in our stomping grounds. Paulina and Jack are back here working and excited about the kids' return."

"Honeymooning? Not house hunting?" *What lies has Sara told you?* The burden of responsibility for Sara and Ethan weighed heavy on her shoulders.

"They're doing both, but they're living in Ulvene. They'll have a vacation home in Atlanta, thanks to your friends Nicholas Carson and Jeremy Hunter who are funding it. Sara will have the best of both worlds. Isn't that what you want?"

"I need to see what's going on for myself." *Sara's lies are catching up to her.* "I shouldn't be there long." She glanced down and her feet sparkled silver. "Can you show me how to get rid of this glitter? My skin feels normal, but jeez, I look like a walking disco ball."

Lainie's cheeks puffed out like a squirrel trying to hold a mouthful of nuts. "Well, it doesn't really go away so easily. I can get you some makeup to cover it for now. Sometimes it fades a little, but when things get heated, it sparkles all the more. It's kind of permanent. You and Dietrich really went crazy marking each other up. Does he have a matching heart on his cheek?"

Mere ran to the full-length mirror. "Sonofabitch. I'm going to kill him. I can't kill him. It might have been my *brilliant* idea for all I know." Mere exhaled. "If you could go get the makeup while I take a shower, I would really appreciate it. The last thing I need is to draw anyone's attention."

Lainie lifted her hips and pushed up from the couch. "This baby is kicking my bladder. For something so small, he or she knows where to focus to make me pee. I'm wearing a dang pad so I don't wet myself. Ugh, I'll call my pilot to get the jet ready. Dietrich will meet you at the—"

"No Dietrich. I need to see Sara alone. He can't be around when I see Jeremy either. And Jeremy is first on my list of people to visit." Mere walked toward the bathroom. "Take my keycard, and let yourself in."

"Mere, you can't leave Dietrich here. You will need him in Atlanta."

Mere gazed at her best friend. *Please don't side with him.* "Lainie, if he shows up, I'm going to find another way to get there without him. Please, do not tell him about this. Jeremy and I are not on good terms right now. They are about to get so much worse, and I will not have some guy I slept with *one time* thinking he has the right to step in and fix it. He's not my boyfriend. He's not my husband. He's not even an American."

"You don't understand. You need him, and he needs you. You can't just go on as if nothing happened."

"Forget the flight. I'll find another way home. If I could borrow the makeup, and, well…just tell me where to buy more." She walked into the bathroom and slipped out of the robe in front of the vanity.

Oh, my God. Her skin shined as brightly as the large diamonds on either side of her nipples and between her legs. Gold glitter shimmered over the blood-bonded crest Jeremy gave her what seemed like a lifetime ago.

She looked like an amped-up version of herself from the visions she shared with Jeremy and the ones with Dietrich, minus the pregnancy and the gold glitter over the bond.

"I'm getting the makeup," Lainie shouted.

The click of the door opening and closing seemed louder than normal. The room seemed clearer, brighter, more vibrant. *Sex with Dietrich made my vision better. Maybe sex with me made his better.* She giggled. *He might not need glasses. I hope his vision didn't improve. I like his glasses. Maybe I'll buy him another pair, one that highlights those gorgeous ice-blue eyes.* She gripped the edge of the vanity counter as a vision closed in on her…

Dietrich slipped the belt from the loops at his waist. "You are not allowed to leave me again."

With her naked body draped length-wise over a leather bench, Mere moaned. She glanced to the side. "I'm going to come hard if you touch my pussy with that thing."

Dietrich's gaze dropped between her legs. He licked his lips. "Then I'll make sure to barely miss." He unzipped his black slacks. "This is supposed to be punishment, darling."

"Then why does it feel like a reward?"

His slacks dropped to his feet. He stepped forward.

Thwack.

"Yes," she gasped. The very tip of the wide leather belt tapped her clit piercings. "Dietrich…"

Thwack.

"I'm coming," she screamed. "Fuck me. Please, I need you."

He lifted her hips and slammed his cock into her. "I need you too. I need you with me, by my side, in everything I do."

Mere stumbled back and nearly fell to the floor, but steadied her legs and shifted, finding balance. Her heart raced, but not erratically. No signs of an episode onset. "That is messed up." *I need to avoid him. Seeing him again would be a mistake. A terrible, potentially deadly mistake.*

She turned on the shower spray and stepped inside. Her pussy throbbed as though she'd just had sex and needed more. The warmth of the water flowed over her hair and traveled down her body in tributaries over her curves and between her bottom cheeks. *I bet he took me there. I bet we did things I've never done with anyone else.*

She shuddered as the spray hit her chest.

Widening her stance, she shifted and leaned back against the tile wall.

I shouldn't even think about him.

She closed her eyes and imagined Dietrich in the shower with her.

She caressed her clit like he would. Hard. Harder. Fast. Faster.

In her mind, her fingers morphed to his. She nuzzled his wet neck and licked the water from his clean skin.

The jewelry caressed her clit…back and forth…back and forth…circling, tapping, massaging until his fingers, his hands, his body, his voice joined her under the warm spray of the shower.

He gripped her hips and spun her around, facing the tile wall. His big cock replaced his fingers.

Mine, she heard him whisper in her mind as if they were linked as one in mind, body, and soul. *Pinch your nipples.*

She pressed her face to the tile wall, wishing this wasn't a daydream, but real. *You feel so real. Fuck me harder.* She cupped her breasts and clamped down on her nipples with her fingers and held them, waiting for his next order.

He grunted and her pussy stretched with each inch he gave. He thrust, and she countered.

The heat of his body pressed flush against her. The glide of the water over them. The rush of his presence.

She arched her back as pleasure rose. *I'm going to come for you, only you. Come with me. I want to feel you coming inside me.*

Meredith, he growled in that sexy voice she remembered him using, but couldn't place what they had been doing at the time. *Drop your hands. Squeeze my cock.*

I'm so wet. I'm going to come. Dietrich, I can't stop. She released her nipples as he dove deeper into her center. Gritting her teeth, she moaned louder. *I feel you inside me.*

Cum spurted from his cock and she gasped as

her pussy clenched and warmth rose inside her.

Yes. Yes. Yes. She trembled with the most intense orgasm she'd ever had.

The moment ended with a sweet kiss on her cheek, but her legs shook so hard she slid down to the floor, the daydream complete. *I bet sex with you is so much better.* She sighed as she caressed her pussy. "No more sex."

For the first time since she took on the responsibility of raising Sara, Mere's thoughts were dominated by someone else. The man she didn't even remember sleeping with gave her a reason to stay in Ulvene and a reason to keep living.

CHAPTER THIRTEEN

THE WOMAN JEREMY LOVED LAY on the wooden pew in his church as though she slept on the most comfortable mattress ever created.

Nicholas stood beside him. "She's a warrior, Jeremy. How many times have we walked in on her sleeping on the floor instead of her bed?"

Jeremy nodded and gripped the red blanket...*her church blanket*. "I'm going to change that habit. She deserves the very best of everything. Now that Sara is one of us." *Sara needs to get her shit together.*

"She will apologize to Mere," Nicholas whispered. "She has to get the nastiness out of her before she can move into my bed. She's strong-willed."

Yeah, strong-willed is you being polite. "How are your lovers?"

Nicholas grabbed his cock. "The growing plague and Sara take up all my time. Do you know when Dietrich is going to visit and help us end the plague? His messages are so noncommittal."

"I don't know, but they are losing wolves in large numbers. I've never heard or seen so many diseased. It reminds me of the stories Mere tells of her life before me, only this is worse." *We've already lost a portion of our army. We can't lose more.* "Dietrich will come. He won't let us fight his fight."

Mere rolled to her side and curled into a ball. "Please, no. No. Please, stop." She whimpered and her body trembled. "Cold. So cold."

Jeremy left Nicholas's side and unfolded the soft blanket. He gently covered her with the cashmere blanket he had made for her. "Shh, my beautiful Queen, you're having a bad dream. You're safe in my church. You're on holy ground." He placed his hand on her shoulder. "I'm here. You're home."

"Jeremy," she mumbled. She adjusted and curled her fingers around the edge of the blanket and drew it up to her nose. "Mine. My Jeremy."

Nicholas lifted her head and placed a pillow underneath. "I'll remove it before she wakes." His hand dropped back to his groin. "I feel really strange around her."

A gentle breeze like a whisper from the old brick-and-cobblestone walls of the passageway implored Jeremy to return to the heart of the Coven. He knelt on one knee before her. "I'm waiting for your eyes to open."

She tilted her head and the strong throbbing of her vein in her neck called him to drink. Their blood-bond surfaced, making her skin form his family crest. The golden energy of their souls he'd woven through their bond sparkled as if she had already turned, but she hadn't.

He kissed the flesh over his crest prominently displayed on her neck. *Does this mean you're ready to be one of us?*

She sighed and ended in a delicate moan. "I missed you."

He licked over the pulsing vein he wanted to sink his teeth into and drink until she became his Vampire Queen.

Nicholas tapped Jeremy's shoulder. "The warrior wolves are here. Dietrich must be close."

"Mmm. Love you," she whispered.

He kissed the crest and the golden energy sparkled even brighter. His body buzzed with excitement. *You're ready. You're finally ready.* "I'll be back soon."

He stood up and walked to the passage to his chambers as Nicholas followed. "Let's go see who Dietrich sent from his army."

"Everyone, my King," Nicholas said. "All of them are here. Six hundred. Luke isn't out fighting, but Michael is. Something is happening. He never sends all of them."

"Let's join our old friends tonight as we eliminate the diseased from our city, and thank them for coming." *Dietrich must be worried about me.* He held in a smile. The man who raised him always came through when things got dangerous for the Coven. *I will have my Vampire Queen ready to meet you by the time you arrive. All her humanness will be gone and you will approve of her.*

Chapter Fourteen

THE ROUND ANTIQUE TABLE DIETRICH had given to Luke and Lainie as a wedding present stood as the focal point in the center of the open foyer of Lainie's home in Atlanta.

Dietrich glided the pads of his fingers over the smooth, curved edge of wood he'd carved hundreds of years ago from the rosewood tree the Madagascar Pack Alpha had given him as thanks for buying them the land they continue to nurture and live on. The Alpha dealt with feral beasts and lost his life when he and his mate were overtaken by the diseased creatures almost thirty years ago. The evidence of a plague carrier's birth appeared with the sudden transformation of healthy wolves to feral, but the diseased beasts turned to ash within a week, indicating the carrier had died. He paid little attention to the cycle he'd witnessed hundreds of times over thousands of years.

An isolated outbreak of disease popped up sporadically and ended almost as quickly. A carrier's birth and almost immediate death remained the norm. No reason to interfere with the natural order of life. The werewolves who fell to the plague usually killed each other on their journey to the carrier, and all died when the carrier's spirit entered the afterlife. Calls for help came from the same areas of the southern United States over recent years, but within a few days the disease vanished, ending the frantic cries for help.

I should have checked out the signs myself. Verified the death of the carrier. I would have known the vampires unwittingly saved the carrier—my mate Meredith. Draining the infant girl to the point of almost death and continuing to do so over and over eliminated her natural scent that carried the virus throughout the world and saved her life in the process.

He gazed at the tall ceiling where an Irish crystal chandelier made by the Wolfson Pack of Ireland hung. The crystal gently shifted and reflected rainbows on the white walls from the sun's rays shining through the beautiful windows as the fiery globe ascended in the sky, marking another day.

Luke loves his Irish crystal. The werewolf subtly brought his Irish roots into the house and showered his living presence through the home without disturbing the memory of the man who had built it.

He had to take a lesson from Luke. Thousands of years had passed since he'd been taught something by his apprentice. *Just because Mere loves another man does not mean she doesn't love me too. Her love for me isn't diminished by his presence. Her love is strengthened by my love. Her love is empowered by my own.* He repeated those words over and over as Lainie and Luke chatted in front of him, probably to him.

"I want to be on record as saying that this is the

worst thing you could do right now," Lainie said.

Dietrich sighed. "I've warned you to stop questioning my decisions, Lainie. I'm much older than you. I know what I'm doing."

The woman huffed. "Mere is private. She's going to take your involvement the wrong way. You can't sex your way out of everything. Luke tries that and it—"

"It works." Luke stepped behind her and wrapped his arms around her. "Stay out of it. Mere and Dietrich can work things out. Couples do that." He kissed the side of her face.

"He's got her moaning with her hands in her panties in public. It's not fair. I remember when you did that to me. I had no idea what was going on, but I remembered most of our first night together. She doesn't even realize it's been three dang weeks. She's going to hate me for not telling her what is going on. Like, seriously hate me. I can't live with that." The dark blue eyes staring at Dietrich filled with tears. "Please, I know Mere. Don't show up at her first meeting with Sara."

"Mere will need me by her side, if for no other reason than to keep everyone involved calm. Ethan needs me there too. He's done recovering. Being near Sara will only weaken him now."

Luke, keep Lainie out of the loop on this. What happens when we leave here stays with us. Michael Flanagan is driving us to Jeremy Hunter's church. Meredith is blood-bonded to Jeremy.

Oh, shit, Luke replied. *I've got your back.*

"Stop doing that," Lainie said. "It's rude and I'm getting angry."

"Shh," Luke whispered. "It's just work. We've

got to go. You stay here and listen to some music. Do that cleansing thing you do for Mere when she comes over so she doesn't get upset when she accidentally touches something with historical significance."

Lainie turned around in his arms and clung to him as if she were hanging off the edge of a cliff and he was her last hope for rescue. "I can't lose my best friend."

"You won't," Luke whispered.

"Blame me," Dietrich said. "She will be angry you lied to her, but she'll forgive you when she glimpses a sample of my power. She'll understand you had no choice."

"But I did," Lainie whimpered.

"No, Lainie," Dietrich said. *You have so much to learn.* "You've done exactly what I wanted you to." He opened the front door and stepped outside.

The crisp air invigorated him. The sun greeted him with a blinding smile.

Dietrich tugged the bill of his black baseball cap down closer to his brows. He slid his fingers over the small chip on the edge of his glasses and pushed them up along the bridge of his nose. *I'm coming, Meredith. Jeremy will survive. He has to survive.*

"Alpha," Michael Flanagan, the Alpha of the state of Georgia and Luke's Beta, opened the passenger-side door of the idling black SUV. He lowered his head and nodded. "I'm glad you're here to guide us in this matter. I have Danny Wedekind en route and he should arrive at the airport as expected."

Dietrich climbed into the vehicle. "Thank you."

Michael closed the door and trotted to the driver's side. He hopped into the driver's seat as Luke climbed into the back.

The doors closed.

"Is there any other way to handle this?" Luke asked.

"No. As soon as Jeremy sees me, he will know there are three options and all of them are miserable for at least one of us."

CHAPTER FIFTEEN

SITTING DOWN IN THE PEW on the front row of the empty church, Mere watched Father Ryan enter from his office door to the left side of the altar. He placed new candles on the Remembrance tray.

"It's not like you to avoid confrontation." He lit a candle and mumbled a prayer.

She glanced beside her at the red blanket she'd folded minutes before. "Yes, sir." *I've never had so many conflicting feelings.* "Thanks for the blanket."

"You should thank Jeremy, not me." He lit another candle and prayed.

I will. Being here, praying, reflecting on things…The signs of Sara's interest in Nicholas and his interest in her. I was so busy trying to make ends meet, but I see it now. I see so much. I should have listened to Jeremy. I wish I had.

The aroma of sandalwood and soil settled over her along with the constant scent of the ocean, the sand, and the crisp mountain air that hovered around her every second of the day and night.

Father Ryan walked to the twelve-foot golden

cross on the back wall. He knelt down and prayed like she'd seen him do hundreds of times. On occasion, she would join him, but not today.

Most of the night, she'd spent praying on her knees about what to do, where to live, and whether the desire to go back to Dietrich was real or imagined. Avoiding the initial rush to see Jeremy, only to argue about things that wouldn't lead to resolution, seemed like a smart move last night. With so many epiphanies all at once, she had no clue what to say to Jeremy.

Handling the situation between Sara, Ethan, and Nicholas seemed impossible. God, Nicholas saved Sara's life, but what happens with Ethan? Would he become a vampire? She'd heard of vampires having two spouses, but it was rare. They were as territorial as werewolves, but they liked group snuggles and caresses. Vampires appreciated the art of touch, of moving fluids through the body, warming the muscles. Maybe Sara and Ethan would do okay as vampires.

"Let Your will prevail," he whispered. "What is done, is done."

True words, Father. There is nothing I can do to undo what has already happened. But what kind of accident would have sent Sara into the afterlife? Why didn't she want me there? None of the events that transpired add up.

Father Ryan stood up and fluffed his robes. He bowed his head and backed ten steps from the cross and then turned around and gazed at her.

"I'm scared to see Sara," she confessed. *I'm terrified to see Jeremy. I blamed him when I should have probably blamed Sara.*

He nodded and pursed his lips as if he understood but was frustrated by her lack of total acceptance of Sara's new life. Unfortunately, Mere'd experienced all his expressions, especially this one. "She will become a better version of herself."

"What does that mean?" She crossed her legs. "She's always been a good kid." *Kind of. On occasion. When she got what she wanted.*

"No, she hasn't always been good. She sees that now, most of the time." The shuffle of his slippers over stone and the swish of his robes as he moved toward her seemed so normal, so comforting. "She blamed you for things *she did*. More than half your overnight moves from apartment to apartment were because of her loud mouth or her involvement with the wrong kids. Nicholas has set her straight, and Ethan has a gift of showing her what real battles looks like. I don't know how he does it, but she's confessed to some very bad things. She has a ways to go, but once she apologizes and asks *your* forgiveness, she will truly be on the right path. She's already confessed and asked Jeremy's and Nicholas's forgiveness."

How could she have confessed to anyone after turning two days ago? "She must have recovered quickly."

"It's gentler than people think." He adjusted his robes and sat angled, facing her in the pew with his back against the armrest. "She is a little gaunt still, but once she consistently follows the rules of her people, some pink will return to her cheeks."

"Does Ethan know about her *new life*?" she whispered.

"He does. Nicholas and Jeremy believe him trustworthy." He rested his arm on top of the backrest. "Jeremy worried about her relationship with Ethan, so he and Nicholas flew to Arizona. If they hadn't been there, we'd be lighting candles for Sara."

"Will you tell me what happened? Did she try a hand at cooking and slice an artery by accident? She's clumsy like that. Drugs? She's done that before. Is she too embarrassed to tell me?" She gazed into his bright blue eyes for any sign she'd hit the nail on the head.

The same tight-lipped expression as before blanketed his face. "That's a conversation you need to have with Sara."

She closed her eyes and inhaled. "I'd like to know what I'm walking into. Lainie won't tell me. Jeremy…" She exhaled so deeply her heart began to ache for a truth she feared would never come. For some reason, Father Ryan's spiritual side was locked down tight, and until recently, she hadn't wanted him to open up or touch him to see what he knew. "If I walk in and no one will tell me anything because Ethan beat her to an inch of her life—"

"Ethan did nothing of the sort," he said. "Ethan was helpless to save her. You could not have saved her. Nicholas was her only option, and she came back for him."

"I see now that those calls and texts between Sara and Nicholas were more than homework. But what would make her want to be one of them over dying a human?" *I love Jeremy, but I'd choose death before I'd ever choose life as a vampire.*

"Love." He leaned back against the armrest. "She found a love worth running through a lifetime of obstacles to hold onto. Nicholas found the same love with her. I'm not sure that Ethan feels the same, but he's here and doesn't want to leave, at least not yet."

Tears filled Mere's eyes. She looked down at her hands clasped tightly in her lap. *A love reciprocated, something I will never know. I ran through Hell to save her life and she can't even—*

She shook her head and refused to go down the path Jeremy always showed her when it came to Sara. *She's a teen. They make mistakes.* "Do you think she wants me to move back here? Does she even want me in her life?"

She gazed up at him only to see the pained expression and hear the sucking in of air through his clenched teeth.

She raised her hands and lowered her head. "Don't answer that."

"Do you want to live here? Have you let go of the past to move forward with Jeremy?"

"I don't know what I want." She shrugged. "I guess I thought I'd always be near Sara but the future I hoped for her is not possible now. I don't know where I fit in or if I do at all."

"You could accept Jeremy's offer and move in with him. Sara would visit you and you would visit her. He could turn you and—"

"I'm not doing anything to change my humanity. I won't budge on that, and he won't budge on his refusal to move or even consider buying a house." *What happens if I did become a vampire for him? He would finally win the last battle in the game he's been playing, and I'd lose the last piece of myself worth keeping. He'd get tired of having me around and throw me out on the streets like I was trash.*

"Are you seriously considering staying in Arizona without Sara?"

Am I? "I guess I am."

"But you lost your job."

"I found a new one." *I'll probably lose it within a few weeks, but maybe I won't. Maybe I need a new beginning away from werewolves and vampires and everything else that seems to reside in this city.*

He tilted his head and raised his brows so high they seemed to almost hide within the deep wrinkles of his forehead. "You need to talk to Jeremy. You need a run-in with Faith. You need…" He kept talking, but the man she loved took her breath away as he strode into the room from the private entrance on the right.

Jeremy halted near Father Ryan and unbuttoned the collar of his black silk shirt, revealing pale skin flushed a light pink.

The ache in her chest expanded as Jeremy's gaze dropped to her chest and he frowned.

She crossed her arms over her chest. Her nipples tightened to hard beads at the pressure. Her belly heated. She straightened her back, and her clit rings pressed in as they slid against the hard wood of the pew and made her pussy quiver. *Dietrich.*

"Father Ryan, I need a few moments alone with my wife," Jeremy said.

"I'm not your wife," she said. "No rings. No marriage ceremony. No license filed with the State of Georgia."

Father Ryan frowned at her. "Mr. Hunter, take as long as you please." He stood up, keeping his frown and disappointed glare on her. He walked to the left side of the sanctuary and disappeared through the door into his office.

Jeremy took two strides forward. "You disobeyed me."

"I don't have to obey you." She uncrossed her arms and lifted her T-shirt over her breasts. "They're nice and sparkly. I think they're sexy."

He licked his lips and his fangs extended. "Is that a church offering?"

Warmth spread across her cheeks. She pulled her shirt down. "That was a bad call. I'm sorry." *There goes my stupid mouth and actions getting me in trouble.*

"No, no. Take it off. You kept my rules. No bra. No panties?" He dropped his gaze from her breasts to between her legs.

She uncrossed her legs and stood up. "Are you here to chat or to inspect me?" She tugged the hem of the denim skirt down a little farther as the color of his eyes swirled with a mosaic of green hues reminding her of the first night they made love. *You were so gentle. That night was the most magical night of my life.*

"I wasn't sure you'd come back home." He knelt on one knee as he continued to gaze at her.

"What are you doing?"

"I love you more than you'll ever believe I do. Meredith, will you marry me? Right here. Right now." He held a red velvet jewelry box in the palm of his hand and opened it. "Please, Meredith. I don't change easily or quickly. I'm willing to compromise a little. You don't have to become a vampire for us to be married legally in your world. I vow that I will love you exactly the way you are for the rest of my life."

I've waited for this moment for twelve years. Twelve years and you do it when I've finally decided to make a home where no one but humans dwell?

He took her left hand in his. Their surroundings faded as a vision pushed forward…

The lights of the city carried a glow into the dark clouds hiding the skyline she knew like the back of her hand.

The terrace door opened behind her. Jeremy slid his hand under her silk robe and over the heavy curve marking her pregnancy. "Come back to bed."

She glanced into the sky for the harvest moon she knew hid behind the darkness. "The moon is calling me."

"You're in labor." He brushed the blond hair covering her neck behind her back and kissed the pulsing vein at her neck. "Come to bed where everything is prepared."

She gazed at his pale hand over her sparkling silver sun-kissed skin. She placed her hand over his and leaned back against him. "A few more minutes."

"I'll leave the doors wide open, as long as you stay in bed." He guided her from the private terrace to their bed stripped of everything except the soft crimson sheets and pillows.

The bedroom door opened. Nicholas peeked inside. "Elisabeth is finally sleeping. She giggled every time I talked about her baby sister being born tonight. Everything okay?"

Jeremy gently slid her toward the head of the bed until she rested against the pile of pillows. He sat at the foot of the bed. "Elisabeth will have a baby sister in a few minutes."

The need to push overwhelmed Mere. She grunted and groaned as her body opened with ease, so different from the other times.

Stretching. Burning. Bones shifting. A gush of blood

and the relief of pressure…

A baby cried.

Black hair like Jeremy's. Tiny nose. Pink lips.

Jeremy placed their daughter to her breast.

A hard contraction hit and in seconds her breasts enlarged and her body shifted back to normal.

The baby suckled her breast.

Jeremy kissed Mere's lips. "You're about to get hit with another—"

"Darling," Dietrich's voice cut through her vision and brought her rushing back to reality.

She pivoted toward the sound of his voice. *He can't be here. Jeremy will hurt him.*

Black baseball cap, black athletic shirt stretched tight across his muscular chest, and black jeans highlighting his powerful thighs couldn't hide the god-like appearance of her sexy man.

"What are you doing here?" she asked. *You have no idea what you're walking into.*

Dietrich strolled down the center aisle of the sanctuary as if it were his home. "You're here. I'm here." He wrapped his arms around her and she returned the embrace. "I missed you cuddled up next to me last night."

"I missed you too," she whispered before she realized what she'd said in front of Jeremy. She quickly pushed him away. "You shouldn't be here."

"Why?" Dietrich asked. "Churches are sacred. Jeremy doesn't mind. Do you, Jeremy?"

She glanced at Jeremy. "Do you know Dietrich?"

"Yes," Jeremy hissed. "Is your clit double pierced with the same types of diamonds as the ones on your nipples?"

"Yeah, but what does that have to do—"

Jeremy looked at Dietrich. "We're blood-bonded as husband and wife and have been for fourteen years. For the last twelve she has taken the role of my wife according to our laws. Our life together is documented in the history of my people. Meredith's name is written as my only heir in vampire law."

"Yes, I've recently become aware of your relationship status," Dietrich said. "You've hidden it all very well."

"I am not your wife, Jeremy. We've never made vows—"

"We have," Jeremy said. "I vowed to protect you, give you my blood and my body for eternity. You vowed the same. It's written inside the crest of our blood-bond on your skin and on mine."

"That isn't marriage—"

"It is a vampire marriage ceremony," Dietrich cut her off. "Blood-bonds are rare."

"How do you know about vampires?" Mere looked for the best escape route. *Jeremy hasn't attacked him. Dietrich seems too comfortable.* "Are *you* a vampire?"

Dietrich released a hearty chuckle. "No, darling. I'm not one of them. Let's go see Sara and then we'll deal with your situation with Jeremy."

"You're not breaking our bond," Jeremy said. "I will never allow it. And if you kill me, Meredith will be bound through our blood-bond to end your life."

Dietrich sighed and frowned. "Jeremy, who sends you birthday cards every year?"

Jeremy slouched and lowered his head. "You."

"Who raised you when your parents passed

away?" Dietrich asked.

"You, sir," Jeremy said.

"Who taught you how to lead your people?"

"You, sir," Jeremy whispered.

"Who didn't tell me anything about the woman you fell in love with?" Dietrich's voice carried a hard, chastising edge.

"I'm sorry. I should have." Jeremy hunched over as if he were being slowly beaten down over all his transgressions.

"Who is to blame in this predicament?" Dietrich asked.

"I am," Jeremy said.

"Who the heck are you?" She asked. *Warlock? They live hundreds of years as long as they take the potions for longevity.*

Dietrich pushed his glasses up the bridge of his nose into place. "We can talk about all the specifics of me after we deal with what is happening with Sara."

Jeremy lifted his chin, straightened his posture, and gasped. "You didn't tell her who you are?"

"We were busy," Dietrich said.

"Is that why it took her three weeks to get here?" Jeremy asked.

"She has a strong sense of responsibility." Dietrich gazed at her with a smartass grin. "Or it might have taken much longer."

"Three weeks?" she gasped. "What are you talking about? It's been a couple days." She hurried to the front pew and rummaged through her purse for her phone. She tapped on the screen and it came to life. In smaller text under the time… *December seventeenth. It can't be. I missed Thanksgiv-*

ing? "What are you?"

She sucked in air as Dietrich pressed his front against her back and slid his hand under her shirt.

He curled his fingers around her hip under the waistband of her skirt and sent a heat wave of desire racing through her. "I'm Dietrich Wolfgang, partner in Luke's hotel ventures. I'm independently wealthy and live in Germany where I'd like for us to live, although I have come to accept that moving to my home won't happen immediately. Living in Ulvene is a good second choice."

Her pulse accelerated as her pussy prepared for his cock. "How could you have raised Jeremy? He's older than you." She turned around in his arms and her brain seemed to shut down most of its functioning. A mist of confusion set in as she tried to make sense of their conversation. "Are you two related?"

The light blue of his eyes dilated and turned almost white, reminding her of something so familiar, something she should recognize, but her thoughts scattered farther away. *I love you. I want you to love me back. Show me you would walk to the ends of the earth to be with me.*

"You really don't know who he is?" Jeremy said.

She wanted to look at Jeremy, but those commanding eyes kept her attention. "I don't know." *You came all this way to be with me, to support me in a situation you don't know anything about. Or do you know?*

"He's the ruler of all of us," Jeremy said. "Dietrich Ulvene Wolfgang is the oldest living alternative being on earth. He is the supreme judge over all conflicts that happen between factions of all of us except humans. He rules over all alternate beings. He is the Alpha over all werebeasts. We call him World Alpha. He is *The Werewolf* that everyone fears. *Everyone* fears him, Mere. If we all gathered against him, *he* would win. If you, with all the power you are capable of unleashing, went up against him, *he could crush you without raising a finger.*"

Dietrich wet his lips with a slow, sensual glide of his tongue as if he were caressing hers. "Darling, I am holding back from making love to you in this church so we can visit with your niece, the girl you raised as your daughter."

She lifted her chin and curled her arms around his neck. She burned to make love to him. "Sara can wait."

He nodded. "She can." His nostrils flared. "But you came all this way and it would be irresponsible to ignore the meeting."

"Meredith, Dietrich is a werewolf. He's. A. Were. Wolf," Jeremy shouted.

"That's not possible," she whispered. *Why is he lying? Does he know I love you?* She blinked, but she caught Dietrich's gaze. "You can't be. I'd know. I'd never have slept with you." *I'd never fall in love with a werewolf. They go feral at the drop of a hat. They kill. They're not…*

"I love you." Dietrich glided his hands over her ass, and his chest rumbled with the sexiest vibration that sounded like a man's growl, not a wolf's.

"Meredith Teresa Kilpatrick," Jeremy hissed. "Get. Over. Here."

Something snapped into place, and she turned tail and ran to Jeremy. She slipped her hand in his.

"Baby," he whispered. "Keep your head in the

game."

She gasped as a jolt of electricity surged through her hand holding Jeremy. "I'm not myself, Jeremy." *I've got to get out of here and away from both of you.*

"Darling." Dietrich took her other hand.

Energy so powerful washed over her, she collapsed under the massive weight. He and Jeremy moved as one, supporting her and keeping her upright.

"Power and wealth hold great responsibility," Dietrich said.

"Stop showing off." Jeremy squeezed her hand. "Walk. Take control of your mind. He's controlling you."

"Love is controlling her," Dietrich cooed. "We're passionate. Our bodies and spirits react to the ones we truly love." He kissed the side of her face. "I'll carry you." He moved more quickly than Jeremy and swept her up into his arms. "I will always protect you."

The power Dietrich unleashed slowly absorbed into her system as he guided them into Jeremy's secret passageway from the church to the underground chambers leading to rooms she knew were there but never accessed. The rooms with things she didn't want to know about, or see, or hear. Rooms that she wouldn't consider going in. Not under any circumstances. Not even for Sara. Never.

CHAPTER SIXTEEN

THE STENCH OF DEATH NEARLY made Meredith retch. She covered her mouth and held her breath.

Dietrich placed her on her feet and stood silently beside her inside the entrance. The only light came from the dim gas flames attached to old copper sconces in the dank, ominous hallway.

Chains made to haul heavy equipment were connected to immense rings bolted to stone walls stained with crimson and black blood. Floor to ceiling remnants of the basest of actions vampires had performed remained etched in the history of the room.

In the right corner, mostly hidden in the darkness, a chained figure hunched behind the man who changed the course of Sara's natural life.

"She's sensitive to light," Nicholas said softly. "Please, if you would, close the door behind you. Your eyes will adjust quickly." He stepped forward, but kept his gaze lower than hers. "I fear your wrath, Meredith. Are you seeking vengeance?"

The necessity to breathe won out over the desire

not to. She inhaled the horrid aroma and moved her hand from her mouth to grip her belly. Her body trembled from memories stored within her muscles and bones. She rocked back and forth seemingly glued to the spot. *Not Sara. Not Sara. Oh, God. Oh, God.*

She opened her mouth to protest Sara's placement in the wretched room, but nothing came out.

Neon green eyes peered out from behind the formidable Nicholas Carson, Jeremy's right hand man, and lit a path as exact as a laser straight to her.

"I thought it best Ethan not be here for this," Nicholas said. "She tends to lose control when he's in the room."

Jeremy took Mere's hand. "New vampires have issues with impulse control. She's learning skills here she hadn't learned in the life she lived prior to now."

Anger burned through her. "Is that a dig, Jeremy? You don't think I did a good job raising her? You want to argue? Is that where this is going, because…Damnit. Bring. It. On." *I did the best I could raising my sister's kid. I loved her as if I gave her life.*

"You didn't hold her accountable, Mere. She walked all over you," Jeremy yelled. "You let the guilt you never should have had run your parenting. So, fuck yeah, it's your damn fault she's in here. It's your damn fault she told Nicholas and me instead of you about transforming into a fucking werewolf. She hated me. Hated. Me. And she still told me over you because of your werewolf bigotry." He cupped the sides of her face. "The only reason she's not dead is because I love you and allowed Nicholas to do what he's wanted to do for years, and that is take her as his wife and turn her. I never wanted her in *my coven* because I knew this is where she would start her life – in the torture cell."

"I will not allow you to—"

"You will," Dietrich said. "She'll be out of here when she realizes manipulation doesn't work. She's not that slow, and she enjoys her creature comforts."

"You don't speak for me." She tried to glance at Dietrich, but Jeremy held her head in place.

"I do," Dietrich said.

"The hell you do," she shouted. The haze in her brain lifted and Jeremy smiled.

"There's my girl," Jeremy whispered.

She pulled his hands from her face. "I'm not your girl or his girl or anybody's girl. I don't have a ring on my finger." She pushed him to the side and crossed the uneven floor. "Sara, stand up. I need to see you."

A sharp hiss echoed in the room as the shadowed figure rose behind Nicholas. "I'm stronger than you."

"You wish," Mere said. "Stop hiding behind Nicholas."

"This is not going well." Nicholas ran his hand over his bald head. "Let's try this in a few hours after she's fed again."

Mere halted midstride. "Wait." She glanced over her shoulder at Jeremy. "Did you say she wanted to be a werewolf? *Ethan is a werewolf?*"

Jeremy nodded. "I've never lied to you, Meredith. Dietrich is a werewolf too. Is it finally processing?"

"Yeah. I'm following you now." *I'm the only*

human in here. Mere turned her head and stared at the delicate hand covered in dried blood clasping Nicholas's pant leg.

If I didn't buy those damn concert tickets, you never would have met Ethan. We would have gone to Tempe and started over. No vampires. No werewolves. But I bought the tickets and your shitty friends ended up being there, bringing those thugs to harass us. I don't know how they could have known we'd be there. You wouldn't have told them. Or would you? Did you?

The beautiful girl with long brown hair and cozy brown eyes that sparkled with life was gone. An ashen face. Unnatural neon green eyes. Dark circles. Skin hung on bone. Stringy hair covered in blood. Every inch of her body showed traces of what she'd become.

"You're never going to touch my husband," Sara hissed. "Touch me. See in your visions how I will kill you in a heartbeat."

I am fucking cursed. Love will never be returned.

"I wouldn't harm Nicholas or Ethan, Sara. I respect your choices." *I've never hurt you or anyone you loved. How many times have I told you I love you unconditionally? I've told you I would love you if you turned into a zombie. Why wouldn't I love you as a wolf? I'd be shocked. I am shocked. I don't understand why you'd choose that life or this one.*

Sara's vampire fangs extended as her gaze at Mere seemed to intensify. The fury inside Sara seemed to grow and fester like a plague rising from her soul for the world to see. So much anger. So much hatred.

Have you always hated me? The girl for whom she moved across the country. The girl she'd raised and showered with as much love and understanding as possible. The girl she'd worked horrible jobs and hours to protect and love. The unspeakable things she'd done just to give Sara the chance of a real life, a husband to love, a big family. Keeping Jeremy at arm's length, when she'd wanted to live in the safety of his home and sleep in his bed. *I wanted marriage. I wanted Jeremy.*

"Why would you lie about Ethan being a were-wolf?" Mere asked. "I know he told you. Had you told me, I could have helped you with your transition. I could have given you my blood to strengthen you." *I bet any love you might have felt for me was lost in the turning. But you came to me. Begged me to protect Ethan. Was there no love then?*

A few more steps and she'd be within touching distance. *If you attack, I won't fight. Not you.*

One. Two. Three steps forward.

Mere wrapped Sara up in her arms for possibly the last time.

Before Sara could escape Mere's hold, the room fell away and a vision came to life…

Mere shivered as the sprinkles from the gray clouds turned to a mixture of rain and sleet. She gazed at the shackles on her bruised wrists and then at the chimney puffing out the scent of burning pine. The glow of warmth radiated from the large log cabin fifty yards away. Dirt trickled down from the tangled strands of hair that looked like clumps of dirt hanging from matted yarn. She leaned against the wooden pole she'd been tethered to like an animal for longer than she could remember.

Her sister Kate opened the front door, slipped into white furry boots, pulled the hood of her long fur coat over the top of her head, and walked over to Meredith.

The pretty caramel of her eyes…the full lips…the rosy cheeks…her plump fingers buttoned the beautiful snowy white coat closed from her neck down to the tops of her boots. Kate was and had everything Mere dreamed of being and having, always beautiful, clean, and lavishly clothed and fed.

"The hail should stop soon. Then it's supposed to rain all week." Kate took her hand from her pocket and tossed a small, white, square bar of soap at Mere. "If you survive, clean up when it rains. You stink."

She lifted her heels and pivoted with the grace of a prima ballerina toward the house. "Pray that God will end your life. I know I do."

The stone walls returned. The stench of blood and death filled Mere's nose. Sara stood trembling with Nicholas's strong arms wrapped around her.

"She looked like me," Sara whispered. "That was you. That was you as a little girl."

Mere stared as shiny emeralds chased the neon green from Sara's eyes. A painful lump in her throat wouldn't allow words.

"Was that my mother?" Sara asked. "That was you?"

Mere nodded. *One of the better moments with Kate.*

"You told me my mom was the best mother in the entire world besides your own," Sara said. "You *lied?*" She tilted her head to the side like Jeremy always did when he was confused. "You never lie."

"Doesn't everyone want a mother who is kind and loving and nurturing?" Mere whispered. "Someone who is forgiving." She bit her bottom lip. "Someone who will love them no matter what they are, or end up being, or choose to be." She held her heart as it ached so miserably that it felt like someone was tearing her apart from the most vulnerable place in her body. "I'm going now. I didn't want you to see that." *I didn't want to remember those days.* "I want the best for you. Always."

Mere hurried to the exit. "Nicholas, I'll check in with Jeremy. Please take care of her. Clean and clothe her. Get her out of this room. I don't care what she's done. Punish her another way." She placed her hand on the door over Jeremy's. "Sara, close your eyes. Even dim lighting will hurt, and…" *I don't want you to hurt like I do.* "Jeremy, open this door or I'm going to break it down."

The door opened. She stepped into the hallway and ran faster than she'd ever run in her life out of the secret passageway, through the church, and outside into the bright sunlight. She shielded her eyes as they adjusted to the sudden change.

Running nowhere fast, she searched her surroundings for a place to hide and regroup. She darted into a corner grocery and over to the checkout counter.

"Hey." Mere looked at the girl with neon pink hair wearing a dress to match behind the counter.

"Hey," the girl said. "You're Mere Kilpatrick. I thought you moved west."

"I did. I was just visiting…Things…uh…" *Do I know you?*

"Things went bad. I know how that goes in this neighborhood." The girl rubbed the scar line from her freckled shoulder to her elbow and dropped her hand. "Type in the code: 344556. The office is in the back. My purse is on the desk."

"Thanks. May I use your phone?" Mere asked.

The girl grinned. "You don't remember me, but

you showed me this day seven years ago. Hurry and get in the office. Leave through the emergency exit. I cut the alarm and turned off the video camera this morning." She fluffed her hair. "Today, I'm going to win enough money for my life to change and meet my dream man."

Not questioning destiny, Mere followed the girl's directions and typed in the code. She opened the door and saw the purse and a pink card with her name on it. She closed the door and read the note.

Take the phone and envelope inside the purse.

I never got to thank you for saving my life from that crazy man who cornered me in an alley on the way to school when I was twelve. Thank you.

-Faith

Mere folded the note. *I remember you now. Little mousey girl with pale skin and dirty-blond hair with a compound fracture when I showed up. I killed that man right in front of you and you never told the police.* She took the phone and pink envelope from the purse and pushed open the door to the outside.

Dietrich stood at one side of the exit and Jeremy stood at the other. Lainie sat in the front passenger seat of Luke's black luxury SUV blocking any chance of getting away.

Lainie rolled down the window. "Get in. I'm going to mediate this mess. If you want to leave once we're done, Luke and I will take you anywhere you want to go."

"And if I refuse?" Mere asked. *How are you involved in this? Is Luke a werewolf? No. He can't be. Shit. The vision. All those women. War. He's too young to have lived through all those conflicts. He seemed so normal that I ignored the signs. No werewolves I've ever met were like him. He's not feral, not even after we met. He never hit on me. He sent the I'm-not-interested vibe every time I moved close before I found out he was in love with you. How is that possible? What is different about him?*

Luke stuck his head next to Lainie's. "Climb into the car or this will end up being more uncomfortable than it already is."

A black limo pulled up behind Lainie's car. Another SUV and limousine joined the line of vehicles, and then another pairing filed in two at a time down the street as far as she could see.

"This is a serious situation," Lainie said.

"Yeah, I can see that." Mere opened the car door to the backseat and climbed in.

Jeremy and Dietrich joined her in the back, sandwiching her in the middle.

"Where are we going?" Mere gazed at Jeremy. *Have you been right all these years? You took me on all those trips to see Sara's grandparents. They said I was cursed. You kept telling me they were lies. Lies humans tell to explain things they don't understand. You hate them, and yet you take me every year to their home. You even protected them because I asked.*

Jeremy placed his hand on her thigh. "There's nothing sinister about this mediation, Mere. No matter what happens, I will always protect and love you. I don't need a blood-bond to love you. I loved you the first moment we met, and I will love you into the afterlife and beyond. You burned your love into my soul and not even World Alpha Dietrich Wolfgang can take it away. I've been Soulburned by you, Meredith Kilpatrick."

The heat of Dietrich's hand on her knee caused

Mere to twist toward him. He slid his hand under her skirt until his fingers grazed her clit jewelry. He whispered in her ear, "We'll see if he is Soulburned. Darling, it doesn't matter if he is. You and I are mates."

She whimpered and spread her legs. *Show me.*

Dietrich moved in a blink of an eye. His hand on the back of her head. His lips on hers. His tongue slid between her teeth and stroked her tongue. Her clit tightened for his touch, his attention.

She trembled inside as her heart beat faster and her breathing labored. *More.*

His lips left hers, but puffs of his fresh breath kept her in rapt attention. "You might enjoy hearing *his* words, feeling his familiar touch, but make no mistake in thinking your feelings for him are more than yours for me. You, Meredith Kilpatrick, are *mine. My name* is written in the fabric of your DNA. Your body will bear *my children.* You belong to *me.*"

CHAPTER SEVENTEEN

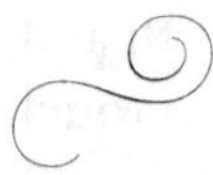

MERE HANDED LAINIE ANOTHER JAVE-LIN from the shed on the opposite side of the track field behind her house. "What are we doing?"

"Order me not to tell anyone about this conversation, not even Luke," Lainie whispered.

"I shouldn't have to order you not to tell about our private conversations, Lainie. I expect you never to tell anyone else anything I say unless I specifically tell you it's okay. Come on. What is with that ordering thing anyway? Is Luke that controlling? Do I need to have a conversation with him?" *What is going on with you?* "It's the werewolf thing, isn't it? Luke asks, you tell?" She handed Lainie the last javelin.

"Yeah." Lainie nodded. "It's really great, but it does have its drawbacks in situations like this." She closed the shed and walked to the front of the metal cart with the equipment in containers organized in groups for each activity inside. "There are things that Dietrich will have to tell you because he's not like other werewolves."

Mere glanced at the three men on the track. "How much do you know about my background?"

"Almost everything now. I didn't have a clue until a few days ago. But once Luke told me, all the bruises, the cuts, the stitches…" Lainie gently touched Mere's arm. "All your injuries over the years suddenly made sense. I have never experienced a feral werewolf attack. I've never even seen one, but Luke said they are insane and terrifying. He's in awe of you."

"I don't really want to talk about it." Mere continued watching the men. Luke and Jeremy kept shaking out their arms and legs as if it were a part of their warm-up. The awkwardness of it all highlighted Dietrich's utter calm.

Dietrich met her gaze and smiled as if she lit up his entire world. She returned the smile, but held back from lifting her hand and waving like he was the captain of the football team and she was the girl no one ever noticed—no one but him.

She would get her heart broken before she invited him over for dinner. He would leave for greener pastures and a woman with less baggage. "What are they doing over there?"

"Luke is nervous, so he's…I don't know what he's doing. He looks like an idiot."

Luke glanced at her and immediately stopped moving. He rolled his shoulders and then stood motionless.

"It's like he knows what you're thinking," Mere mumbled.

"He does," Lainie said. "The benefit of being mated. We can communicate with each other without speaking. We do it through a spiritual web of sorts that is connected to our thoughts. There is the mating link, and then there are pack links which include everyone in your specific pack. I'm in two, the Georgia Pack and the Nevada Pack, but I'm also in the International Alpha Pack, which is made up of all the Alphas over each sectioned area of the world. It's an intense group. There are private links and so many others that I haven't connected to yet. The mating thing happens over years with the kind of power Luke has inside him."

Lainie squeezed Mere's arm. "Please don't let your past experiences influence what is about to happen here."

"Are you one of them?" Mere stared at Laine's hand gripping her bicep. Nothing seemed different about her friend. Mere continued searching along Lainie's arm and shoulder, jaw and ears looking for any sign of the wolf lurking inside. Lainie's human-ness seemed fully intact.

Lainie dropped her hand to her side and nodded. "Luke saved my life when he changed me. I would have died with Frank that day, but I had to live. I had to live for Frank and for Luke…and for me." She placed her hand on the black rubber handle of the cart. "I grew a couple inches, but I'm much shorter than the born werewolves. I'm as lean as them, though."

"You've always been lean. You don't look taller. I don't understand how it works."

Lainie pulled the cart across the track to the center football field as Mere joined her at her side like they'd done for years. "I don't understand it, but it was like when you told me Frank needed to go to the doctor immediately or he would die within a month. You gave me a year more with him than I would have had. I can't explain the gift you have. I don't understand why or how one day I can be human and the next I'm a werewolf, but I don't have to today and neither do you."

"You don't seem different. I was so stressed out at the wedding thinking if we were attacked, I couldn't save everyone, and I was in the middle of an entire pack." She glanced at Dietrich, but his back faced her. He lifted up his shirt and the way the sun hit the silver sparkles on his skin made a mirrored disco ball effect which highlighted the broad and ripped muscles over his back and neck. *Every inch of you is magnificent.*

He turned his head and caught her ogling him. He parted his lips and dang if she didn't want a taste of him.

She lowered her gaze. *Get a grip. He's a damn were-wolf, and he wants to change me. I'm not changing for either one of them. I was born human, I'm dying human. But if I were to change? What am I thinking? No.*

She raised her gaze and swallowed hard. Dietrich slid his hand down the perfect rectangles of his abs. His hand explored lower, dipped into his shorts and adjusted the hard bulge.

You could make me agree to anything. I'd probably beg for you to change me if I believed you loved me.

She blew an exhale. *I am more fucked up than I thought. I'm considering the unthinkable.*

Lainie sighed. "Yeah, Dietrich is on another level of perfection."

"He's not wearing his glasses. He needs to wear his glasses. The man is semi-blind, and as a were-wolf, he'd be picked off pretty quickly in a fight.

Please tell me they aren't going to fight. I'm against some kind of testosterone-induced domination game. I don't respond well to that." *Do werewolves lose their sight as they age? I've never met one who wore glasses until—*

"He can see," Lainie said.

"I highly doubt that."

Lainie dropped a handful of javelins, making a racket. "When two men are interested in the same woman they aren't willing to share, but they prefer a peaceful resolution, they set up a mediation. Luke told me they used to fight to the death, but in the last few hundred years they changed the rules to games of strategy and strength."

"How civilized." *Not.* Mere picked up the long-bow stand from the back of the cart and placed it on the lush green grass. *I'm not a possession. They want to beat each other, not win my heart.* "When will this be over? I'm ready to go home or on vacation or anywhere but here."

"They're going to race on the track, throw the javelin at the red mark on the ground on the other side of the field near the fenced-off garden, and then try and slice my arrows down the center wherever they land."

Mere laughed. "That will be fun to watch. I hope you get creative."

Lainie hung quivers filled with arrows on the bow-stand hooks. "Me and my daddy used to have so much fun practicing. He'd take me out in storms and…I've told you this story. He was so awesome. Luke is so much like him." Lainie placed her hand on her belly and smiled. "This baby is going to have a wonderful life."

"That's for sure," Mere said. "So, after you blow their minds with your skills, I can leave?"

Lainie nodded. "I don't want to lose you, Mere. Please don't hate me."

Mere wrapped an arm around Lainie. "I'd never hate you. I don't want you to hate me and…" She glanced at Dietrich. *You need your glasses.*

"Get your glasses, Dietrich," she shouted. "You shouldn't run without being able to see or you'll trip or break something." *Dumbass. You're just as handsome with them as without. Maybe more so with them. Definitely sexier with them. I really like the glasses.*

The man grinned and stared at her as Luke stepped off the track.

"One loop around," Luke shouted. "Ready?"

Jeremy seemed totally focused on winning.

"On your mark. Set. Go," Luke shouted.

Jeremy took off, but Dietrich left the track and jogged to Mere.

Mere dropped her arm to her side. "What are you doing?"

"Seeing if you need any help." He curled his arms around her and dipped her backward. "I missed you."

"You did?" she whispered.

His hot lips gently touched hers. "So much, dar-ling."

She closed her eyes and parted her mouth. "How much?"

He licked her lips. "So much I can't think about anything else." He slid his hand to her bottom and pressed his bulge between her legs.

"But you'll lose the race," she said, panting.

"Fuck the race," he growled. "You are my top

priority. If you want me to run, I'm going to carry you. I never want to be away from you."

Her heart pitter-pattered in a steady but different rhythm than ever before. Cream rushed from her pussy onto her running shorts.

"Yeah?" she cooed like a teen in love.

"Yes, my beautiful Meredith."

She made a whimpering sound filled with such desire that she would have run, hidden, or been embarrassed with anyone else. But not him.

A vibration that half sounded like a purr rumbled in his throat. "Wrap your legs around my waist and pull the crotch of your shorts to the side."

She obeyed. *I shouldn't do this. I want you inside me. I shouldn't want you.*

Currents of electricity surged through her and seemed to bounce around inside and along her sex. She rolled her hips and rubbed her folds against his abs.

Rushed breathing caressed her mouth like a rough kiss.

Fuck me, Dietrich. I want you now. Right now. Oh, God, I wish you could hear me.

"I want to bury my face in your pussy," he whispered. He sucked her bottom lip into his mouth and slowly released.

She opened her eyes and panted. "Yeah, I want that. I really want that."

"I can't until this test is over."

"Fuck the test." She nearly hyperventilated as she tried to kiss him.

"We can't." He straightened up with her wrapped like a blanket around him. "Stay by my side for the rest of the games."

"Okay. Yes. Absolutely." *Anything you want.* She dropped her legs and slid down his taut body. "Wear your glasses."

"Yes, darling," he whispered. "As long as I have you, I'll wear them."

"Jeremy wins the first race," Luke shouted.

Jeremy walked toward them. "And I will win the rest." He stopped beside Dietrich. "You're going to lose, so you don't even try? That is not the Dietrich I know."

Dietrich shrugged. "What's next?"

Luke took the glasses hanging from the collar of his green athletic shirt and handed them to Dietrich. "Javelin. Six throws. Get as close to one red mark as you can."

"I'm great at this." Jeremy picked up a javelin, rocked back and forth, then ran and released. The flight and arc of the metal rod was beauty in motion, a lesson in perfection. One after the other landed on the mark.

With his glasses in place, Dietrich held her hand and squeezed. "Any advice?"

She tugged his hand and he bent over with his ear near her lips. "Can you see your mark?" she whispered.

He nodded.

"Have you ever thrown a javelin?" she asked.

He nodded. "It's been a long time."

She kissed his cheek. "Good luck." *You are so screwed.*

He held her hand with his left hand and picked up all six javelins with his right.

"Dietrich, you can't do it like…" She watched as he coiled back his arm and flung the rods with almost no effort. "Holy shit, you're strong."

The sound of metal scraping against metal ended with a loud clatter and thunk. One hit the mark, but the rest of the javelins formed the shape of a heart, which melted her own at the sweet sign of affection.

She raised her gaze to the man holding her hand. "I don't know what to say." *You don't care about beating Jeremy. Are you trying to impress me?*

"Yes," Jeremy hissed. "I win again." He moved to the bow stand and picked up the black bow and quiver as Lainie picked up hers. "I know what to do."

"Are you hungry?" Dietrich asked. He pushed the middle of his glasses up along the bridge of his nose and seemed to inspect her. "Thirsty? Are you feeling okay? You're perspiring."

"I'm hungry, but I can wait until this is over." She swiped away the sweat from her forehead. *It's not hot. I shouldn't be sweating. I shouldn't have allowed them to bully me into coming here.* "I can't hold your hand through this."

"Stand behind me and hold me around my waist," he whispered.

Luke handed him the wooden bow and leather quiver. "Lunch is waiting in the sunroom." He gazed at Mere. "You okay?" He sniffed and frowned. "You're hungry and thirsty, and you're ignoring your body's call to action."

Mere closed her arms around Dietrich's waist and pressed her body against his. *Why isn't Jeremy asking me to hold him? To kiss him for good luck?*

He barely moved as the sound of the shaft against leather signaled the release. His arm seemed like an extension of the bow. The string vibrated, yet he took no notice as he swiftly emptied the quiver of its contents. Arrows flew across the field forming a pattern as they silently entered the target. In seconds, the event was over.

"Again," Jeremy bragged. "I win."

Mere gazed at the two targets. Jeremy's arrows all centered in the middle, perfectly splitting all of Lainie's arrows down the middle, where Dietrich's formed a heart with the bullseye as the top dip that connected to the two sides as one like in the Javelin throw. Lainie's cluster of arrows were left untouched at the top right corner.

"You're my heart." Dietrich swept her up and carried her across the field to the sunroom off the kitchen entrance.

"Why didn't you win? You clearly could have," she asked.

"This is a learning experience for Jeremy," he said. "I hope I don't have to explain the lesson when this is over, but I have a feeling I will."

"Lesson?" *I am not following you. I thought the loser had to walk away from me.*

"Actions of love are the purpose of each event," he whispered. "Don't tell him. Let him figure it out on his own." He opened the screen door and walked to the dining table.

"I can sit in my own chair," she said.

"I know you can," he cooed. "I'd like to hold you for a while longer."

"She's more than capable of eating on her own." Jeremy took a sip from his black thermos and set it on the table.

"She is." Dietrich picked up a steak and bacon

slider and held it to her lips. "I made these earlier this morning for you."

She opened her mouth and took a bite. His lips parted and the tip of his tongue slid forward as though he tasted what she ate.

"You're beautiful," he mumbled.

She chewed as his hand slipped between her legs and his sly fingers moved the soft fabric between her thighs to the side.

"Mmm," she moaned as the tips of his fingers opened her wet folds.

He nuzzled the side of her neck and dipped into her sex. "Good, huh?"

"Sandwiches are overrated," Jeremy said.

I can't do this. Mere slid her hand over his, but instead of moving his hand away as she'd intended, she pushed his finger along with her own farther into her center. *I am going to come if you curl your fingers and press against that spot.*

He slid his hand from between her legs and stood up with her in his arms. "Mere has to use the ladies' room."

Jeremy huffed. "She can do it on her own."

"I know." Dietrich picked up the tray of sliders and carried her and it through the house to the first bedroom they came to.

He closed and locked the door. "You have to be semi-quiet."

She nodded. *What are you going to do?*

He carried her to the bed and placed her on the pastel-yellow comforter. He climbed up and knelt between her legs. With his hands on the waistband of his shorts, he pushed them down. "Take off your top."

She lifted the hem of her tank top up and over her head as she arched her back and his hands drew down her shorts. He dragged the fabric along her legs and tossed them on the floor. She opened her mouth for the hard cock jutting out between his legs.

He shook his head. "Pussy."

Her heart raced. She spread her legs and lifted her hips. "Make it quick?"

He gazed between her legs. "Quick and more than once."

She nodded a bit too enthusiastically. *We can do it twice before anyone starts looking for us.*

He chuckled. He dropped down to the bed as she tightened her abs and curled up.

They clicked teeth when their mouths met and laughed.

"Is this the awkward first time that isn't our first time?" she whispered.

"Yes." He crushed his mouth to hers and, when his tongue met hers, true love bloomed unexpectedly. She freefell into an abyss with no end in sight. He held her life in his hands.

A swipe of his tongue over her teeth brought her closer to him. A thrust of his hips and fear of the curse's continuation crept out of her soul. *Real love isn't possible. Not with me.*

She bucked her hips and threw him from the bed. *He's going to leave or break my heart like everyone else. Cursed to love but never experience it in return.*

He growled and leapt on her. "You're mine."

"No, I'm not." Glancing from side to side, she tried to find a way to escape. *I can't do this again. It hurts too much.*

He pinned her to the bed. "Yes. You're mine, and I'm yours. I'm all yours. There is no one else and there never will be. I'm nothing without you." He kissed her nose. "I'm nothing without you, Meredith." He pressed a kiss to her forehead. "I am nothing without you, love of my life."

She turned her head. "I'm new and sparkly." She cracked a smile. *Have you rubbed off enough of the makeup on my neck to reveal the silver glitter matching yours? We sparkle now, but it will fade with every wash, eventually leaving nothing but an old memory.* "You'll get bored and move on as soon as the silver begins to tarnish."

"Darling, you couldn't be more wrong. The longer we're together, the stronger our love will be."

"I want to believe you." She gazed at him. *I'm such a mess I'm hanging on every word of a werewolf…a werewolf…who has stolen my heart.* "Did I break your glasses?"

He nodded. "I don't need them. I can see just fine."

"Can you?" *I don't believe you.*

"I really can, but I think you like them." He smiled so big she almost believed he loved her.

The desire to run eased the longer she gazed into his eyes.

"You do like them. I'll get another pair."

"I'll buy you a pair." She turned her head and stared at the framed swirls of pastels hanging on the cream wall. The gentle, smooth curves of soothing soft hues flowed from the canvas like the meandering line of the beaches in her visions of the future with him.

His grip on her wrists loosened as he rested the

side of his face to her chest and lay atop her. "I saw the vision you showed Sara earlier today."

She stiffened. "I only touched Sara."

"I have powers that you can't comprehend, but one day you will." He traced the inside line of her arm down to her breast. "Trust me, Meredith. Open up to me. I will show you ways to control the visions instead of them controlling you."

"You want to be my mentor?" She inhaled and exhaled. *I don't want a mentor.*

"No. I want to be your husband, lover, mate, and partner for life." He lifted his head and licked her breast.

She shuddered and her body thrummed with the need for more. "I'm going to regret this."

"Choose me, Meredith. End the current blood-bond you have with Jeremy." He kissed her beaded nipple. "End it and make love to me."

She shook as the fear of rejection, of abandonment, roared through her. The memories she'd locked away the day she'd left Sara's grandparents' cabin in the woods when she was barely a teen opened. The worst of her memories flooded her mind in a vision only the two of them could see.

"It's okay, Mere," he whispered. "I'm here. I'm never leaving. I love you."

"Do it." Her voice trembled. *Please don't break my heart.* "If you can do what no one else could when they bit me…I know biting is part of it."

"Biting starts the process. My saliva is what carries the ability to transform my true mate — *you*. Making love will complete the initial ceremony. Your transition to wolf will be immediate, although you most likely won't fully physically transform until the next full moon." He licked around her nipple. "Normally there is a question as to whether a human would survive, but there is no question with you. And each mating comes with challenges."

"Your bite will hurt. I know it will. I probably won't survive, but I want to believe you." *I'm ready for whatever happens. I want you in me. I want you to love me the way you say you do. The way I already love you.*

He pushed up and flipped her over onto her belly. "My bite won't hurt. The sound of your bones cracking will trigger a painful muscle memory experience, but it's just the sound. I'm going to make this good for you." He thrust his cock deep inside her.

She moaned and whimpered. Her arms and legs shook as her chest constricted with each intake of oxygen.

He licked her shoulder. "My love is yours, forever, always."

I should stop you. I should—

His teeth sank into her flesh, cut through her muscle and crunched into her bones, jarring a memory she'd forgotten. *We've done this before. In the bar. In the bedroom. All over the hotel. But I didn't transform. Did you stop it from happening? Are you that powerful?*

He grunted and thrust. Heat swarmed her shoulder and he released his jaw only to do the same to her neck, and arms, and legs.

The heat turned to a burning fire inside her. Rich reds and passionate pinks swirled around her in thousands of ribbons of energy. Blues and greens joined the other colors and banded together into thick braids. Silver and gold combined and circled the others until everywhere she looked was silver and gold. Sheets of glorious glistening gold and silver formed letters, numbers, and symbols. Those wove together forming pictures of people and places from the past, the present, and the future.

Power surged outward from him as his tongue licked over the blood-bond crest on her neck. "Bonds must be broken. The soul must burn. Death turns to life." He thrust and tore out the crest Jeremy formed from their flesh, blood, and souls.

She collapsed. Her spirit rose from her body like it had done so many times over the years when her heart stopped beating, but her heart continued to pump in a strong and steady pattern. Veins, muscles, cartilage, fascia, and skin regenerated along the path where the bond had developed and grown and Dietrich had ripped out.

She gazed at her body, but floated toward the ceiling covered in the web of silver and gold. Everywhere she tried to go, the energy he'd formed as a barrier to the afterlife stopped her. He had trapped her in a state of limbo.

The body healed and the crest diminished along with the golden sparkles of energy, but remnants remained. Seven times he repeated the removal until nothing but silver shined in its place.

"Mine," Dietrich growled. "Come back to me."

She fell from the spiritual realm he'd confined her in and crashed into her body.

CHAPTER EIGHTEEN

MERE OPENED HER EYES TO the same cream bedroom in Lainie's home, but the comforter and linens had been changed to white and a piece of her soul was missing. *Jeremy. Jeremy, please don't die.*

"Don't talk," Dietrich whispered. "I'll return in a few minutes."

The click of the door signaled his exit.

A familiar hand held hers. "It's going to be okay," Lainie whispered. "You made the right decision."

Got to get to Jeremy. Mere wiggled her toes and pain like she'd never known vibrated inside her, ripping her organs, muscles, and bones. Burning flames seemed to travel through her in the same miserable pattern and leave through the place Jeremy's crest used to be.

"Don't move," Laine whispered. Tears filled her eyes. "I'm so sorry. I wanted to tell you. I wanted to tell you this was the only way, but you had to agree to it on your own. Dietrich will be back in a minute. He's helping Jeremy heal."

Thank God, he's alive. "I need to see Jeremy,"

Mere whispered. *What have I done?*

"You can't see him," Lainie said. "Luke said it was the strongest vampire blood-bond he's ever seen. You can't be in the same room alone with him right now. I'm not joking."

"I've got to get out of here. Help me."

"I can't," she said. "I would massage you, but I'm only allowed to hold your hand. Dietrich is controlling. I had no idea he…" Droplets of tears fell from her eyes. "Please, just do as he says. I can't lose you."

The bedroom door opened.

"How are my two favorite massage therapists?" Luke asked. He towered over Lainie and placed his hand over both of theirs.

"Good?" Lainie whimpered.

Luke clenched his jaw. "I see. Mere is speaking and trying to move. Am I correct?"

"Yes, sir," Lainie said.

The scent of salt water filled Mere's nose.

"Already scheming with Lainie?" Dietrich said.

She turned her head toward the door and broke into a miserable cry as her body revolted against her movement.

"Do. Not. Move," Dietrich growled as he approached. "Your body is healing. It won't be long." He tilted his head and smiled. "I can see you're working overtime trying to figure out an exit plan." He kissed her forehead. "It is difficult to be vulnerable like this, but you are safe."

"I don't feel safe." She pushed through the pain and rolled to her side.

"Meredith, you're stubborn. You're making the recovery more difficult." He knelt beside the bed and rested his chin on the mattress. "I don't want to order you the way I'd have to so you would stay in one place."

"You can't order me to do anything," she said.

"I can, but I'd prefer not to." He traced the hairline of her forehead, pushing away strands stuck with sweat to her skin as he followed the line to her ear. "I'm sorry this hurts so much. I'm easing as much of it as I can."

"I want to see Jeremy."

"Not yet, but you will very soon." He inhaled. "He learned the lesson of the challenges, Meredith, but it took the bond breaking for it to sink in."

"Go away," she whispered. *You don't love me. You wouldn't have broken the bonds if you did.*

"We'll be leaving Lainie's soon," he said. "You're too defiant to stay here much longer."

"I'm thinking clearly now," she said. "You're not controlling me."

He sighed. "I don't want to control you. I want to trust you."

She swung her leg forward and twisted. She screamed as a lifetime of pain came rushing forward in one damaging blow from such a simple movement.

He grabbed her leg and forced her onto her back. "You want to get moving so badly you are willing to harm our child? You want to end his life?"

"I am not pregnant. I will not…" She glanced at Lainie and the tears, the apology, the vocalization of her best friend's fears of their friendship ending, and the fear for her safety made sense. "You didn't tell me I was already one of you, and you knew?"

Lainie nodded, but turned away and cried into

Luke's embrace.

What kind of power do they have over you? "I want Lainie to stay and bring my phone. I have clients I—"

"Lainie had her assistant cancel the appointments," Luke said. "Your schedule is filled at The Ulvene Fitness Center when you return."

"Is Lainie off limits to me too?" Mere growled. *I'm going to beat the hell out of both of you bastards as soon as I get out of this bed.*

"No, but phones and tablets and everything electronic is unavailable to you until you're..." Dietrich paused and his eyes widened. "You want to beat the hell out of me *and Luke?*"

"Yeah." Mere squeezed her hands into fists with no ill effect. "Watch out, because I'm feeling better. Much better."

He grabbed her wrists and slid them toward the headboard. "Ahh, anger heals you faster. That's a good gift to have." He inhaled and lowered his eyelids halfway. He rested his cheek against hers and whispered in her ear. "I have the same gift. It's rare, very rare. Luke is the first in a thousand years to have our gift. I'm the only werewolf that can dominate him. Now, you might be able to dominate him too. I'm not sure, we'll have to see when you try to beat *the hell out of us.*"

She breathed in so deeply her nostrils flared and fury burned inside her. "I fucking hate you. I regret ever meeting you. I'm going to take you down and rip out your—"

"My heart? My lungs? My man parts?" he smirked. "You are a feisty one. Are you going to try and throw me in jail again? I'd love that. Only this time, I'm going to fuck you in that flimsy cage."

She fought against his hold. "You wish you could fuck me. Your sex life is about to be nonexistent."

"I don't think so." He moved her hands together, and he switched and held her wrists with one hand. He maneuvered the covers and her. Nothing but his clothes separated them. "I think sex is about to happen multiple times a day, every day, for the rest of my life."

"You wish." She bucked, but he countered. She tried every move she knew to get out from under him until exhaustion set in. *You're impossible to beat.*

Yes, he answered. *You can't win like this. But you are healed.* He kissed her lips. "I love you."

"I want you to leave," she said.

"It's time for me to check on Jeremy." He hopped off the bed and sauntered over to the door. "Lainie, get my mate ready to travel."

Mere sat up. "I'm not going anywhere."

He glanced over his shoulder and grinned from ear to ear. "Enjoy the time with Lainie. You're about to get hit with a very intense hormone rush. Clothes will be an issue for a few weeks." He walked into the hallway with an extra spring in his step.

"Do not even think about leaving this room." Luke growled. He strolled out of the room failing to sustain his usual calm confidence.

Lainie's lips trembled. "I don't understand what is happening."

"You're my babysitter. Luke is responsible for keeping you in line. Dietrich is testing your husband's leadership skills. You have nothing to worry about. If you have a dress I can wear, grab it, and

I'll put it on." Mere swung her legs over the edge of the bed and stood up, feeling better and stronger than she'd ever felt before.

Lainie walked to the white dresser and opened the middle drawer. She placed a black cotton dress on the top of the dresser. "Do you want help?"

"No, thanks," Mere said. "I'll let you know when I'm done."

Lainie walked out of the room and closed the door.

Mere slipped the soft cotton dress on and ran her fingers through her hair. A quick trip to the bathroom and she found everything she needed to be presentable.

"I need to see her," Jeremy shouted. "I have to see her."

"You are forbidden to see her," Dietrich roared.

The foundation of the house shook, but Mere ran to the door and nearly tore it off its hinges opening it.

Dietrich and Jeremy stopped and stared.

The man she loved and counted on for backup during a fight stopped and stepped toward her.

The pale face she loved was covered in purple bruises.

She gasped. "What did you do to him?"

"Turn. Around. Darling." Dietrich stepped in front of her and blocked her view of Jeremy.

"I want to see him. You can't st—" The glare from Dietrich held her vocal cords in a vise.

"I'm fine," Jeremy said. "I was worried about you. I'll see you soon."

"Dietrich, did you do that to him?"

"No," Jeremy said. "When he stripped the bond,

he blew out most of my veins and arteries. I'm not fully healed, but I will be by the time I see you again. I love you."

"I love—"

The house shook with the growl that grumbled inside Dietrich. "Think hard and long about the words you use and the consequences from that which comes from your lovely lips, my darling."

"I…am sorry." Her chin quivered as she chose her words carefully. "I…" The crevasse in her soul from Jeremy's loss widened. "Jeremy, you are going to fall in love with a beautiful woman. You'll love her so much you will take her to your church and marry her immediately. No waiting. No hesitation."

Tears welled in her eyes as the man she barely knew showed the side of the werewolf she knew too well. Possessive. Controlling. Total domination.

Her breath hitched and the emptiness within held the unbearable knowledge that one decision caused her to permanently lose her long-time love. "Dietrich is right, we can't see each other for a while." *But I will always love you, and my soul will remain void where your love once lived.*

"Good girl," Luke whispered. He stepped in front of her and joined Dietrich in forming an impenetrable wall between her and Jeremy.

She retreated into the solitude of the neutral space of the bedroom.

Luke closed the door and stayed inside the room with Mere.

"You did the right thing," Luke said. "It hurts. It's going to hurt, but as time passes, the experience will make you stronger."

"Hand that bullshit to someone else," she said. "I want the truth."

"What do you want to know?" Luke asked.

"Am I a prisoner?" Mere asked.

Luke laughed. "No. We're trying to manage your security."

The door swung open and Zoe Geroux strutted in like a model on a fashion runway.

"I've missed quite a bit." Zoe frowned. "Never would have guessed you'd be Alpha's mate. I'm glad Sara found a way to survive and save Ethan. Losing Ethan would have been felt across the world." She held out her hand to Mere. "It's good to see you again."

I want to know exactly what you are, Zoe. Mere shook her hand and the room darkened as she willed a vision to come forth.

Dietrich and Zoe stood under the chandelier in the foyer of his hotel room in Ulvene, Arizona.

"I missed you," Dietrich whispered. He kissed the beautiful blonde like they'd been together for a lifetime. He picked her up and hauled her over his shoulder. Her pale blue dress shimmered with threads of gold. The sheer top layer of her skirt fell over his face as he carried her down the hall toward his bedroom. "How did the meeting with Sara Kilpatrick go?"

"As if you don't already know," Zoe said. She rubbed his bulge with her nose. With her hips perfectly held at the top of his shoulder, her long legs flowed down his back. She tapped her toes against his ass as she lifted her head and unzipped his black slacks. She pulled out his cock and covered the top with her mouth.

"You give the best head." He stopped at the door to his bedroom and inhaled. "Sara is young and weak. She's

not fit to be an Ulvene."

Zoe released his cock and gazed at the bed. "I did what I could to prepare her."

"Odds are against her." Dietrich guided her mouth back to his cock. "I'm already late for the wedding, but I want to take the edge off with you."

Zoe straightened her leg and moved it to the other side of his face. The dress flipped over and uncovered her bare ass. "I don't want this to end."

He pushed her back against the wall and buried his face in her wet pussy…

The vision ended and Zoe's beautiful blue eyes widened. "It's not what you think."

"And how should I interpret that?"

Luke stepped between them. "You better leave, Zoe.

"Luke, if you don't move, I'm going to rub all over you until my scent is embedded into every miniscule thread of your clothing. And then I'm calling for Dietrich."

"Rub away," Luke said. "I have nothing to hide from my Alpha. You'll have to explain your behavior to my wife. She might not appreciate your affection."

Zoe laughed. "Reduced to babysitting, I see."

Mere spun around and walked to the other side of the room, lifted the window, and climbed out. As soon as her bare feet hit the thick, manicured grass, she took off toward the woods. She'd navigate the land until she found a road. She'd hitchhike and start over wherever the driver stopped. She lifted her gaze to freedom.

Enormous men, three rows deep and at least a hundred across lined up shoulder-to-shoulder and strode from the woods to the edge of the lawn and then stopped, blocking her path.

"Move," she yelled. *I'm running right through you.*

The front line shifted. Clothing ripped and fell from their bodies to the ground as the men instantly transformed into wolves the color of the desert and as tall as the old Georgia pines behind them.

The appearance of the fiercest wolves she'd ever seen knocked the wind from her lungs. She slid to a stop. *Oh, my God. I'm screwed.*

CHAPTER NINETEEN

WATCHING THE WOMAN HE LOVED more than his own life stand in defiance of his personal army worried him more than he cared to admit. All because of one vision. One infinitesimal moment in time. One decision to postpone the meeting of his mate. Meredith chose to run.

Dietrich closed his eyes and focused on the private beach Mere's vision brought him to when they were locked up in the jail cell. *You love me. You chose me in the vision. You chose me in the bar. You chose me in the test. You will choose me over everyone, and I will choose you. I will use every means I know of to protect you whether you want me to or not.*

"Are you going to try and prevent me from leaving?" Mere shouted.

Dietrich opened his eyes to see his gorgeous mate standing before him. The beautiful pale skin of her body was flushed crimson while her eyes lightened to the golden brown of her growing wolf.

"Don't bust any veins, darling," he said before he could stop himself. *You think like a human, not a wolf.*

"Don't go there." She drew her hands into fists

and widened her stance. "Not after what you did to Jeremy and me. And I know about Zoe and what you said about Sara." *I never want to see you with another woman, not her or anyone else. I believed you wanted me. I was so wrong.*

"I don't know what you're talking about. Zoe is here to help you navigate through some of the differences in your new world. She's our historian and the Alpha over the rare humans who carry the compatibility gene. Lainie carries the same gene. Sara's DNA was compromised for some reason, but she was saved by the vampires. You carry the gene made especially for me. Human compatibility is incredibly rare, survival even more so. Zoe heads up preparation, and for those already transformed, assimilation into our society. As to my comment about Sara, what did I say that has you so upset?" He reached out for her hand, but she slapped it away.

"You know damn well what you said and what you did." She shook like a Chihuahua getting ready to lose a fight. The red in her face turned a strange shade of purple the longer she glared at him. "I don't want that bitch near me or Sara or Lainie or any human or fucking anyone I know or care about." Her voice rose as she complained about Zoe without saying anything specific.

"Darling," he said. *You are stunning when you're furious. Attack me. I will take you down to the ground and grapple with you until we're making love.*

She stepped forward and grabbed his wrists. "You're a liar. You're worse than a liar. Whatever you did to me, undo it. Undo it," she screamed. "I don't want any connection to you. I want you out of my sight. I want you out of my life. I want you and"—she released his wrists and pointed to his army—"them to disappear and never return."

"You're upset, darling." *You're blocking me from all your thoughts, feelings.*

She glared at him and poked his chest. "Don't you *darling* me."

He grabbed her hand and held it. "I'm not lying to you. Open your side of our mate link, and we'll talk privately."

"Aww, no. I don't do private. Everyone needs to hear about your sexual relationship with that woman. You need to know that I. Don't. Need. You."

"What woman?" *You're the only woman in my life.*

"Zoe. Zoe. *Zoe.*" Her eyes widened to the point she looked as though they were going to pop out of their sockets and hit him. "That woman. Your woman." She turned around and leaped, but as her feet left the ground, he grabbed her.

He spun her around in his arms until she faced him. "She's not my woman. Whatever you were told is not true."

"I saw it. She confirmed it. You tried to have sex with me after you rolled around in the hay for hours with *her.* You pursued me, and I was stupid enough to open up and believe you wanted me. Only *me.*" A heavyhearted whimper rumbled in her chest. She quit fighting and rested her head against him. "I listen to my heart, and my heart is a fool. I'm a fool."

"Darling, you're not foolish. You had a vision of one snapshot in time. As you mature, you'll understand our ways, our drives, the things that matter to us and those that don't. Zoe is one of thousands."

"Oh, my God," she growled. "That was not the right answer. That was so far from the right answer, I don't know how to respond." She pushed to leave the embrace, but he held her tighter.

"Meredith, I've lived a very long life, and werewolves are not celibate. You weren't celibate before you met me." *I wish you would open up to me.*

You hate Sara, Meredith shouted through the werewolf bond. *Jeremy hated Sara. You expected her to die and did nothing. You did nothing. Getting me in bed was more important than trying to save her life. Jeremy loves me, not you. He saved Sara's life so I wouldn't have to grieve her loss. Now, Ethan is married to a vampire. Poor Ethan. What is going to happen to him?*

She licked the center of his chest. *Salty man. Sexy man. You're so warm. I want you. No. Because of you I can't have Jeremy. I can't protect Ethan. I can't stand the things Sara will have to do now that she's one of them.* Mere's mind raced and jumped all over the place broadcasting her thoughts through the Alpha Pack Link. *I'm going to kill everyone who did nothing to help.*

The silence on the other ends of her mental rant relayed the other Alphas' fear of Meredith's retribution.

The warriors protecting Meredith shifted their basic line to an advanced battlefront. They would die guarding her from the feral wolves approaching from the woods. They'd keep her surrounded until the first wave of wolves fighting alongside Jeremy's Coven eliminated the first round of diseased canines. Saving Mere came first.

Dietrich held silent through the ebb and flow of a youth's tantrum until logic and exhaustion took over Meredith's mind and body.

It was her choice, Meredith continued communicating her thoughts. *Nicholas wouldn't have turned her without her permission. She chose not to tell me. She chose everyone else above me. I am cursed to love and never be loved the same in return.*

I love you, Lainie replied through the Alpha Pack Link. *I will always be here for you. I consider you my sister and have since the day we met. I will stand by you through good and bad times. And, Mere, Zoe is harsh. She's a pain. But she's honest. Whatever went on with her and Sara was probably similar to what happened with Zoe and me. And her dealings with Dietrich before you don't matter. World Alpha loves you more than anyone else. It's the way of the mating. Just so you know, Luke has fucked Zoe too. I'm pretty sure all the Alphas that weren't mated when she came into puberty had sex with her—*

Lainie, quiet, Luke interrupted. *Get a private link with her. Don't spread all that around so mates can get all riled up again.*

I forgot, Lainie answered. *Sorry, y'all. I am still new to this.*

For the record, I have not had sex with Zoe, Michael Flanagan announced to the group. *Neither has anyone in the Georgia, Tennessee, Texas, Florida…ok, none in the central to eastern half of the United States. There's more coming in. Wow, she's less prolific than I thought. Meredith, I am your Georgia Pack Alpha, and I am honored to tell you that I have your back in good and in the worst of seasons in life. I can also handle your taxes and set up a plan for your financial future. I am proud to say my Packs are both physically and fiscally strong.*

Really, Michael? Daniel Wedekind, Luke's best

friend, chimed in. *You're pitching your financial consulting services now?*

Yes, Danny, Michael replied. *Meredith doesn't know my gifts, and she deserves to be aware of what her Georgia Alpha can do for her. She's not angry with me. The rest of you are going to have to clean up your business. Meredith is perfect to lead the females. With Lainie by her side, who is also a solid member of my Georgia Pack and calls me Alpha, they will set the standard for all females.*

Michael, this is not a business pitch or a reminder of the power you hold within the Georgia Pack now that Lainie and Meredith are in it, Daniel said. *Lainie is part of the Nevada Pack also.*

Yes, but she doesn't call you Alpha, Michael replied. *Or does she?*

Daniel growled. *I never slept with Zoe either. Meredith, as the Nevada Pack Alpha, I would like to welcome you to my Pack. I would love for you and World Alpha to visit Nevada. If you've never been to the state, I would be happy to show you around.*

Now who's buttering her up? Michael retorted.

Meredith's side of the Alpha Pack Link severed. Michael closed off his side too.

Devoid of Meredith's presence, the Alpha Pack Link blew up with fears of Meredith's reckoning over Zoe, over Sara's werewolf transition fail, over all the feral wolves they let live within their territories, especially the ones who worked in small packs as nomads traveling the country. So many journeyed from all over the world through border after border toward Georgia. Michael had asked for help, but received little. Now his territory remained a battleground to be cleansed.

Dietrich addressed his Alpha Pack. *My mate will forgive as she matures. Show her your loyalty, your faithfulness, your patience, your love. Be the leaders I know you to be. Work together. Be kind and she will return your kindness. Honor her and she will honor you.* He closed off his side of their link as Mere's body softened against his.

The front row of his warrior wolves relaxed and one by one lay down with their heads between their front paws, taking their cue from her body language.

Meredith Kilpatrick, what are you thinking? He didn't expect an answer, and he didn't get one. "We need to take a detour to a friend's home."

She shook her head. "I'm not going with you."

"Why?" *It better not have to do with your human jealousy.*

"What I do and where I go is none of your business."

"Everything you do is my business. Mates stay with mates. It's what we do."

She gazed up at him.

Meeting her brown-eyed stare, he searched for the wolf living silently inside her without calling the beast to surface.

There's a side trip, Michael Flanagan said through their private link. *She hears Ethan's distress. She is seeing the kind of person Sara truly was. Sara had been slowly tearing the boy and his beast apart, finding ways to torture them. Nicholas broke the mating bond to save Ethan's life, but Ethan is confused. He blames Nicholas when he should blame Sara.*

Nicholas will remove the evil inside her and bring her into the light, Dietrich replied. *She's weak and Nicho-*

las is stronger now that he has her. Jeremy will make sure Sara does not enter society without a full soul transition.

I was going to pick up Ethan at Nicholas's home alone, but Mere wants to go, Michael said. She wants to face Nicholas and find out the truth. Now is the perfect time to meet privately with Jeremy. Should I move forward with your plan or wait?

Set up the meeting with Jeremy. Keep Luke in the loop. The feral situation is about to end abruptly. Burn any feral wolf remains prior to the plague's cleansing. Once the world has been cleansed, the ashes will disappear. Keep our part in the cleansing out of our history books. We'll be written into the vampire history by Jeremy on secret scrolls of which only the Vampire King and the Queen have access. Meredith will be safe and no one will know the correlation of events but those of us in the inner power circle.

Yes, Alpha, Michael replied.

"Michael Flanagan is taking me to Nicholas's to pick up Ethan. I don't want you there. I will not lose my temper." She gathered in a cleansing yoga breath as if her sanity depended on staying calm. "Michael explained why the wolves are guarding me and why my choice to have sex with you wasn't really a choice at all. It was inevitable. The attraction. The mating trance. The mating ceremony. I know you blocked my memory of our original mating ceremony and only you can restore it. Now might be a good time to return my memories."

"We'll discuss your memories when we're back in Ulvene. I'm going with you to Nicholas's. Michael may attend the meeting." *You're smart to choose Michael instead of Luke to accompany you. Your relationship with Lainie would cloud Luke's judgments.*

"I'm using my privilege as the Female World Alpha and executing my right to have a private meeting with my hometown Pack Alpha Michael Flanagan. Others in attendance is up to my discretion and will remain a private matter. The location is a secret. I will stay within a relatively close proximity to you, so if you are needed, you will quickly be able to"—her shoulders slouched and her eyes rolled—"*come to my rescue*. There, I said it."

He held a stoic expression, but his heart soared with joy. *You know you need me. You know I will come. You know my love for you grows by the second.* "I see you're learning the rules quickly and assimilating to our ways. Darling, I'm proud of you."

"Are you trying to see how many bullshit endearments you can dish out before I lose it?"

The rage burning in her eyes made him smile. "I've said it before, and I'm sure I'll say it a thousand more times—you are so sexy when you're angry." He cupped the back of her head. "I'd like you to lose control. I'll take over, my love."

His cock got so hard the world around her faded into nothingness. He lifted her up and those strong legs he wanted spread open on his bed wrapped around his waist. He thrust and ground against her bare pussy. *Open my pants. Hold my cock.*

Yes. Yes, Mere moaned through their mating link. *No. Shit. It's the mate connection. It's not real.* Human logic vanished. His needs became hers. She unbuttoned and unzipped his pants. *I want you. I need you.*

He crushed his lips to hers. Sweet magnolia fragrances swam across his senses intensifying his carnal desire to mark her as his all over again. His tongue met hers with a spark and tingle racing to the tips of his toes. A leisurely swirl and soft dive deeper into her mouth softened her jaw. A lingering stroke and a retreat wouldn't be enough to quell his rising need.

Her magnificent fingers caressed over the tip of his cock.

He broke the kiss. *Legs straight. Hands on the ground. Get that dress off you now.*

She went down to the ground into position so fast, his head spun. Pink pussy shined silver with his claims and glistened with her juices perfectly poised for entry.

He grunted as he tunneled farther within her pussy. She took all of him. Every inch. His balls landed at her clit and her walls clenched around his cock so deliciously, he nearly lost his balance and tumbled over her. Her pussy vibrated and her orgasm sent juices around his cock base and dripped down his balls.

"Come for me again." *I am going to come so fucking hard.*

A growling purr rumbled through her, sending her limbs trembling and more cream slipping from her sex. "Dietrich," she whimpered. "I need you."

He gripped her hips and slammed into her over and over and over like it was the first time. *You're mine. Mine. Mine. Only mine.*

She lifted her legs and curled them around his hips.

He thrust, and she squeezed, countering his movements. He bent over and slid his hand down the middle of her chest and lifted her against him like she was poised as a figurehead at the bow of a boat. She arched, pushing her breasts into his palms, and reached behind her, finding his neck to hold on to.

He opened his fingers and closed his index and middle between the jewelry at her nipples and dove his cock into her depths.

"I'm going to come," she roared. "I can't handle it. It's too good. It's too intense."

She panted as she extended her arch and bounced up and down on him.

"Fuck my cock, beautiful." *Open your body more and I will give you everything you ever wanted.*

"Oh, God. Dietrich. Dietrich. Yes. Right there. Right there." Mere stiffened, shuddered, and then relaxed. *I love you. I love you. I love you. Only you. Forever you.*

He thrust as the world seemed to stop spinning. Cum rose through his shaft and spurted into her. *I love you, Meredith. I love you.*

Making love to her strengthened him. The sun seemed to shine brighter in the sky. The grass seemed greener. Life was better. Soon they would be spending summers in Germany making love, ruling together, and raising their children.

He gazed at the wolves surrounding them. Adjusting her so his wolves could see her, he slid his right hand down between her legs and opened her folds with his fingers, showing off the markings on the flesh of her pussy around the jewelry announcing her position in the Pack as Alpha over all females. Only her face was left without his claim, except for the symbol of love on her cheek. "Mine." *No one touches you but me.*

She shuddered and another rush of her juices flowed from her sex. *No one?* she whispered into his mind.

Not even a handshake without my permission.

The delicate touch of her hand skimmed along his right arm down to his fingers sliding the diamonds back and forth at her clit.

With her fingers over his, he traced around and over her clitoris.

"Feels so good," she moaned. "You're going to make me come again, aren't you?"

"Later." He glided her hand with his as he traced her folds around the front of his cock. "My mouth is going to be here."

"Uhn," she moaned loudly. "Yes."

He drew his hand up the center of her body to her lips. "My cock is going to be here."

"I want that." Her pussy tightened and pulled cum he hadn't known was inside him out, giving him a mini-orgasm. He shuddered. *Holy shit. You're still ovulating. We're going to have multiples.* He sniffed and, sure enough, scented two more babies being created.

"Dietrich," she whispered in a sultry southern drawl. "Let me go with Michael alone, and I will—"

He nuzzled under her ear, silencing her. "I'm territorial, darling. I have to strut my stuff and show everyone I am the boss."

A soft whimper left her lips. "What if I promise that I will not let anyone touch me, and I will not touch anyone? Will you let me go alone then?"

"You're in danger. I am your protector, warrior, lover, and mate. You will not go without me." He flexed his cock.

Another delicious whimper escaped her lips. She

angled her neck to the side as he rubbed his nose behind her ear.

He blocked his thoughts from everyone as her neck offering carried the desire for Jeremy's mouth on her and the connection he'd removed.

"Okay," she said. "But let me speak with Michael privately."

"Mmm." He licked behind her ear. "Soon."

She slid her legs from around him and he carefully guided her to stand.

Her lids lifted and she gasped. She spun a hundred and eighty degrees and faced him. "You jerk. That was a territorial wolf thing. Making love to me in front of everyone. What is wrong with you?" She twirled away and picked up her dress. "You're fucked up. Fucked up with a capital F." She pulled her dress over her head and down, covering the naked body he wanted to see.

"You're ovulating, darling. I'm making love to you every chance I get." He grinned. *Damn straight. I'm showing my army you are mine, and they will never have you or be able to control you.*

"Stop talking into my mind. It's weird." She walked toward the house instead of toward the woods.

Her hips had a sexier swing and each swish of her dress gave him a precious glimpse of her bare ass.

She grabbed the skirt of the dress and lifted it over her head. "Why am I so itchy?"

"You're pregnant," he answered. "You're going to prefer being nude for a few months. You didn't see Lainie much after she told you about Luke. That is why."

"I wasn't talking to you." She tossed the dress down and walked into the house. *I need clothes, Dietrich. No more sex. None.*

There is a wrap dress on the bed. If you ask nicely, I will take away your discomfort. He held his cock as he strode toward the house.

Not. Going. To. Happen, she answered.

He followed her into the bedroom.

She pivoted and gazed at his cock.

"You want to suck it?" he asked.

She dropped to her knees and opened her mouth like a born werewolf ready to please her mate. "I need to taste you."

He gripped the back of her hair and fed his cock to her. "Yes. Do it."

She was finally reading his needs and acting like a werewolf. Falling to her knees. Sucking his cock. Opening her legs for his every desire.

He thrust and she accepted all he offered.

He gazed out the open windows at his army's eyes fixed on Meredith. Each and every one of the men wished they had her. Finding an appropriate guard for his mate would be difficult.

She swirled her tongue back and forth along the base of his shaft.

His balls clenched so tightly the beast inside him rose to howl, but held off as he demanded more of her. "Swallow my cum."

He grunted as wolf teeth grazed the edge of his balls. "Mark me again. Show everyone I'm yours."

The wolf inside her rumbled her pleasure.

He thrust and shuddered as his wolf called to hers. The pierce of her canines started his sperm to rise up. *The more you mark me, the more you will bond with me, desire me, need me, and obey me.*

I need you too much. You're going to send me away. You're going to—

"Stay," he roared, completing her sentence with the word she refused to believe as truth. Cum spurted from his cock into her mouth.

She swallowed over and over. She gazed up at him in a sex-induced werewolf high. She opened her mouth and sighed. "That was…I've never…I think I might…"

She collapsed in a sexually satisfied exhaustion, and he caught her and carried her to bed. *You can't use sex to negotiate with me, but I hope you don't figure that out for a while.*

CHAPTER TWENTY

OPENING HER EYES TOOK EFFORT. Rolling off Dietrich seemed monumental. A new
ache in her chest nearly toppled her as she moved
from the bed to the bathroom without him. Her
vision blurred. *What is wrong with me?*

You're mated to the most powerful being alive,
Michael Flanagan said through their private link.
*Being mated to a regular werewolf causes pain when one
of them is away from the other, but Dietrich has waited a
long time for you. He adds connections and links to your
mating bonds every time you make love. Being without
Dietrich is not an option for you, and he knows it. Ask
him to come to Nicholas's home and stand guard outside
while we talk to Ethan and Nicholas. He may or may
not agree to the distance that would separate you.*

The ache disappeared and her vision cleared.

"Darling." Dietrich took her hand. "We need
to be within touching distance until you fully
awaken. The blood-bond interfered with the com-
pletion of our mating links. I've cleared up most of
the problems the bond created. You can have more
distance as soon as your head clears, but it will be a

shorter distance than before yesterday. I'm not joking when I say that mates stay with mates. There are no short cuts, unless I allow them."

And you'd never allow them. "But Lainie told me yesterday that she left Luke after they went through their mating ceremony."

With Dietrich beside her, holding her hand, she walked to the vanity.

Dietrich stood behind her at the counter and slid his hands around her waist. "There were extenuating circumstances which I thought important enough to give both of them the strength to get through the separation. Please don't tell Lainie or Luke of my interference. Lainie needs to think she has more control than she does."

"How much are you controlling my actions?" She kept her gaze on the caramel granite counter as his body pressed flush against hers, his hard erection pressed firmly against her back.

"I'm giving you opportunities to do what I want you to. You decide whether my offerings are worth your time." He ground his cock against her.

With her palms against the counter's edge, she stepped back into a wide stance and rose onto her tiptoes.

He placed his hands next to hers as his cock glided over her folds. "That was all you, darling."

She gazed up and met his light-blue eyes in the mirror. "It feels like you."

"Mmm." He rocked his hips back and forth, sliding his cock against her slick slit. "It was you, my beautiful mate. All you." He rolled his hips and thrust into her pussy. "Your ovulation period ended. You're no longer in a werewolf heat. This is all *you* wanting *me*."

"Pull out of me," she whimpered.

He withdrew from her. "You don't want me to stop." He kissed the back of her neck. "I don't want to stop."

"But you did." *I need an interruption. I need to refocus. I need you fucking me into oblivion again.*

"Yes. Oblivion sounds wonderful." He spread delicate feathery kisses along her back to her bottom and rubbed his cheek against her inner thigh. "A small taste to start the morning right."

"Yeah," she moaned. *I shouldn't agree to this.* "Okay. A taste." She rested her head against the counter and spread her nether lips for him. The need for him to touch her, make love to her, be inside her overwhelmed her body and mind. She slid her fingers into her pussy. "I'm so wet, Dietrich."

"Show me your fingers, and I'll decide if you're wet enough." He exhaled against her clit.

Her legs trembled as she glided her fingers from her center and held open her folds.

"Mmm," he whispered. "Very wet." He swiped over her center with his tongue. "I want more, but I need some attention, darling. Sex is so much better when we're both getting what we need."

Her pulse quickened. Her heart pumped faster and faster, warming her chest to cheeks to toes. Words she reserved only for Jeremy rushed from her mouth. "I'll do anything. Absolutely anything."

He maneuvered under her into a crab crawl. "Hold your pretty pussy open for me and suck my cock. I'll do the rest."

She pushed away from the counter and placed a hand flat on each of his thighs. "Like this?"

"Find your balance," he whispered. "You're going to have to get closer."

She curled her right arm around his thigh and then the left. The strength he possessed seemed unreal, unnatural for his height and build. *You hide your power so well.*

"Give me your pussy. I'm hungry."

She caressed along his thighs over his ass to his heavy balls. She nuzzled his long cock. "You're huge."

He seemed to vibrate a purr. "Suck the top. Massage my balls. And do whatever you need to so I can eat my preferred breakfast."

She lifted his cock with her tongue and sucked as she shimmied her bottom closer to his face.

"A little farther, darling." He shifted his weight to one hand and grabbed her hip. "Now."

"Oh, my God," she squeaked as his mouth covered her sex.

"Uhnn," he rumbled.

She sucked in the head of his cock and dipped, taking more. Bobbing her head up and down and up and down along the length, she worked to get as much of him into her mouth.

He dipped his tongue into her sex. Her entire body tingled and vibrated with his every swipe over and into her center.

An odd, rumbling purr similar to his, yet different, emanated from inside her ribcage. Pleasure rose faster and filled her from her chest to belly, to legs, arms, and head until that something inside her roared.

Her gums tingled. Her teeth sharpened. Heat poured from her flesh as she writhed against his face. His tongue dipped and penetrated deeper than should have been possible. He nipped and sucked her folds, then clit, and thrust into her pussy.

She left his cock and pushed up against his abs. She humped his tongue. His teeth cut into her pussy and held her in place. He wiggled his tongue into a sensitive spot that seemed to be made just for his tongue.

"Dietrich," she screamed as the first wave of orgasms crashed through her. "Fuck me, please. Fuck my pussy with your big cock."

She landed on the hard tile floor on her back.

He held her thighs wide open and thrust and thrust and thrust and thrust.

The earth shook under them as the first spurts of liquid heat erupted from his cock. She soared into the heavens. Silver threads of energy spun around her as if she were a spindle on a sewing machine, spinning and spinning, faster and faster as words and pictures formed and wove in and out of her flesh. In and out, the energy flowed in layers upon layers, disappearing inward, meeting her muscles and bones and repeating the process again and again. Layer after layer of silver energy transformed her from her innards out until her body and mind buzzed with a new power, a strange awakening of her new life.

He stretched his legs and his cock slipped from her. He shuddered. "That was incredible." He shuddered again. "I didn't know you would open up like that. I've reconsidered your request. I'll stand guard at the meeting you've set up."

There was something different about his eyes, the blue hue lightened to almost white. *There's a softer side to you that hides—*

Abruptly, he stood and tugged her hands.

She caught air as the force behind his hands lifted her. She landed softly on her feet.

He let go of her and strode into the bedroom like a man who ruled the world and all who dwelled on his land.

"Hi, Michael," he said.

"Hey, Alpha," Michael replied. "The car is ready when y'all are."

"I see you're using the local slang," Dietrich said. "You assimilate easily, always have."

"Uh, thank you?" Michael said.

"Meredith, clothes are in the car. Come, darling. Hurry. You don't want to be late for your own meeting."

Mere looked into the mirror. She ran her fingers through her thick hair and didn't look half bad. "Give me a minute."

"Darling, you're beautiful," Dietrich said. Inside the doorway, he stood wearing jeans, a T-shirt, and a baseball cap. He held his hand out to her. "There are clothes in the car for you."

"I really should take a shower."

He grinned. "We'll have to tackle the shower later." He sauntered toward her. "I'd have you naked all the time, everywhere we go." He picked her up and threw her over his shoulder.

"Hey, this is not okay. I smell like sex."

"As you should." He walked into the bedroom.

"Hey, Mere," Michael said.

She slapped Dietrich's firm butt. *Mmm.* "I do not want Michael seeing me like this." *Naked is not okay right now.*

Dietrich slid his fingers into her pussy, and damn it, she moaned.

"It's fine, Mere. Nudity doesn't bother me," Michael said. "And sex is a necessity of werewolf life. There is nothing to be embarrassed about."

"Why isn't Michael the human compatible liaison? He seems to have the only state that has them. He's nice, unlike your bitch."

"Well, darling." He bent over and plopped her down on the seat in a modest sedan with leather interior.

Must be Michael's car. Financial guy. Future builder. Setting the example for his Pack. Probably always doing the right thing. Why couldn't I have been mated to him?

Michael and Dietrich whipped their heads in her direction, their expressions the same. Jaw dropped. Chin lowered. Eyebrows up to the middle of their forehead. Their eyes screaming disbelief.

Crap. "Did you hear that?"

"Yes, darling," Dietrich said.

"I didn't mean it like that. Well, I kind of meant it. He had the decency to—"

The growl Dietrich let out stopped her cold.

"Sorry." She lowered her gaze to the floorboard. She hadn't been chastised in a long time for something she actually did wrong. Her stomach churned with guilt. Acid burned her throat. *Now my thoughts are getting me into trouble. I am so fucked.* "I really am sorry."

Two doors closed and the car immediately rolled forward.

"Michael, I agree with Meredith about you being a wonderful liaison between humans and werewolves, but Zoe will remain in her position for reasons we are not discussing. And Meredith, we do not disclose our feelings through public mental pack links. One word or thought can and does change the dynamics of our overall and individual packs. Humans worry and so do werewolves. We worry and plan and strategize for the survival of our race. Your words and thoughts carry the weight of my status. Your actions, physical or mental, are taken as sanctioned by me. I expect mistakes. You're new. You're very young. You've experienced the worst of our race and the worst of yours."

She swallowed, but the bile bubbling into her esophagus kept splashing and burning as it rose higher and higher. Ripping pain tore through her chest and into her heart.

"Michael is one of the top three strongest and most powerful werewolves in the world. He is *humble* which allows him to say and do things others cannot. He *hides* his *thoughts. Controls* his mouth. You seem quite capable of the same when you *want* to."

Each word hung in the air like a noose. The longer he held his tongue, the tighter the rope cinched around her neck until she could barely breathe. *I'm sorry. I'm so sorry. I love you. I like Michael. He's nice, but he's not you. I was mad at you. I'm sorry. I was wrong. Very wrong.*

"I forgive you," Dietrich whispered. "Close off the largest connection you have and speak through only the strongest ones – Mine, Lainie's, Michael's, Luke's, and Ethan's. Yes, I know about your newest, and barring Michael's and mine, the strongest bond you have within the Pack—Ethan's. Use those channels to vent your feelings. Although, I'd prefer you to exclusively use our private connection to rage through."

The gentle touch of his hand on her thigh loosened the noose around her neck.

She leaned against him. Scooted her hips toward him. Twisted her torso and pressed her chest against his. Nuzzled her nose along his meaty shoulder.

He slid her into his lap. His rigid body softened with each of her kisses over his shirt on her way to his neck.

"You should have just had me arrested and thrown in jail," she whispered.

"Now is not the time for jokes."

The lack of his usual endearment "darling" at the end or beginning hurt her heart. "What can I do to make this up to you?"

Michael handed Dietrich a gift bag.

The car gained momentum as it merged onto the interstate.

One by one, Dietrich pulled strips of white fabric with ties out of the bag. "This drapes over your breasts and ties around your neck." He handed her the first piece and tied it.

She looked down at her chest. The soft material left little to the imagination. "Are you serious?"

His non-reaction forced her to eat her words as he passed over two thin slips of nearly translucent white silk with ties on either side to "make it up to him."

"This is like those ancient Egyptian whore clothes," she mumbled.

"No." He gritted his teeth and growled.

Oh, God. I screwed up again.

"This is the traditional dress of the Female World

Alpha when acting in an official capacity, as you will be doing at Nicholas's home. You are going to wear this or nothing at all. There are some things that are *negotiable*, and some that aren't." He placed it around her waist and tied the strings at the sides. "My mother wore this same outfit. My sister wore this at the ceremony when she became the Female World Alpha. You are the third FWA in our history. You will wear this with pride."

"I am trying to." *I'm sorry. Okay!?* She scooted away from him. *I'm screwing up left and right. Damn it. I don't need to be kicked when I'm down.* "Please, don't give me that look."

She pulled the sides of the barely there fabric, attempting to gain more coverage. "Is this silk?"

He nodded. "If you tug too much, the fabric will rip."

She let go of the fabric and gritted her teeth. "It's soft."

Michael gave a hand mirror to Dietrich. "Show my—" He cleared his throat. "Show your mate how beautiful she looks in the dress."

"Sit against the door, feet flat on the seat, and your legs bent and relaxed open."

She scooted over and obeyed him. The fabric didn't cover her lower girlie parts.

Dietrich's lids fell to half-mast. He licked his lips. Lust and love poured out of him like syrup over waffles onto every nook and cranny of her body. *Mine. You will always be mine. Submitting to me first. Running to me first. Needing me first. Always. Forever.* He held up the mirror.

She gazed into it and shut her eyes as the transparency of the fabric highlighted her red nipples, her shimmering diamonds, her glittery silver sparkles marked with *his*…

With her teeth clamped together so tightly they threatened to crack, she closed off all the links but the strongest. *I could kill you right now. Kill you as in rip your fucking head off. What is wrong with you, Dietrich Ulvene Wolfgang? I can't believe you did this to me.*

She opened her eyes and dared to look between her legs. She drew her hands into fists as his name written in a thicker silver glitter than the rest of her skin popped as if it were a different color. Everywhere her eyes traveled his name rose like a hologram from inside the sparkles. "How the fuck did you do that? This better wash off. It better or I'm going to—"

"It's permanent. We sparkle like the stars when we bite our mate during our mating ceremony. It's a werewolf thing. The more sparkles, the more powerful the bond. Each person decides how the bond is weaved, how the sparkles are configured, how others will see his or her mate. They fade only when around humans, but as soon as a werewolf is in the area, they sparkle. The more werewolves, the more they—"

"Lainie's don't look like—"

"They do. You haven't seen them as a werewolf." He lifted his shirt. "Look at me."

His skin sparkled, but not as brightly as hers.

She rolled her eyes and huffed. "I don't see"— she lifted her hands and motioned at her chest as she shimmied—"your chest with—" She gasped as her eyes focused on the almost-white sparkles. *Well, dang.* Her name jumped out at her. Everywhere she looked, her name was written into his skin in the whiter shades of silver. She left no area of his chest untouched.

He unzipped his jeans and his cock rose. "I didn't remember you doing this, but I love it."

She covered her eyes with her hands. "Put that away."

"We are territorial, darling. There is strength when a person knows what is theirs."

"Yeah. Yeah. I don't need a lecture. I got it." *I'll wear the transparent silk. This is embarrassing. Nicholas has never seen me naked. No one but Jeremy had seen me naked until you came along.*

The car slowed and then stopped.

"Nudity is nothing to us. Bodies are bodies. Although yours is perfect." He inhaled. "The lecture you don't want is happening now. Listen so I don't have to repeat myself. Ruling through strength and strategy have not changed since the beginning of time. You have the power to wage war or to keep the peace as long as you stay the strongest. You're wearing the white silk to show you expect a peaceful resolution. The show of skin reveals you are a wolf and a mated one at that. You also display the depth of your connection to me by exposing the birthmark of my baby wolf's paw. You have accepted your new life and the responsibility that goes along with it and they need to know it. You're walking into that house with my permission and harboring no ill will toward any vampires, even though they kept you a secret from me."

"So this is about you?" She gazed out the side window.

"This is about us and the entire world of werewolves."

"So, are you going to tell me what to do and say during the meeting too?" *You seem to be controlling everything anyway.* She swiveled in the seat and looked at the house she passed hundreds of times walking to Jeremy's.

"Darling, you seem to be an all-or-nothing kind of woman. You're going to have to learn the art of negotiation." He placed his hand over hers on her lap. The heat of his body encroached upon her space until he snuggled against her. "Look at me."

She kept her gaze on the house. "I've learned you can't negotiate with werewolves." *But vampires listen to reason. They understand laws and order. They have been good to me over the years. They like clothes. They get hungry when they see skin.*

"You can't negotiate with feral werewolves or any diseased alternate being, for that matter, my dear. I've kept the peace between the species for thousands of years through negotiation." He gently guided her chin toward his.

She closed her eyes. *I'm not going to look at you. I can't resist you when you're—*

"I love you, Meredith." His breath seemed to blow feather kisses onto her lips. "You're stronger than any woman I've ever known. Come on, sweetheart. Open those pretty brown eyes and look at me."

She shook her head and lowered her chin. *I don't want to wear this. I'm sorry about earlier. I have a loud mouth and even louder thoughts.*

"Darling." He kissed her forehead and brushed his lips down the side of her face to her ear. "Wear the traditional dress. This is important to me."

She curled her arms around his neck and rested

her head against his. "I've known Nicholas for a long time. This isn't about your kind. It's about me talking to Nicholas and Ethan about Sara. I want to be clothed. Werewolves don't care about nudity, but vampires do. The more skin exposed, the hungrier they get. Please don't make me walk in like this."

"Clothing is a sign of weakness around vampires. You don't know all their laws," he whispered. "You've been on the outskirts of our kind's society. Jeremy doesn't break his rules, so I know he didn't bring you into his inner circle or you would be one of them instead of one of us."

He seemed to hit her where it hurt the most. Jeremy didn't love her enough to marry her. He didn't love her enough to make things work for her and Sara to live with him. He loved himself more.

She made the mistake of opening her eyes and showing the real vulnerability inside her to him, hoping his love wouldn't be short-lived. "You're not coming into the room, right?"

"I will stand guard outside the room."

She nodded. "I'm changing as soon as this is over."

"Yes, darling." He opened the door. "Keep your head in the game."

"As long as you're not there, I'll get what I want." A whiff of sweet peaches in the air took her attention from the house. She cocked her head to the right. Ethan's strong scent of cactus blooms rose and mixed with the scent. *Ethan has a mate nearby.* She strode with new purpose into the house. *My life might be a mess, but Ethan, I'm going to clean up the disaster Sara engineered for you.*

CHAPTER TWENTY-ONE

THE WOMAN HE LOVED WALK into his best friend's house under false pretenses, something Jeremy would have died before allowing, but when World Alpha requests a private meeting and demands the place, players, and outcome, choices are limited.

The flimsy fabric Dietrich had her wear molded to her sparkling flesh. Dietrich's signature along with his sweat, saliva, and sperm marked her skin as the Female World Alpha – Dietrich's mate.

Territorial bastard. Bringing her here. Marking her. Showing her obedience. Flaunting her pregnancy with your child when that child should be mine. Jeremy closed his eyes for a second. *Her visions always come true. There will be a miracle. You're worth the wait, Mere. You've always been worth waiting for.*

The door closed behind Michael Flanagan, locking Meredith and Michael inside the room with Nicholas and Ethan.

Jeremy strode to Dietrich. "Nicholas will keep her occupied. Ethan is unaware of what is happening. Sara is with one of my guards outside the door. She will be going back to the cell as soon as this is over. Without Ethan readily available to side with her, she will experience the full weight of Nicholas's dominance." *Shit. I overshared. Damn it. Mere will be furious. And now he knows Sara isn't fully bonded to Nicholas. Fuck. Fuck. Fuck.*

Dietrich nodded.

Jeremy cocked his head to the side and narrowed his gaze at the man who never agreed to anything until he got what he wanted first. The white eyes of the warrior wolf stared back at him.

Jeremy raised his left brow. "What is going on?"

Dietrich glanced at the door to the private bleeding room. He held up his finger to his lips and without a sound walked over and opened the door.

Like he'd done thousands of times over the years, Jeremy followed the powerful leader and closed the door.

Dietrich's bored expression held strong, but his wolf's gaze softened to the wise and compassionate old wolf who took him for rides and curled around him after a long day of lessons. "Mere is the carrier. She is the cause of the feral outbreaks. She's the one who carries the virus and spreads disease to all beings, except vampires."

"What? No," Jeremy said. "Carriers die before their second birthday. She's thirty. You're wrong on this one."

"She was an infant bleeder. I am not going to tell you anything you don't know. Infants don't survive vampire feedings. Yet, she survived vampires, the elements and…" Dietrich's stoicism faded and his watery gaze drifted upward. "She survived one of the worst feral wolf attacks ever recorded in our history. She lost so much blood and still gave a transfusion to Sara so the little girl could live. Ethan and Sara reacted like they were mated because of Meredith's blood inside Sara. The mating ceremony didn't work because Sara wasn't Ethan's mate, she wasn't compatible. She didn't carry the gene, but remnants of Mere's blood made her smell and react like she did. Ethan hasn't died because he bonded in a spiritual link he formed through Mere's blood within Sara and then transferred the bond to Meredith who cemented it to her chi. Ethan bonded to my mate as if she were his without consummation. Ethan can survive, will survive, as long as Meredith lives."

"What does any of that have to do with Mere being a carrier of the plague?"

Dietrich's nostrils flared as he lowered his gaze to Jeremy. The face of total control burned red-hot like he was about to explode. "My mother was like Meredith. She could bear any being's child who procreated like us, but was fully compatible as a mate to only one – my father."

"She lived a long time, right?"

The heat radiating off Dietrich cooled and his face drained some of the bright crimson blood to more of a heavy pink flush. He glanced around the room and sat down on the black velvet couch.

Jeremy followed his lead and sat beside him. "She had you and your sister and a few other brothers?"

"My brothers were two years older than I. My sister was even older. My father witnessed his pack getting sick year after year. Whenever my mother traveled, feral wolves would come for her, hunt her. Other beings came. Wars broke out. My mother carried a scent unknown to them—magnolia blooms so fragrant, so intoxicating, so strong even the Vampire King could smell her wonderful aroma."

"Mere," Jeremy mumbled. "I can smell Mere coming a mile away, even further. I followed her scent across the country, but smell nothing else."

"Nicholas, enough of this bullshit," Mere's voice carried into their room. "Damn it. Talk to me. I thought we were friends."

Dietrich sighed. "She's hot-tempered like no one I've ever known."

Jeremy laughed. "Nicholas can handle it. He'll rile her up and then calm her down. She's brought so much life back into my Coven. We miss her. All of us miss her. Me most of all."

Dietrich smiled and nodded. "She's got most of my Alphas squirming in their shoes. High alert has new meaning for them."

"What happened to your mother?" Jeremy asked.

"She got pregnant with me. My father went to the Vampire King. They figured out the problem and the cure. I assumed I would be having this discussion on behalf of one of my wolves, not me." He bowed his head.

Jeremy glanced around the room to see if anyone more important arrived. The two remained alone in the room. "What do you need? My blood?"

"I humbly ask for secrecy first."

"Of course," Jeremy said. "Second?"

"A blood-bond between me and you, and then you and my mate."

Jeremy bolted upright. "Hang on there. We don't blood-bond. That's not done. Werewolves are toxic to us."

"My father did it with your ancestor. You are a descendant of my mother. We are related, although the line has been thinned tremendously over the many generations. Why do you think I took you into my home? Why do you think I watch out for your people as if they are my own?"

Jeremy backed up. "It's not in our history. He had a wife. Her name was—"

"Akiva Hunter. She was a blonde until she turned. Her hair blackened, but her eyes stayed the lightest of blues, almost white from her wolf. She bore seven children with the Vampire King. Three survived."

"My father told me we were immune from the plague because only the strongest of us survive childhood."

"That, and you don't breathe to live. Your body functions differently. Nothing airborne can harm you. Zombies are similar in that they don't breathe or have working hearts, but they're already diseased and attack everyone."

Jeremy nodded and stepped forward. "Akiva was your mother?"

Dietrich nodded. "She was pregnant with me when she was turned into a vampire by the King. She had more werewolf children, but the years and the wars took their toll on my family. The Ulvenes are descendants of my beloved sister and her mate."

"How do we keep what you're inferring we do a secret? I thought you were coming to work out a solution to Sara's torture cell. I'm not sure I can do what you're about to ask."

"The history of my mother will remain a secret

along with the way the plague ended. What we will do with Meredith tonight will be a secret between our worlds. Sara must never know the history Meredith played in ending the plague. And you better straighten that girl out tonight regarding Meredith, or give me three minutes with her and I'll do it for you."

"She will be my Vampire Queen in every sense. How will I explain it to my Coven? How will I explain my children? This can't work." *My people will not stand for lies. I will not deceive my people.*

"Your Coven is small," Dietrich said. "Hold a gathering. The Coven gathers for baby showers, correct?"

"You know they do," Jeremy said. "Ohh. Nicholas's line is expanding" He nodded. "Gotcha. But then what?"

The frown of disappointment Jeremy knew too well spread over Dietrich's mouth.

"Tell them you are saving the Queen and the wolves from the plague. But because she is mated, the Coven must stay silent to protect her. I will be forever grateful and join your Coven for all pregnancies and births as I do the Ulvenes. Your people are already special to me, but saving my mate…" He whimpered. "I don't ever want her to know she is the cause of the outbreak. Please, she must never know."

Hearing the strongest man he'd ever known suffer brought Jeremy to his knees. "If she asks, I will be forced to tell her the truth."

"She will never ask." He inhaled. "You will take her last breaths from her. The plague will die along with all those she infected when her heart stops beating. Your blood-bond will save my life, and in turn, save hers from following me into the after-life."

Jeremy bowed to the man who raised him. The man who taught him to lead. The man who taught him to follow the law and helped him change as the world changed. "Alpha, I have never been more honored in my life. You saved me, protected my people, forgave me countless times, and now you've given me the woman who Soulburned me." He took Dietrich's left foot and lifted it. "I will protect you and your mate, I will honor you as my family, love you as I always have, and I will give you my blood to complete our bond." *Please do not let your blood kill me.* Jeremy sank his teeth into Dietrich's heel.

Dietrich reached down and grabbed Jeremy arm. "I will not kill you when you are alone with my mate or if she gives birth to your children. I prom-ise I will protect you and your people as long as they honor our bond and hold fast to the secret of the plague's origin. If anyone breaks the law we declare through our eternal blood-bond, I will rain down hell on earth until all those involved are wiped from the face of the planet."

Blood rushed into Jeremy's mouth, and fear set into his bones as the bond solidified into some-thing altogether different than a vampire crest or a werewolf spiritual link. *You're different. You're a wolf-bonded vampire and created as one unique being. You're different in every way.*

Canine fangs dug into Jeremy's wrist and sucked once. He dropped Jeremy's arm and pulled his foot from Jeremy's mouth.

"You have to turn her tonight or Atlanta will fall within a week. Your Coven and my wolves will lose ninety percent of our ranks." He tilted his head and gazed out the window to the backyard. "My entire Ulvene Army is here. Do whatever you have to with Sara. She does not want to experience the full weight of my wrath." He walked out of the room and left the door open a crack. "Darling, I'm so proud of you."

"Really?" she whispered. "Ethan is sick, but I know where his mate is. I didn't know there could be more than one."

"It's rare, darling. Very rare. Let's go find her and celebrate."

Jeremy stayed frozen on the floor. *He got every-thing he wanted.*

I got everything I needed, Jeremy, Dietrich's voice said into Jeremy's mind. *I'd prefer never to share my mate, but this is the only way to protect her, and she has an advantage my mother did not. My mother held no affection for the King, but Meredith has been Soulburned by you and you her.*

You can hear me when I think?

Of course, Dietrich said. *Taking a taste of your blood allows me to do many things. Get up and get moving. Time is not on our side.*

Jeremy pushed up from the wooden floor. He managed to make it to the couch and sit. His blood buzzed with energy. *I can't function with your blood in my system.*

Push through the power surge, Dietrich said. *There is no time for your childish whining. Give yourself one of those pep talks or get someone to give you one. Either way, get your shit together.*

"Nicholas," Jeremy shouted. *I can do this. I can get through this. My Coven will stand with me. They love Mere and want her back.*

The man he depended on to lead his army when trouble arose stepped into the room and closed the door.

"Hey. That was crazy. Mere's skin shimmered with Dietrich's name everywhere I looked. It was hard not to stare at places I shouldn't have stared."

"Yeah. Well, we've got a situation we have to keep secret form Sara and Meredith and I need the Coven gathered here tonight. Tell them it is for Claymora and Spatha's pregnancies."

"That's going to be hard to do. The women are barely pregnant. Jeremy, secrets and vampires don't mix." He pressed his lips together and crinkled his forehead.

"I know, but circumstances demand it."

"Are you okay?" Nicholas ran his hand over his freshly shaven head and strode forward. "You're shaking strangely like you've overdosed on caffeine or you've been drugged or—"

"I blood-bonded with Dietrich," Jeremy whispered.

"We don't do that. You don't do that. We don't drink werewolf blood." Nicholas crouched down and placed his hands on Jeremy's thighs. "Sara didn't transform. It was messed up and that was the only reason I could save her."

"We can blood-bond, *if* it serves a higher purpose and that werewolf is the World Alpha." He leaned forward and wrapped his arms around Nicholas's neck. With his lips to Nicholas's ear, Jeremy pulled him closer. "We can turn them with

Dietrich's help."

Nicholas slid his hands from Jeremy's thighs to his back. "Are you sure? I once drank from a werewolf and puked for days. It almost killed me. Your reaction has to be from his blood. It's toxic. You could be dying."

"I'm not dying. I barely took a sip, but I can't take more from him. He's too powerful."

"Please don't think you can take Mere's. She's *his*."

"I have to turn Mere. She's going to be the Vampire Queen. There has been one other like Mere in our history. She birthed the Hunter Line."

"Mere is like the ancient Queen Akiva?

"Mere wasn't born a werewolf, Akiva was," Jeremy whispered.

"Before my father passed away, he told me that Akiva carried the plague and the King saved her," Nicholas said just loud enough for Jeremy to hear. "When her spirit left during the turning, all the diseased died with her. But when she had risen, the plague didn't return. Could that be true?"

Jeremy nodded. "It is true. I've been saving Mere all these years, protecting her by drinking her blood, thinning her scent, slowing down the spread of the plague. Since she mated with Dietrich, the disease has exploded, spreading like a world-wide forest fire."

"Please don't tell Mere. It will kill her," Nicholas pleaded. "Dietrich hasn't told her, has he?"

"No. He wants secrecy, as do I."

"I will gather the Coven immediately. Sara will never know about any of this," Nicholas assured him. "We will save the wolves. We will save the others. We will celebrate our Queen's return to our Coven and your bed." He kissed Jeremy's cheek. "My King, may your soul burn with her fire for the rest of your days. May you be blessed with many children and our Coven be blessed with new royal life."

"Thank you, my friend. We will celebrate new life tonight."

CHAPTER TWENTY-TWO

"TAKE A RIGHT AT THE next street," Mere said to Michael.

The car rolled past the street. "I'll make a right down the next," Michael said.

Mere leaned over the console and grabbed the steering wheel. "Make a U-Turn. You can't go down the next street." She sniffed. *Peaches and blood. Formaldehyde. Soil. Rotting flesh. Woods. Beasts.*

Michael removed her hand. "I'm driving, Meredith."

She glanced down the streets and behind her. "They're here. *They're* here. Call Jeremy. Call Jeremy now. He'll come with Nicholas and help." She slapped the dash. "Stop the car. We have to help. We have to stop them before they reach Ethan's mate and kill everyone in their path."

Dietrich laid his hand on her back. "My wolves are here. Can you pinpoint the girl?" *Luke is working with Nicholas. War has been declared by the diseased. We have this under control. Focus. We need to get the girl first. We will deal with the rest afterward.*

Mere shook as the memories of the feral beasts

fought for control. *I'm stronger. I can do this.* "I feel her calling as if she's one of us, as if I know her. Can't you smell the sweet peach scent?" *She's from here, but isn't connected to the land.* "She's connected to"—she gazed at Ethan—"you and me."

He smiled. "Us. Me and you forever." *I love you,* Ethan said into her mind. *You're amazing.* "Her connection isn't as strong as ours, but I like it."

She glanced over her shoulder at Dietrich. "Is that strange?" *I'm talking to Ethan. He's acting really weird. Can you hear what he's thinking?*

He nodded. "You have a unique connection. Close your eyes and see if you can visualize his mate."

Can you really hear what he's saying to me? He's telling me he loves me. He seems to be puffing his chest out like he did with Sara before things went bad. Am I imagining that, Dietrich?

He nodded. *I can hear it all. You two have an uncommon bond. Let's find his mate. I want you to tell us exactly where she is located. Stay focused on her.*

With her eyes closed, an image of a young woman with blond hair, carrying a pink wig and wearing a neon-pink dress with matching heels appeared as if she stood before her. *I've found her.*

Dietrich rubbed her back. *You're doing great. Tell us where to go. I'll make sure your path is cleared to get her.*

"It's Faith from the Quickstop."

"Do we know her?" Michael asked.

"I do. You don't." Mere rocked forward. "Hurry and turn around."

"We can't at the moment," Michael said.

She glanced out the back window.

The guests from Ethan and Sara's wedding marched shoulder-to-shoulder down the street, clearing the road of pieces of the feral beasts and decayed zombies that littered the sidewalk.

A sleek flash of black ran past the car.

Her heart skipped a beat. *Jeremy. You came.*

Streaks of black and red and green zipped past them as Michael turned the car around. A sea of vampires arrived.

My people. My friends. Tears filled Mere's eyes. *They came.*

"Darling, stay with Ethan and Michael until you're in front of the shop where Faith works. I'll meet you there." He kissed her cheek.

She blinked and he was gone. His clothes lay folded on the seat beside her.

A magnificent wolf taller than the skyscrapers with spindles of some type of sparkling silver metal rods resembling fur all over his body marched forward. The Ulvene warriors had transformed into wolves, their rows expanding to form barriers three stories tall. Jeremy grew taller, rising like a giant with his army filling in the gaps between the wolves. They gathered beneath and behind the sparkling silver beast and followed him.

The car accelerated forward toward her mate.

The head of the magical beast moved in a sweeping arc over his shoulder. The white eyes she recognized gazed down at her as she stared out the window at him. *My Dietrich. Do you need your glasses?* She shook her head. *Forget that. Stupid question.*

The wolf half-jumped, raising his front legs, and threw his muzzle up like a rearing horse. A low, bellowing roar rumbled from deep in his chest and shook the ground, cars, and buildings with his volume. His front paws landed on the pavement. A shockwave spread like a tsunami outside their safe bubble.

The car came to a screeching halt.

Jeremy stood perfectly poised and back to normal at the entrance to the shop, a lopsided grin on his handsome face. His black silk trademark shirt was unbuttoned enough to see the ripped muscles of his chest. His black slacks were slim enough to show off his bulge, but loose enough to give room for a full range of motion.

Put on my shirt, Dietrich ordered her. *Then go get the girl.*

Following his order, she slipped his black T-shirt over her head and hurried out of the car.

Jeremy opened the door to the entrance. "Hey, sweetheart."

She gently closed her hand around his, squeezed, and let go. "Hey." She glanced down, feeling the old fire burn as strongly as it ever had, and hurried into the shop.

He slid his arm around her back and tucked her into his side. "You're sticking beside me until you're back in the car."

"I don't want D—"

"He knows. It's fine." He kissed the top of her head. "I told you a blood-bond doesn't make my soul burn for you. You did that. You. Your love for me. My love for you. It doesn't go away."

"Hey." Faith stood behind the counter and stared out the window at the Michael's sedan. "You shouldn't be outside or inside here. The city is under Marshall Law. The National Guard is on the way."

She removed the pink wig from her head. Long, blond curls bounced over her shoulders and down to her waist as she pulled out one brown bobby pin after another, releasing the spiral tresses woven like flower petals around her head.

"I need to leave while the street is cleared."

"Faith." Mere stepped out of Jeremy's protective cocoon. "I'm here to help. I want you to meet someone."

Faith gazed at her. "Meredith?"

"Yes, sugar. It's me."

The young girl sucked in her bottom lip. "I won money in the scratch-off you showed me in your vision." She gazed outside. "But I got mugged outside the store where I redeemed it. The money is gone. I will never get out of here."

"I want you to meet a friend of mine," Mere said. "He's in that car outside."

Hurry up, Dietrich ordered.

"Faith," Jeremy said. "Get in the car outside. Now."

"Yes, sir." Faith walked to the end of the counter. "I thought you two broke up." She lifted the side of the counter.

"We did," Mere responded as Jeremy said, "We didn't."

"We're still together," Jeremy announced. He tucked her against his side.

"No, we're not." She elbowed him. "Come on, Faith. It's not safe here."

The clear blue in Faith's gaze lightened as a blurry haze unrolled like a sleeping bag covering her eyes. "Today is the strangest day I've ever had. People dressed up as zombies and half-wolf/half-man surrounded the shop. I saw a wolf balloon that sparkled and shined, and it rose so high into the sky I couldn't see the top. Is there some kind of paranormal parade going on?"

"Yes, Faith," Jeremy said. "There was a parade, but it was stopped because the city is under siege." He held out his hand. "It's time to go."

Faith rolled up her sleeves and placed her small hand, palm up with a small black dot inked in the center, over his. Blue and purple bruises covered her arms and legs.

Mere zeroed in on Faith's face. Caked-on makeup couldn't hide the swelling on her cheek, or the fresh bruise underneath.

Jeremy tucked her into his other side. "We're going to take care of you. You're finally safe." He led them outside and helped Faith into the car. "I will see you again, young lady. You're in good hands."

Mere slid into the car and sat next to Faith.

Jeremy stuck his head in. "Michael, follow us to the church." He closed the door and ran toward his people.

"He's almost as fast as Dietrich," Michael said.

Ethan managed to crawl into the backseat. He placed his hand on Mere's thigh and then pulled Faith into his lap. "I'm Ethan Ulvene. Do you like the age you are? Do you like wolves? Do you want to marry me and become my wife?"

"You're the quarterback from Arizona. You didn't go pro. You like training people to fight." Faith opened her mouth and smiled. "I want to be with you forever."

"You will be," Ethan whispered. "But you have to know, I love and have vowed to protect the Female World Alpha." He squeezed Mere's thigh.

Mere's jaw dropped. *What the heck?*

Faith shifted in his lap and straddled his thighs. She unzipped his jeans and pulled out his cock. "Make me yours."

Mere climbed over the center console. *She's in the mating trance, like I was. Once it takes hold, there is nothing anyone can do to stop it.*

Ethan slapped her ass. "Pretty pussy, Mere."

"Hey, you can't—" she paused.

Ethan's mouth covered Faith's, but his eyes stayed on Mere. He thrust into Faith and closed his eyes. *I love you, Meredith. Thank you for bringing me Faith. You know exactly what I need when I need it.*

She dropped her bottom into the front seat.

Let it go, Michael said through their private link. *He's been promoted, and you do have pretty girl parts. He's young and will learn quickly to keep his hands off your body and his thoughts of affection to himself.*

I sure do hope so. She squirmed in her seat as Ethan's affection toward her warmed her in places she didn't want it to. *Where is Dietrich? The Ulvenes? Jeremy and his vampires?*

The car turned around the corner. The street was desolate. No people or cars. No homeless. No trash. Nothing.

Jeremy and his kind are offering safe haven at his church and home. Dietrich is there. The Ulvene army is providing security outside the church and the Coven. My Pack is gathering at Lainie's home with Luke while we are strategizing our next move.

Michael drove up to the front of the church and parked the car. "You won't see me or Ethan for a short period of time, but I will remain available for anything you need."

The door opened.

"Darling." Dietrich slid his hands under her and carried her from the car. "I had a talk with Ethan about swatting your bottom."

"Thank you." She kissed his lips. "I never imagined a wolf could look like you. You're more magical than artist renderings of unicorns or dragons. You are amazing."

"Do you finally believe me about not needing glasses?" He stumbled on the first stair and quickly adjusted as he continued into the church.

"Uh, no."

"Okay. Maybe I could use a little help seeing." He opened the doors to the sanctuary and entered. "I need you to do something for me."

Jeremy stood at the altar next to Father Ryan.

Dietrich gently helped her down to her feet.

"What's going on?" Her heart pitter-pattered. Both men stood together as friends and warriors united in one cause. Her stomach fluttered with hope.

"I talked to Jeremy privately today. My mother was compatible with more than humans and werewolves, like you. My father protected her as I will protect you."

Hope that love conquered all vanished from inside her. "You're leaving me?" *But you said that mates stay with mates. That's what you told me.*

"I'm guaranteeing your survival," he said. "This war is serious and the last time a war broke out like this we lost many. I'm the last of the Ancient Ones. To protect you and our children, I need you to become Jeremy's Vampire Queen. He's powerful enough to turn you. You will be changed, a hybrid of werewolf and vampire. None will be like you as none are like me. You will no longer be able to procreate with everyone, only Jeremy and me…" *And Ethan. But Ethan has Faith to calm his desires and you have me or Jeremy to quell your growing interest in him.*

"I'm not turning into a vampire. How can I be a vampire and a werewolf? How can I be your mate and Jeremy's Vampire Queen?" She shook her head. "Werewolves are toxic to vampires. What you're saying is impossible."

"Werewolves are typically toxic to vampires. We don't mix. Werewolves can only have children with their mates. Vampires can only have children with vampires. You're different. You're an anomaly like my mother was. If you went into heat and I wasn't there to get you through it, any being could impregnate you as you are now. You won't be able to control yourself during the next werewolf heat. Each ovulation will get more intense. You will fuck anything that moves. My mother struggled for thousands of years, until she met the Vampire King and he turned her. After she was turned, everything changed for the better."

"But I'm pregnant. You said I was pregnant with your child. He won't make it if I do this. He'll die with me."

He shook his head. "I survived in my mother's womb. I hoped taking out the blood-bond would change your compatibility. I hoped weaving my love through all our spiritual connections would change your DNA enough to avoid this. I hoped so many things, but this is the only way to ensure you live to raise our children, to enjoy a peaceful life, and to experience the kind of love from me, the Pack, and Jeremy and his Coven."

"I want to be with you," she whispered.

"You will be." *You will live with me, sleep in my bed for most of the year and you will have Jeremy in the same way, only at different times. Jeremy and his Coven already love you as you do them. They are a loving and affectionate community. You will thrive with the combination of both our kinds.*

He guided her to the altar and offered her left hand to Jeremy. "The Female World Alpha accepts your proposal."

Jeremy slipped the wedding band he'd bought her for the ceremony they never had onto her left ring finger. Dietrich added a diamond and emerald wedding band that cradled Jeremy's.

"Vows have been made many times over," Father Ryan said. "Love blesses this union in life and death."

"Love is the great equalizer," Dietrich whispered into her ear. "Love makes us sacrifice our selfish desires to protect, shelter, nourish, and nurture others. Love is spoken, and those words spring into action. Love conquers all obstacles."

She whimpered quietly. *This isn't right. I love Jeremy, but I choose you. I want you.*

"Bless this union with love through the ages, passion with every touch, peace that transcends thought, and many happy children. Bless Jeremy and Meredith with health and purity of spirit throughout their lives together," Father Ryan said.

Jeremy handed Meredith a wedding ring. He held his left hand next to the band.

Dietrich, I don't want to do this.

You're doing this for me, for our Pack, for Jeremy and his Coven. You're doing it for Sara and Nicholas, for Ethan and Faith. You're doing this for humans. For your people who will suffer greatly.

She looked at Dietrich. *Why would my people suffer? What aren't you telling me?*

Tears filled his eyes. *You're sick, Mere. Your heart is healed, but there is a virus that is—*

Am I going to turn feral? She touched Jeremy's hand. *The curse. I have the love I always wanted, and I'm going to lose it.*

No, you're not turning feral. You will never lose me. You. Are. Mine. Dietrich placed his warm hand on her cheek. *You are sick, like my mother was. This is the cure. It's the only cure.*

There has to be another way. I don't want to—

There is no other way. You love Jeremy. He loves you. I know what you will do with him. He knows… He grinned. *He kind of knows some of the things I will do with you.* He drew her hand over Jeremy's and glided the ring onto Jeremy's finger.

"The vows spoken over many years of love are sealed forever. Jeremy, walk your bride to your chambers and bring her into your church and Coven," Father Ryan whispered. "I will pray until you send word it is done and the Queen has risen."

Dietrich nudged her forward as Jeremy led them into the passageway.

The entrance to the tunnel closed behind them.

With Jeremy in front of her and Dietrich behind

her, pushing her along, Mere felt like she was walking her last mile. For the first time in her life, she wasn't ready to die. She wanted to live, live for him and her and Jeremy. *What if I don't survive the transformation? What if my blood is toxic, and Jeremy dies?*

You'll survive. Your blood is like nectar to him. Mine is toxic to him or any vampire if taken in more than small doses over thousands of years.

They passed the torture chamber where she'd visited Sara. *What if something happens and I go insane? I won't survive one of Jeremy's chambers.*

No chains can hold you, not once your wolf adjusts to the change.

Jeremy opened the doors to his private chambers. "Meredith, only you and Nicholas are allowed entrance to my inner chambers during the turning. Dietrich will stay here, in my master suite."

He's taking you where only the King and Queen reside. I will be here, waiting for you.

She panicked. "I can't have two husbands. As open and okay with different lifestyles as I am, I'm not like that. I'm traditional. One husband. One family. One…" She panted for air. The room spun. "I'm hyperventilating." She squatted and leaned forward with her palms to the floor. "I can't do this. I can't drink blood for the rest of my life. I can't live without a beating heart. I can't."

Jeremy and Dietrich gently stroked up and down her back and removed her clothes.

"You're going to drink my blood at first. Then we'll test your blood to see whose blood type is ideal for you," Jeremy whispered. "From the history that I could find, you will only be able to consume vampire blood, not human blood. There is evidence within our history that your heart may beat during certain phases of the moon, but your lungs will be absorbed by your body."

"We will figure out a schedule for you and Jeremy to be together. I will find a way for this to work. I promise, we will never be far from each other."

She rocked back and forth, trying not to pass out. "Secrets don't last long with vampires."

"They do," Jeremy and Dietrich said.

"Sara will tell. She'll tell the world," she whimpered.

Jeremy wrapped his hands around her waist. "She will not be told—not for a very long time, if ever."

She moved and Jeremy moved with her until they both stood up straight. He somehow guided her through hallways and rooms so quickly that the short journey became a blur of colors.

He twirled her around the perimeter of a bedroom she'd never seen before. Emerald walls with golden accents. An intricately carved antique poster bed with canopy stood in the very center of the small room.

"Where is Dietrich?" she asked.

"Pacing in my outer chambers." He unbuttoned his silk shirt and tossed it in the corner. "I've waited a long time for this." He unzipped his slacks and dropped them to the floor. "We have to be creative with the placement of our bond." His green irises darkened to match the black of the pupil.

Witnessing the predator in him for the first time pushed her into flight mode. *You're too strong.* "I'm not doing this."

CHAPTER TWENTY-THREE

IN A MAD DASH TO get out of the room, Mere leapt on the bed, but Jeremy's speed won the race.

He grabbed her and took her down flat on her back in the dead center of the bed. "You're not winning this time."

The gentle yet firm hold on her lessened her desire to run away. "This is cheating. I can't cheat on him. I'll lie for you. I'll tell him you tried, but something happened and you got sick. *Really* sick."

"Babe, you're married to me. If you're cheating on anyone, it is me when you're with him." His eyes flashed neon green and settled back to a forest green. "Traditionally, we bond at the neck to allow for discreet feeds."

"We can't do that." *Dietrich, you have to come and get me. I can't do this. I'm scared. It feels wrong.*

Jeremy is saving your life, Dietrich replied. I know you love him. It is okay. I promise, you are mine. We're going to live a long and happy life together. You're going to have the very best of both of us.

Jeremy nuzzled below her ear. "You love me too. It's okay to love both of us, just not at the same time."

She let out a half-laugh and whimpered. *I love Dietrich more.*

"Your feelings are magnified for Dietrich. It's okay," Jeremy whispered. He kissed down her neck to the place his crest marking their blood-bond used to lie.

Sparks of desire delved deep within her belly. "Jeremy, I don't want to die."

"I won't let you die," he moaned. He licked along her neck, over her collarbone and down to her right nipple. "I'm your King. Listen to your body. Listen to your soul calling to be with me and our people who love you. Remember the visions of our future. Trust and believe in my love for you. You want this. You've always wanted this. Let go of the past. My love will light the path your soul will journey. My love will bring you home."

Electricity buzzed within her, muting her fears. Energy swirled in beautiful pinks and crimsons above him revealed the man she'd fallen in love with all those years ago. Truth, faithfulness, and honor defined the man who'd waited patiently for her to join his world.

"I trust you. I don't want my past to rule me anymore. I want you, your laws, your love. I believe you. I believe you and Dietrich have ended the curse." She spread her legs and opened her body and soul for him to take and do as he willed.

"That's it," he mumbled. "Surrender your love and life to me."

The prick of his fangs into the outline of her areola sent fire into her blood. Her pussy clenched, aware of the void within.

He moaned so loudly that the vibration shook her heart into an erratic pattern of beats. He sucked and swallowed, drawing in her blood faster than he'd ever done before.

She panted for air, for freezing cold air, as the fire in her soul burned through her veins. "Jeremy, I need water."

He sucked and swallowed over and over and over. Crimson sheets of energy dropped over her and seeped through the silver webbing of her mating links into her blood and organs, raising the heat in the bonfire living inside her shell.

Crimson and pink appeared as dots of energy in the air. The colors pooled together and dumped like splashes of water over them. The energy soaked in, drowning her. Over and over the dots formed. The fire within extinguished and cold swept through her.

She gasped for air. "I don't want to die."

His hand covered hers as he pulled the last bits of life from her body.

CHAPTER TWENTY-FOUR

"I'M HERE," DIETRICH WHISPERED. "YOU need to—"

"Mine." Wild golden eyes stared into his.

Faster than sound, she launched at him. Her teeth sank into his jugular. She moaned as she swallowed. Over and over she sucked down his blood. She trembled and her teeth elongated and pulled blood from his veins with increased urgency.

"No. Meredith, no," Jeremy ordered. He tore her mouth from Dietrich's neck. "Nicholas, Train, Caleb." He placed her on the bed and pinned her. Lines of black veins rose and bulged under her skin. Black blood wept through her flesh and onto the bed.

Nicholas arrived first and took over Jeremy's position. Jeremy's cousins Caleb and Train pried her mouth open. Her teeth turned black, crumbled, and fell out.

"What's going on?" Dietrich's body ached and burned as if he were dying in slow motion.

"This is not normal. This is more than were-wolf toxicity," Jeremy said. "You can't take her. She hasn't risen. She hasn't risen."

"She called me. I came." *Mere. Mere, can you hear me?*

"Get out. She needs time. She's—"

"Her eyes," Nicholas gasped. "There will be no hiding what she is."

Jeremy bit into his own wrist and forced blood down her throat. "Dietrich, I need you to leave. There are secrets of the Coven that not even you are privy to."

"I can't leave her." *Darling, answer me.* "I can't hear her."

"You will, but I need to take care of her and I can't with you here," Jeremy hissed. "Get out."

Warning growls rumbled from the doorway.

"Alpha, she's fighting for her life," Ethan said. "Let them do their job. They let us do ours."

He walked out of the room, his entire world shattering. *My blood should have strengthened her, but it's killing her. It's killing her.*

CHAPTER TWENTY-FIVE

THE SMOOTH, SUGARY SWEET LIQUID coated her tongue and the excess slid down her throat. She swallowed and more of the delicious nectar flowed into her mouth.

"Good girl," Jeremy whispered. "Take a little more."

She obeyed and lazily sucked and swallowed.

Hard cock pressed against her pussy. *Mmm.*

"That's enough for now," Jeremy said in his sexy southern drawl. "Lick to heal the wound. An enzyme in our saliva heals any cut on a human or vampire."

She licked her lips of the leftover fluid. She tried to open her eyelids, but they refused the order. "Am I dreaming?"

"You had a challenging turning," Jeremy said. "Your body doesn't function the same way it used to. We speak by manipulating the air that naturally flows into our mouths and down our throats. The vocal cords are no longer cords, but muscles we can flex. Our necks are incredibly strong. All the ligaments and tendons are now surrounded by muscles and veins. Open your mouth and gargle."

She opened her mouth, but quenching her thirst took precedent. "I need a drink."

"Slow, lazy sips, Mere," Jeremy cooed.

Skin brushed her lips and, without thinking, she sank her teeth into the flesh. Beautiful springs of luxurious, creamy liquid with a hint of vanilla beans and honey filled Mere's mouth.

"Mmm," she moaned.

"Good girl," Jeremy said. "Sip and let me hear the pleasure."

"Mmm," she moaned louder. The warmth of the liquid flowing down her throat and the vibration of her new sound carried a sense of pride.

She licked the flesh and opened her eyes a hair, just enough to see two men resembling Jeremy. "Who are they? Did I have sex with them?" *Dietrich? Are you there? I feel our bond, but it's weak. Can you hear me?*

Jeremy laughed. "You did not have sex with them. You're mine, sweetheart."

"Good." *Dietrich, talk to me. Please, talk to me.*

"I had your blood tested after you turned," Jeremy said. "For now, you can't drink from humans. That might change as you mature, but I'm not sure. We tested the entire Coven, but Caleb and Train are my cousins and the only other vampires who are capable of feeding you, beside me. They will be your extra donors for as long as you need them. You are not allowed to tell the wolves about our donor system or that some vampires only drink from vampires."

She closed her eyes. "Okay."

"You are compatible with Caleb and Train too,

so if they are injured or sick or need to feed and no humans are available, you will be required to serve as a donor to them. They will feed you, travel and live with you as your guardians when you are away from me. Drinking from Dietrich is not possible. The bond you two share does not make you compatible to feed from him. I'm sorry."

She stretched her mouth and traced the edges of her sharp teeth with her tongue. *I lost my teeth. I got sick and almost died. I remember.*

"Caleb and Train, take a break and go to the bleeder room. When you're refreshed come and join us."

"Yes, sir," the men said in unison.

"They're gone," Jeremy said. "You have to control your pussy action when you're feeding. We are extremely sexual and…" He swatted her bottom. "Quit rubbing the head of my cock with your clit."

A gurgle came from her mouth instead of the huff she intended. "I can't move and you're telling me I'm grinding you?"

"Oh, my precious flower, you've been fucking my cock for weeks. You get a taste of blood and you're bouncing up and down on my cock like it's a pogo stick."

"That's not possible," she shouted. "I didn't mean to yell," she whispered.

"You're testing your voice. It will fluctuate until you're fully healed."

She opened her eyes. Her wrists were shackled with fur-lined cuffs and connected to a ring on a rod hanging from the canopy of a white metal bed in the middle of a white banquet hall. She sat upright on top of him.

He chuckled. "Eating your words?"

"I don't feel my body. I see my position, but I don't…" She trailed off, shaking her head.

"You got really sick when you rose from death. You couldn't keep anything down." He frowned. "Something black seeped from your pores for four weeks. We washed you in rooms, then burned and rebuilt them. You've been on my cock ever since."

"I remember the black tar substance seeping from my pores. I remember being washed over and over and over." *The Coven gathered and cared for me. I remember.*

He held up his hands. "Follow my hands and call your body to action. Feel. Move. Moan. Shout. Don't try to control anything yet. Whatever you do is between you and me. No one else."

She nodded and parted her teeth.

He cupped the outsides of her breasts. "They've grown. They'll stay like this." He caressed over the top and circled the small dimples in her skin where his fangs marked their blood-bonds. The right bond generated the stronger response. "Vampires have better sight than wolves. The pack won't see these without one of us showing them."

"Is this a secret I need to keep from Dietrich?"

"No. He knows. He probably knows all our secrets, but he acts like he doesn't." He glided his hand under her breasts.

She moaned as his fingers caressed her right breast. Tingles sent shivers over her chest. Crimson dots of energy appeared in the room and swarmed over her right breast, then caressed over her skin to the left.

"The new crest is here." He traced the outer

edges of the Hunter Family Shield he'd woven into her flesh marking their blood-bonds. "Call the energy to connect from your right crest to your left."

She didn't do anything, but the crimson dots of energy in the air gathered into lines, spun together and formed a braided rope. The end pressed to her flesh and ran into her crest, shooting electricity and warmth all over her torso and buzzing into her left breast.

"Let the chi expand," Jeremy said.

Embers of energy multiplied and spread into her sex.

"Yes," she moaned. Her pussy squeezed the cock buried deep inside.

"My Queen," he mumbled. "Let the blood in your veins follow the chi running through your body."

Strength returned to her limbs. She pumped her thighs, riding his incredible cock up and down. Up and down. She flexed the muscles in her arms and pulled up, taking her higher and higher. Her pussy and clit swelled and contracted. Nerve endings she hadn't known existed awoke and called to be pleasured.

"My King." She humped and ground, drawing his cock to her most sensitive spot. She slowed her climb to bliss and circled her hips, ground her clit, and relished the new sensitivity of her vampire body. "I feel everything."

"You'll feel so much more as each year passes," he whispered. "Think about my cock. Follow your instincts. Rise, my Queen."

Flashes of black and red filled the room until a

crowd of vampires surrounded them.

She shimmied and her nipples brushed against his smooth lips. "I didn't know I could feel like this." Her pussy closed in around his cock. The smooth skin, the rising veins pulsed against her walls.

"Yes." He licked the tips of her nipples. "Stand and see how your pussy glows."

She rose to her feet and saw the shackles on her ankles. She shuddered and cream trickled from her folds. Waves of golden energy flowed around her sex. "Are you doing that?"

"Yes," he whispered.

Delight washed over her as he manipulated the layers of golden energy fields swarming them. "The Heart is back inside the Coven."

The golden light expanded and shot up into her sex seemingly from his silent order.

She shook as an orgasm rocked her.

"My King," she cried out in a barking roar. Juices gushed from her sex. She dropped to her knees and straddled his lap, his cock buried completely inside her. Up and down, back and forth, she rode him. Moaning, shoving her breasts against his mouth, utterly and completely driven by pleasure.

"Meredith," he hissed. "Squeeze my cock."

She squeezed and bliss rocked her world.

He thrust. The first spurts of cum vibrated against her channel. The second rushed upward, opening the pathway to fertilization that wasn't available. The third thrummed against nerve endings that sent her back into bliss.

She collapsed forward, limp. Her arms stretched backward, the bindings holding her millimeters from touching his chest.

Soft fingers, large and small, drifted over the crest on her breasts and the small marks from Jeremy's recent feeding from her. She leaned into each touch, each caress that developed into a tender kiss. The closeness of the Coven drove away the loneliness she'd always carried with her. The kisses and caresses she had always shied away from and rejected, she welcomed.

She kissed all who offered cheeks and lips, necks and chests.

Jeremy released her hands and she pulled each vampire against her, hugging them, tracing their crests if they had them, exploring the most private of parts. She moaned as their touches grew bold, sliding against her pussy where she and Jeremy were joined, until each and every vampire in the room whispered their love and she returned theirs.

"The Queen has risen," Jeremy announced.

"The Queen has risen with love," the Coven replied.

"The Queen has risen," Jeremy said.

"The Queen has risen with strength," the Coven replied.

"The Queen has risen," Jeremy said.

"The Queen has risen and blessed our Coven. She has saved us, and we have saved her."

"The Queen has risen." Jeremy skimmed his hands down her sides to her hips. "She will bless us with many children."

Mere placed her hands on her belly and the Coven closed in on her again. Hands glided over hers and her belly in a special sense of worship. Kisses covered her, and her body thrummed with a happiness that matched that within her soul.

"I hope to have a big family with my King." She rose to her feet and Jeremy joined her. They held hands and hopped off the bed.

He curled his arms around her and held her back against his front. He grazed his fangs along the length of her neck. "We'll have a very large family."

"Mmm," she mumbled.

"I love you," he whispered.

Caleb stepped forward and bowed. "I am here, ready to serve."

Saliva lubricated her mouth. "I'm thirsty." Her pussy quivered and juices trickled down her thighs.

Caleb rose and offered his neck. She wrapped her arms around him and sank her teeth into his waiting vein. She sucked.

"Slow down," Jeremy whispered. He caressed her breast. "Train, drink from her here."

Sharp teeth sank into her breast.

"Mmm," she moaned. She sucked harder and gulped. *I need to fuck. I need to fuck right now.* She rocked her hips and widened her stance.

"Hold back on the sex," Jeremy said. He pulled her hips against him. "Think nourishment, not orgasms."

She dug her fingers into the back of Caleb's neck. She licked over her marks and gripped the back of Train's head. She pulled him closer. "Take more."

Blood rushed to her breast and into his mouth. "Jeremy. Jeremy, I'm going to come. I'm…" She shuddered so hard the room turned dark.

Jeremy held her up and Caleb and Train stumbled back, then quickly righted themselves.

The Coven erupted in applause.

A smile pressed against the back of her neck.

"You've brought so much life back into my Coven."

Caleb stepped forward and offered his neck again. Train knelt before her.

"Try again," Jeremy whispered. "This time without the orgasm."

She curled her arm around Caleb's neck and kissed. She caressed Train's dark brown hair and guided him to her left breast. She gently pricked Caleb's skin as Train's teeth sank into her flesh.

Jeremy stepped to her side and the desire for sex shifted to the need to fill her belly.

She drank. The flow of Caleb's blood down her throat coupled with the way Train pulled the old blood from her body seemed to strengthen her.

She slowly withdrew from Caleb, licked the wounds and kissed his neck, nuzzled him and kissed his lips. "Thank you."

Train licked over the wounds then kissed her breast. He rose to his feet and kissed her lips. "Thank you."

The two men stepped back and bowed.

"That's how your feedings will proceed when you're with Dietrich," Jeremy said. "The time with your Queen is at an end." He led her out of the room and into an adjoining room with three beds.

Caleb and Train undressed and crawled under the sheets of the two smaller beds next to each other.

Jeremy turned down the black duvet and helped her under the covers. "The sunlight won't kill you, but it will burn your skin until you're stronger and can heal quickly. I'm handing you over to Dietrich tomorrow. Work indoors during the day. Get to your job before the sun rises or just as it starts to rise." He continued to tell her everything she needed to know about blending in with others not of their kind.

"Dietrich told me you might have protection from the sun when you're in the form of a wolf. He's going to privately help you test his theory, and he will have Caleb and Train on hand, if you need immediate healing."

She yawned. "Cuddle me."

He curled around her. "I will spend the rest of my life making sure you know how much I love you."

"I feel good," she whispered. "I have never felt better. I love you." *I don't want to leave.*

CHAPTER TWENTY-SIX

D RAPED IN A BLACK SILK dress, Mere walked into the hallway leading to the outer chambers of Jeremy's master bedroom. She stood outside the door. *I can do this. I've got this.*

Jeremy held the handle and looked to her for the nod to open it. She glanced to either side. Caleb and Train stood wearing black silk dress shirts and slim black pants like Jeremy.

She traced the edges of the silk fabric from her neck down her chest and pushed it out to show more of her breasts. Her breasts had enlarged after the Coven's welcome. She'd grown to five feet eight inches, barefoot. The small curve of her belly showed off the baby growing inside that survived the turning.

The small button at her side held the fabric together. She'd wear the dress or one similar for the rest of her life because of her skin, because of the blood poisoning she'd had after her turning. So much went wrong, yet still she survived.

So much had changed. Her long brown locks had grown in such a light blond it looked almost white. Her eyes were now a light blue with no sign of the natural brown and gold she'd once had. Toxicity had marked her as strongly as the blood curse had claimed her life, as powerfully as the virus had lived inside her body since conception. The scrolls in Jeremy's library told her everything she wanted to know and even more that she didn't.

She nodded at Jeremy. *Dietrich? Can you hear me?*

The door opened and Dietrich stood a few feet inside the room. His cheek twitched, lifting the bottom of his new black-rimmed glasses up and down.

He patted his chest over the white silk shirt he wore and slid his hands into the pockets of his black trousers. He sniffed and smiled. "Darling." He nodded and added a slight bow.

Jeremy led her and her guards forward into the room. "Hey, Alpha."

Meredith flipped the skirt of her dress up, out, and threw it back as she curtsied, in accordance with vampire law when she entered a room where another person resided.

Caleb and Train bowed beside her.

She rose and walked forward and stood before her mate.

"You've grown," Dietrich said. He sniffed. "How long has it been since she's fed or been fed from?"

"Two hours," Jeremy said. "She has another hour before she must quench her thirst. Day feedings will be difficult to manage at work."

"Her work schedule is flexible." Dietrich sniffed again and glared at Train and Caleb. "They have the same scent as *my mate.*"

"They are her guardians. You cannot feed from

her. She cannot take nourishment from you. I can't suddenly drop my Coven and start traveling or living with you and *my wife*," Jeremy said. "This is a special circumstance." Jeremy closed his eyes. "Alpha, your wolves know we saved her life. They don't understand us. They should let the scent thing go."

"Do I smell bad?" She asked. "I've lost my sense of smell, but I can taste things and distinguish the type of…well, I have an amplified sense of taste."

"You smell lovely." As Dietrich exhaled a rosy glow covered his cheeks and a big smile spread across his face. "Your aroma is like a spring breeze gathering up fresh wildflowers for a bouquet. I'll gather the flowers you smell like so you can taste them."

She lowered her gaze. "I'd like that."

"May I kiss you? Or do we have to go to jail first?" He smirked.

Jeremy laughed. "She's the one who got you arrested?"

"Yeah, my sassy mate challenged me in from of my warriors," he said.

"You deserved it," she whispered.

"I did." He enclosed her hand in his. "What about that kiss?"

She glanced at Jeremy.

He nodded. "I'll visit Ulvene soon. If her scent changes or she starts sleeping instead of feeding, don't wait, call immediately. The first two years are the toughest." He kissed her cheek. "It's all working out, Mere. Don't worry. You know where I'll be."

The door closed, and he was gone.

"How about that kiss, darling?"

She nodded. "I'm nervous."

"I almost lost you," he whispered.

"I'm here." She licked her lips as hunger rose and her belly grumbled.

"You need to eat." Dietrich cradled her head and dipped her back. He gave her a peck on the lips. "Can you last thirty minutes?"

"She can," Caleb said. "But we need privacy to feed her properly."

Dietrich swept her up and carried her out of the suite and through the house to the foyer. Doors opened and closed so quickly that the sunlight didn't touch her, not even as she moved into the car.

She sat on Dietrich's lap in the backseat with Caleb and Train on either side of them.

"Missed you," Ethan said from the passenger's seat. "You're looking extra sexy this morning."

"Ethan," Michael growled. "The comments have to stop."

"She is sexy. Women need to know how hot they are." Ethan winked at her. "Growler over there missed you too." He held out his hand to Train. "As you may have figured out, I'm Ethan. I'm her guardian like Mike over here. If you need anything, let us know. If Mere stops acting vampy or something we wouldn't know about, you get us and we'll make things happen. Got it?"

"Vampy?" Michael groaned. "Ethan, I can't tell whether that is an insult or not."

"So not." Ethan shook Train's hand and then Caleb's. "You guys smell damn good. Not like normal vamps. They smell like death and compost."

He pinched his nose. "Not so pleasant." He let go of his nose. "I have a mate. She's gorgeous. Blonde, blue eyes. Hot as fire. I'll introduce you. She's making some human friends in Ulvene. It's rare because we have like forty humans in our county."

"Ethan, less is more," Dietrich said.

"Right." Ethan leaned over the center console of the SUV and kissed Mere's forehead. "I'm happy you're coming home."

Mere's body warmed. "Thank you." *Dietrich? Can you hear me? I need sex before I eat.*

He didn't answer her thoughts.

"I need sex before I eat," she whispered in Dietrich's ear.

Dietrich turned his head and growled into her ear, "Yeah? Every time?"

She swallowed. "Yeah, pretty much. About every two to three hours."

He drew down his zipper. His cock sprang to life.

She gazed down at the engorged thing and licked her lips. She straddled his lap and pulled apart the fabric covering her legs. *I'm nervous. Can you hear me? I need this, but—*

"No panties?"

"Sensitive skin. Jewels get caught in the silk as it rubs between my folds. Spontaneous sex is more difficult. Hiding sex in public is a challenge." She nuzzled his neck. "I'm hungry."

"You can't drink from me," he whispered.

"I know. But I wish I could." She lifted her hips.

"You're so wet," he said.

She leaned forward and pressed her chest against his. "I learned that I'm a breeder." She kissed his cheek. "I spent hours in Jeremy's library researching others like me."

"And?" Dietrich said.

The car stopped. Everyone emptied out, except them.

"Breeders die during infancy, most of us—really, all of us do. Except your mother and me. Most of what I read, I figured out when I was much younger." She took his hand and placed it on her wet inner thigh. "Since I've become a vampire hybrid, I need a lot more affection. A lot more touch. More sex." She guided his hand to her pussy. "I understand why Jeremy needed—no, he *demanded*—*sex* wherever we were, whenever he wanted it. Sex for us is like oxygen for everyone else."

She unbuttoned the side of her dress and the silk fell open. She caressed her belly. "Our child is growing inside me. He will be just like you. Strong. Powerful. Intelligent."

"What else did you learn?" He dipped his fingers into her sex.

"I will happily kneel before you and Jeremy."

"You want me more," he whispered.

Her pussy squeezed his fingers. "Tell me you still love me."

He gripped her hips. "I never stopped loving you. I will love you until I die. I will love you whether you're carrying my child or his."

"Really?" she whimpered.

He pulled her down onto his cock. "Yes, darling. *You're mine.*"

She thought her heart would beat again, but her body didn't come alive. Hunger raged in her system, overriding the desire for him to spur her into bliss.

Dietrich's face blurred. She focused more intently, but the harder she tried to clear her vision the worse it got until there was nothing.

"Hang on, Mere." Dietrich ran, carrying her onto the private jet. He shoved her into Caleb's arms. "She blacked out for a few seconds. There's a bedroom at the back of the plane."

The faint squeak of a door opening filtered into her consciousness.

"Leave us now," Train shouted.

Her back landed on soft sheets.

The sweet taste of blood coated her tongue. Teeth against her flesh. Jaws moving, tongues gliding. The nourishment she needed to live.

She bent her knees and pulled them to her sides.

She sucked and swallowed over and over.

Slow down. Think nourishment. I can do this. She lowered and crossed her legs. *No sex. Food. Only food.* The hunger inside her eased. She licked, closing the incisions, and then nuzzled Caleb's neck. She kissed his skin and gazed into his dark eyes.

He kissed her lips. "You have to listen to your body. If you start to sweat or your juices wet your thighs without an orgasm, you're on your way to dehydration. You have to drop whatever you're doing and come immediately to us."

Train kissed her breast and met her gaze. "You have to manage your body." He kissed her lips. "Go to your mate and tell him the signs he needs to look for. Your baby will suffer if you wait for food, and that is the last thing any of us want."

She scooted to the edge of the bed and sat up. "I feel different than I do at home."

"You're a new vamp and you're a werewolf mated to *Dietrich*. You're going to feel different." Train sat next to her and leaned against her. "Go into the cabin, climb on his lap, and fuck his brains out. Come back to us, and we'll feed you for another round with the World Alpha. We'll be fine."

Caleb sat on the other side and put his arm around her. "Let the sex happen. Don't force it. You're not the same as you were." He whispered into her ear. "Vampires are better lovers than were-wolves or humans."

She giggled and nuzzled against him. "I think Dietrich can hear you."

"We hear and see better than them," Caleb whispered. "They have us on smell and taste."

"Represent us well," Train whispered. "Sex him up good."

Caleb hissed. "All men are not like you."

"All men want sex. And they want sex with our Queen." Train licked his lips. "*He* wants it bad."

"I'm feeling pressured here," she said. "What if my heart never beats again? What if my wolf doesn't survive?"

"Then it doesn't." Train patted her back. "You're the first of your kind. We saved you twice." He grinned. "You're *ours*. He knows it."

Caleb nudged her forward.

She stood up.

Train slipped the black silk dress, marking her as the Vampire Queen, up her arms and wrapped it around her front. He slid the silk button through the hole to hold it together. "Never forget who you are."

Caleb inspected her. "You represent the King

and the Coven in every movement, in every word, in every thought." He gazed at her chest and raised a disapproving brow.

She looked down and adjusted the fabric to show more skin. She fluffed the front of the dress at her legs. The silk draped open and revealed the optimal amount of leg.

Caleb nodded. "Have a mental checklist of the rules and follow each one."

"Thank you." She bowed. "Please, continue to remind me and make sure I'm obeying the rules. There are so many."

Train kissed her cheek. "You look beautiful." He guided her forward and opened the plane's bedroom door to the main cabin.

Dietrich stood. "You don't have to dress for me."

She gazed at the gray carpet under her bare feet. "I have to enter a room that is occupied by another person in this dress. In the privacy of your home, I can't roam naked, unless I'm in wolf form. If I can transform. Um, I'm not sure how that would work anyway." *Dead heart. Dead lungs. I'm already getting cold.*

"Mmm," Dietrich mumbled. "Vampire law. I'll have to brush up on it."

"When we arrive at the house, I will give you a special guidebook of the laws which apply to you and the Queen," Caleb said. "When we're with your kind, should we refer to the Queen as Female World Alpha?"

"Only when we're acting in an official capacity and that includes when we are at your Coven visiting for werewolf business." Dietrich sat on the bench seat and motioned for them to join him. He

buckled in and talked through the rules and reg-
ulations of her obligations and theirs while under
his authority.

She hesitantly joined him while Caleb and Train
sat in captain's chairs at the end of the bench.

Caleb and Train listened intently to everything
Dietrich said and seemed to know and validate all
the information given.

The plane's engines revved and accelerated
down the runway. She covered her ears as the
noise increased. She squeezed her lids shut. *One.
Two. Three. It's going to be okay. I can do this. The shaking is normal. The rumbles are normal. Push the excess
sounds away and focus on his heartbeat. Feel the rush of
blood through his veins. Count the flib, flib of the valves
opening and closing. Isolate the strongest flow of blood.
Remember and categorize each line of life as if they were
skeins of colored yarn mixed and wound into one hot
mess. Clear the mess one by one.*

Hot hands covered her ears. The sound of the
engine roaring made her brain feel like it was
placed inside an out-of-control salad spinner. The
vibrations rocking the plane rumbled through her,
pounding against her organs, muscles, and bones.
She grabbed her stomach as the plane rose and fell
with sudden turbulence. She lurched forward and
dry heaved.

Caleb and Train sprang into action. Caleb's wrist
was at her mouth. Warmed blankets enveloped her
chest and neck.

"Call Jeremy," Caleb said.

She unbuckled from her seat and tore her mouth
from Caleb's wrist.

Dietrich pulled her into his lap. "I'm taking you

to bed. If you get sick, you get sick."

Train hissed. "This is one area you are unfamiliar with, Alpha. Vampire needs during pregnancy vary, but she is unique. We vowed our lives for hers and her children's." He reached for her.

Dietrich growled and stood up with her in his arms. "You touch her right now, and I will rip you apart." He carried her into the bedroom.

As soon as her back hit the sheets, she rolled to her side and curled into a ball. Her stomach churned. "I need Caleb and Train."

"You're nervous and have some motion sickness. Mostly, you're reacting to the distance separating you and Jeremy." He pulled the covers over her and crawled under them. "It will get easier."

He snuggled next to her and slid his hand to her belly. The perfect amount of heat radiated into her from him. The nausea waned. The spinning stopped.

"Turn around," he ordered.

She maneuvered in the bed that suddenly seemed small and faced him.

The smooth flesh of his chest sparkled silver and white with her name, the marks of her claim bold for all to see. She gazed at her pale hands void of his mating claims. Her soul cracked as the loss of his absolute proclamation once written in sparkling silver on her seemed gone forever. He hadn't said a word about how different she looked now. The visions they'd shared couldn't come true, not the ones of them or the ones with Jeremy. The mating claims marking her as Dietrich's vanished in her transition to vampire. The sun-kissed skin gone. So much gone.

Words stuck in her throat as all he'd sacrificed to save her and hide the truth of the worst part of the curse – the scent from her blood spread the plague. Had she not found the scroll hidden under a series of books about vampire saliva healing puncture wounds of all kinds, the secret of the plague would have stayed hidden. But she did find it, and knowing he loved her so much that he tried to protect her delicate heart made her love him even more.

He caressed up her arm and drew a section of her hair forward and down over her chest. "Blond suits you." He glided his hand along the muscles of her neck and cupped the back of her head. "You'll be training with Paulina and Chrissy until your muscles are fully developed." He tilted her head back and stared into her eyes. "Your eyes are the lightest blue I've ever seen. They remind me of my father's eyes. Strong. Fearless. Calculating. Yet, yours have a gentleness his never had."

She stared at him silently. No tingles of love accompanied his touch. No electricity rushed through her veins. No desire flooded her sex, not like it did in the car, not like it had before the curse ended.

His lids drooped halfway. His cock rose and poked her thigh. "Your wolf is adjusting to a new body system. She's in there, covered in our mating bond and huddled around our baby." He rolled and took her with him.

The rise and fall of his chest with each of his deep breaths warmed the skin under her dress. The soft silk drifted open and unveiled the rest of her body.

The temperature of his flesh rose like a fireball,

warming her and increasing the absorption of oxygen from her blood and making her brain function at a higher capacity. Her vampire fangs extended. *Bite. Drink. Fuck.*

Pink flushed his cheeks. He licked his lips. He nestled his cock between her thighs and pushed at her center.

Her teeth dropped farther, forcing her lips to part. She tilted her head and offered her neck. Cream lubricated her pussy.

He nuzzled up and down the strongest line of her neck and nipped at her flesh. "In all my years walking this earth, you are the only vampire I have ever taken to my bed. This is a first for me."

"In Akiva's diary, she said the wolf inside will eventually die from the change," she whispered. "I don't feel the wolf inside me, even though you say she's still there. I don't feel our baby. I am different. I don't feel the same." *So much has changed. The undeniable chemistry between us isn't there. I feel different.*

"Your wolf is strong. She grew from your soul, not your heart. She will survive and thrive once she figures out how to work within her new body system." The grin that made her panties combust appeared on his face.

Tingles sparked her pussy to quiver. "Yeah?" The elongated fangs disappeared back into her gums. She spread her legs.

He growled. "Yes, darling."

Electricity surged through her body. She shuddered as blood moved quickly through her veins. Images of his name covering her skin…the heart on her cheek…his name between her legs…

She gazed into his eyes. Her chest rumbled and, in turn, her belly bloomed with a sense of belonging.

The white eyes of his warrior wolf rose to the surface. "You're going to be almost as big as me when your wolf is fully matured. You have a warrior wolf inside you." He vibrated with power. "Our son…" He contracted the muscles in his legs. "Mere, oh, my Meredith."

"Yeah?" she whispered in the sensual, southern drawl she seemed to have only when speaking to him.

He thrust. "Your wolf and our son are protecting our daughter." He growled. "Our daughter survived. I scented our daughter earlier. I didn't believe my nose. I didn't believe my gut." He rocked back and thrust.

She gripped the thick slabs of muscles running along his sides. "But I…" Heat bloomed deep within her. "We're having twins?"

"Yes," he roared. "Jeremy saved them. He saved both of them."

She wrapped her legs around his hips and he thrust again. Faster.

He grunted and thrust, over and over. Blood surged through her body. Shockwaves of electricity pounded her pussy and her chest.

Her sex pulsed with life. Her fangs dropped once again from her tingling gums. *I need blood. I'm so thirsty.*

Dietrich thrust and she dropped her feet from around his waist to the bed. She lifted her hips as his cock retreated from inside her. Her focus shifted. Brilliant ribbons and rolling waves of gold, silver and crimson energy danced around them.

His thighs flexed, and he slammed his full length into her, into the place only he could find.

The energy expanded, adding a silver glint everywhere she looked.

Power surged. Jolts of pleasure throbbed within her. Silver and gold floated down, sprinkling her skin as if she were in an afternoon sun shower. Crimson ribbons curled around her as if she were being wrapped up as the grand prize.

Wave after wave fell and disappeared inside her. Ribbon after ribbon wrapped and absorbed into her skin. Her gums ached as thick, sharp teeth cut through. Bones strengthened. Precious gold grew over the flesh of her feet like fur socks.

She ground her teeth. The taste for blood rose as bliss begged for release.

"Mine," he howled as he rammed his cock into her channel.

Liquid heat spurted inside her. She closed her eyes and gave him all she had left of her soul.

"Yes," she screamed as bliss released.

She floated in space, bathed in pleasure.

The warmth of his body left her.

She rolled to her side and found the familiar body of her guard. The pulse at his neck throbbed. She licked the flesh and sank her teeth into sugary sweetness.

Warmth flooded her belly as she sipped and swallowed. Liquid life flowed until the desire to moan knocked at the door. She licked the wounds and kissed his flesh.

She gazed up and met Train's dark gaze. "Oh. I wasn't expecting…" She gazed down, not realizing

Caleb drank from her breast. "Oh, hey."

Caleb lifted his mouth and smiled. He lapped the blood trickling from the incisions and kissed each tiny, healed wound. He caressed over the dips in her skin where his teeth had been. "They're deeper, more pronounced."

Her nipples tightened. *I'm adjusting to vampire feedings and my new body.*

Train rolled from the bed and Caleb followed.

Caleb smiled. "Your muscles are stronger. The ports Jeremy formed within his crests for feedings are distinguishing nourishment, which widens the ports, from sex, which narrows it. The first allows more blood flow while the second protects from overindulging."

Train stood at the door to the cabin. "We're proud of you. You controlled your instinct to drink during sex. You chose life instead of death."

They departed from the bedroom cabin, leaving her alone.

She glanced around and found her reflection in a silver-framed mirror over a sink. She shouldn't have looked. But the draw to remember and wish for a piece of the past when Dietrich's claim on her had been undeniable forced her gaze to settle on the features she barely recognized anymore.

Shimmers of silver sparkled on her skin from making love to Dietrich faded in seconds. Defined ribs covered the dead heart that would eventually be fully absorbed into the muscles and veins hidden inside. Her skin was flushed pink, a sign of a recent feeding. The change from brown to an almost pure-white head of hair Jeremy politely called blond that no coloring chemicals could change would be another constant reminder of her differences. The conversion from brown eyes with specks of gold to light blue instead of the green or brown of every other vampire declared the total draining of every fluid in her body before allowing her to rise again from the dead. She'd become both things she'd never wanted to be – vampire *and* werewolf.

"Darling," Dietrich said.

"Hey." She grabbed the dress and slipped it on. "Do you mind if I stay in here for a few minutes alone?" *I need to pull myself together. I look different. No big deal. So my heart doesn't work. I don't breathe air. I pee once a month.*

But, my reproductive organs work like a charm. My brain functions. My eating pool is limited to three men, but I am still here. Dietrich survived. Two of our children survived. I saved the world, in a way. My death would have saved the world, but Dietrich wouldn't be here, and the world needs him.

"You don't need to be alone." He enclosed her in an embrace. "How's Sara? Have you seen her?"

"She's fine. She knows I turned but thinks I'm a vampire because my werewolf transformation got botched up because of my bad heart. She came up with that scenario all on her own. No lies were told. She's not too intelligent, so where I would go and research something, she just accepts." She shrugged. "She calls me Mere or Auntie. It hurts occasionally, but I am her aunt, and vampires are sticklers about rules and bloodlines. I requested she not call me Queen, but Nicholas insisted she use my title when around other vampires."

The heat of his body pumped the blood through

her veins more easily. She nuzzled along his collar-bone. "I haven't seen Sara all that much, and Jeremy has been with me each time, but she told me she had no idea how easy I made her life until she moved in with Nicholas. I guess that's something."

"Does she know Ethan is mated to Faith?" He cupped the back of her head and held the side of her face against his chest.

The sound of his strong, steady heartbeat pumping large volumes of blood reminded her of her lost humanity. She recalled Jeremy's words: *The soul determines the person when they return. A loving soul becomes a vampire who builds peaceful communities. A wretched soul becomes a vampire who destroys everything they touch.*

"She hasn't asked and I haven't told her about him. But Nicholas is demanding and keeps her busy every minute of the day. She needs constant monitoring and, when Nicholas isn't telling her what to do, Nicholas's mother takes over."

"Stop making excuses for her. Ethan hasn't asked about her either, although Ethan has worried non-stop about you. And I know you asked about all of us, not just me."

The warmth of his embrace and the gentle stroke of his hand gliding up and down her back kept her from leaving and ending the conversation.

"I see Jeremy shared with you the art of silence?" he said.

"Yes, he did, and the research I uncovered confirmed the need for silence over conversation."

"Omission will be your greatest weapon," he whispered. "Telling the absolute truth can be difficult, often times hurtful. People ask many subjective things and expect answers."

"There are two hundred vampire books on answers to subjective questions. I'm working through them." She laughed. "I now know when Jeremy doesn't like something I wear, do, or say, but doesn't want to hurt my feelings."

"That can't be often." He rolled his shoulders and rubbed his delightfully warm body against her. "I missed you. Being away from him is challenging for you. He can't move his Coven or take extended vacations away from his home like I can. The world is my territory. His is limited."

"My territory is limited too," she said. *I can't live in cold climates.*

"As you age, your area to roam will increase." He stepped forward, nudging and adjusting her to his movements without speaking. No mental conversations popped up. He guided silently, and she followed.

He opened the door to the cabin. She double-checked her dress and its fit, fluffed her skirt, lifted and tossed it up and behind her as she took a step forward into the main cabin without help. *Head high. Shoulders back. Chest up. Add the swing of hips and show off the legs. Vampires are the most sensual of the alternate beings. Sex plus blood equals life.*

Caleb frowned at her chest.

She quickly pulled apart the fabric and looked for his approval.

The neon gaze of frustration and anger stayed at her chest.

As fast as she could, she lifted each breast and adjusted the silk to show edges of her areola.

His eyes darkened to an emerald green. His gaze

drifted to her legs and the frown appeared again.

She pulled apart the fabric and displayed the diamonds peeking out between her legs.

He nodded and smiled. "Until you recognize the signs of dehydration for yourself, we have to look for them. Newly turned vampires are more susceptible to serious illness."

"I've not seen other vampires required to show their body like my mate is required to do," Dietrich said.

"We keep the humans we turn mostly underground for the first year or two, until they get used to the way their new body functions. Our Queen is needed outside our Coven and has disadvantages that most don't," Caleb said.

"Our King has disclosed the Queen's feeding situation caused by being a werewolf prior to turning *and* attempting to *drink* the *blood of a werewolf* after the transformation. She must feed more often and will be more prone to dehydration due to her pregnancy and youth. We were told she will not be associating with humans for two full years. If that is not the case, turn the plane around. We will take her to the Coven for safekeeping," Train said.

"She won't be near humans," Dietrich said. "I was unaware of the signs of dehydration. Please, sit down and tell me more."

"Please, no," Mere mumbled. She sat down on the bench.

"I need to know," Dietrich said. "Your life is mine to protect."

Caleb unbuttoned her dress and, for the umpteenth time that day, she undressed. He pointed out her feeding ports on her breast. She had no idea there were more than the two sets of bonds or that they were millimeters apart and the farther the dip, the healthier she became. She listened and learned. The crest rose as Caleb and Train touched and explained the rise and fall of each portion of the shield split into sections with a golden glow of a sword. Mini ports that looked more like dimples spelled out the Hunter name and formed naturally for nourishing the children she would one day birth.

Train pointed and guided Dietrich's fingers along her folds where the last signs of dehydration appear. "A sudden gush of fluids that don't cause a hair-curling orgasm is bad. And because you're not capable of feeding her, you have to make sure she can easily get to food within seconds." Train glanced around. "No one can hear us who shouldn't be able to hear us, right?"

"No. Ethan and Michael are listening, but they will keep the information secret. If I'm unavailable, they need to be aware of a situation where you will suddenly take her into a private room." Dietrich slipped his fingers from her and licked them. "They don't and won't touch her like this. We're a touch-driven society, but private parts are off limits for mates, unless the Nevada Pack is involved. They're unique."

"I can't imagine such a cold existence within a community," Caleb mumbled. "We don't have sex with everyone, but we do kiss and lick and touch."

Train's fingers paused at her inner thigh and the feeding port Train used in the mornings to check for changes in her pregnancy. He skimmed over it without saying a word and caressed the curve of her belly. "Any other questions?" He leaned forward and kissed her breast. The crest glowed in a beautiful rich golden color, then faded.

"Does the crest glow when Jeremy is near?"

"The crest glows to show her love for her people," Caleb said.

"Inside the Coven, she glows like the golden angels who came from the heavens and created us," Train said. "We will do anything to protect our Queen."

"And I will do anything to protect my Coven." She ran her fingers through his thick black hair and brought his face to her chest.

He curled his arms around her and grazed his fangs against the curve of her breast.

"I'm fine," she whispered to him. "I'm fine."

"You're sad," Train whispered. "You're not glowing here. There's no color to your eyes."

She couldn't lie. Showing Dietrich how much maintenance she was now embarrassed her. She couldn't go out in public. She couldn't dress in jeans and tees. She lived by new rules, *vampire rules.* She was more vampire than wolf. "We're on an adventure."

"I've designed our homes with secret underground tunnels and chambers connecting one to the other." Dietrich placed his hand over hers on Train's back. "My home is your home. The Ulvene Pack is honored to have two of Nicholas's best warriors training at our gym and guarding the Female World Alpha."

Mere leaned against Dietrich. "Thank you." *Can you hear me now?*

Caleb embraced Mere and Train. He nuzzled

against her neck, grazed his teeth and quietly sank his fangs into her flesh. He silently sipped while she and Train relaxed against Dietrich.

"Arizona is a wonderful place to live," she whispered. "It's safe and warm."

The silence on the other end of the mating link that held on by a thread brought a soft whimper inside her. The beast inside wasn't strong. The diary of Akiva told mostly of the painful death of her wolf and when her wolf passed away, she did too.

CHAPTER TWENTY-SEVEN

"I AM NOT GOING TO WORK like this," Mere shouted at Dietrich. "I don't care that everyone has seen me basically nude for weeks. It's unprofessional."

"I talked to Lainie about it and she said that under the circumstances it would be fine," Dietrich said in the same bored tone he used when he refused to budge.

"I'm not going." She fluffed out the skirt of her dress and tossed it behind her.

"You're getting better at that. It looks like you're making your own air currents." He leaned against the white doorframe of her changing room at the gym. "Darling, nudity is a non-issue."

"Non-issue my ass," she said.

"I love your ass." Dietrich pushed away from the door and walked over to her. He placed his hands on her hips. "You're either going in that dress or you're going naked. It's your choice."

The jerk winked at her. "I'd prefer to see you naked, but I know you're still sensitive."

She flipped him off and spun out of his hold. She

picked up the skirt of her dress and glared at him over her shoulder. "You know I can't go anywhere without wearing my dress."

"You're getting worked up, darling." He pressed his hot-blooded body against hers and caressed her belly. With a slight tug of the silk at the perfect angle, he slipped the fabric from the button of the dress. "Oops."

The dress floated open on a swell of silver energy, *his energy.*

Always in control, Dietrich. Always doing whatever you want. Always pushing me.

He kissed the side of her face before she could move. He slid the fabric from her shoulders and let it fall to the floor. He traced the curves of her hips to her belly and downward to her mons. "I love it when you get angry. You heal faster. You grow stronger. You get me so hard I can't think about anything but fucking you."

"Stop it," she whispered. *Don't stop.* "I can't smell like sex when I go in there. It's—"

He slipped his fingers between her folds. "We always smell like sex."

She moaned. "Dietrich. You don't play fair."

He traced the outside of her clit and growled. "You don't." He huffed and the warmth of him against her disappeared along with the rest of her dress. "You're getting dehydrated. You haven't focused on your health today."

She turned around. "What the heck?" *I just ate. Fuck me. Fuck me. Damn it.*

"I'm sending your client in, so you can explain why there will not be a massage." He strolled out of the room with her dress over his arm and closed the door with no other explanation.

"I need my dress," she shouted. *I can't leave the room without it.* "You're being a total dick. Dietrich Ulvene Wolfgang, get your ass back in here or I'm going to—"

He opened the door and peeked inside. "You're going to?"

"I'm going to beat the crap out of you in front of everyone at the gym. That is what I'm going to do," she shouted.

"Well, that sucks," he said.

"Damn right, it will suck for you," she hissed.

"I guess your visitor is going to have to wait, since you're in such a nasty mood."

She froze. "Oh, my God, is Lainie here?" She hadn't seen her best friend since she arrived in Ulvene. She'd only had alone time with Paulina and Luke, and that didn't really count as *alone time* with her trusty guards Caleb, Train, and Ethan in the room listening and watching for any potential health issue to pop up.

"Not Lainie," Dietrich said.

Mere slouched and walked over to the couch. She plopped down on her butt. "What does Luke want?"

"Not Luke," Dietrich said.

"Michael?" She rolled her eyes. She loved Michael, but she talked to him every day and he visited once a week.

"Not him."

"Faith?" Ethan's mate was a favorite of her guards and not just because Faith was Ethan's, but because the girl's personality bubbled happiness. *I could use some happy right now.*

"No, darling." He opened the door and her King stood beside Dietrich.

"Oh, my God." Her feet began to tremble. Her legs joined in. Within seconds her entire body shook. "Is this really happening?"

Jeremy grinned. "Dietrich called and said you only gained one pound this week. He worries."

She gazed at Dietrich. *You aren't worried.* She tilted her head as a familiar cord seemed to connect to her mind.

I love you more than you will ever believe, Dietrich whispered into her mind. *I wish you could hear me. I want to hear you. I want us to be strong again. I don't care if you never link to the Pack or Alphas. I want you to love me enough to find our—*

Dietrich? Is that you? Is that really you?

Mere, you can hear me? Say aloud my favorite food.

"Bison steak cooked rare," she said.

Dietrich ran over and swept her up into his arms. "I love you." *You can hear me. You can hear me.* He crushed his mouth to hers. *Mine.*

"That wasn't quite the welcome I had hoped for," Jeremy said. "But I guess your mental link finally connected. I told you it would, Dietrich."

Dietrich skimmed his tongue over her fangs and ended the kiss before it began. *I've got to check on Faith. Her ex-boyfriend contacted her. Paulina and Jack want me there when she shows Ethan the email.*

Ethan is going to lose it. We should talk to Jeremy about it. Jeremy could—forget that.

She gazed into emerald eyes. "Jeremy?" She looked around the room as she curled her arms around Jeremy's neck. "Where did Dietrich go?" *How did you two switch places without me noticing?*

"He's walking Faith to her car. The poor girl has been through enough. Her ex will never bully anyone ever again." His fingers circled along the base of her head. "You look beautiful."

"You're ignoring my other question."

"Yes, my Queen. Did you miss me?"

She kissed his lips. "You know I did. Every day. All Day. All Night. What happened that brought you here?"

"Dietrich is a worrier. He took you from me too soon. I should have allowed him access to you while you were recovering. We made mistakes, but we're working together to fix them." He carried her through the gym to the passage Dietrich and Luke built for her to avoid the sunlight. He cut around the underground chambers, and sprinted to his home away from home behind Dietrich's mansion.

He pulled down the crimson linens on the bed and placed her gently on the mattress. "You're not feeding often enough. Dietrich was right." He undressed and joined her. He ran his hands over her neck and chest. The crests glowed gold and the ports for his fangs throbbed for attention.

She splayed her legs and rotated her pointed feet so he could easily see the marks from her most recent feeding on her thigh.

"Your belly should be larger and the ports should be deeper."

She dropped her legs. "Really? I don't see you for almost a month and you're bitching at me?"

He chuckled. "I'm really bitching more at *him*. Caleb and Train have been talking my ear off about the bromances they've got going on with Ethan and Michael. That Dietrich is beyond awesome. And how they're training with the strongest army on the planet."

"They're learning a lot here, but nothing you didn't teach me. Nothing that you don't know." She rolled to her side. "My heart hasn't started up again."

"I know," he whispered. "I don't think it will. Dietrich said your wolf is different. She's alive and growing, but the heart isn't beating and the lungs aren't expanding. Have you talked to him about it?"

She shook her head. "I haven't told him everything I know."

"He knows you know about the virus." He ran his fingers through her hair. "He asked. I told. I couldn't get around it. He wants to know why you're so sad all the time. I want to know too."

She closed her eyes.

"Baby, don't close those pretty blue eyes."

She raised her eyelids.

"Has someone been mean?"

"No," she whispered. "Everyone is nice. It's just...I don't belong anywhere. I'm different. I think my babies are different. I don't know how to talk to Dietrich anymore. I yell and we make love, but we're not as close. He wants to bite me, for me to bite him, but he doesn't. I can't bite him, or I'll drink, and we both know what will happen then."

Caleb and Train entered the bedroom and joined them in bed. They worked together moving pillows, propping her up, and readying her for the feeding they all wanted.

Train settled between her legs at her thigh and

Caleb snuggled at her side and licked at her breast.

"You belong in both worlds," Jeremy answered.

Her body glowed like it did when she was safe and loved inside the confines of the Coven.

Train kissed her thigh and swiped his tongue around her wet folds as he did when they allowed her feedings to be witnessed by the community in the Coven.

"I miss the intimacy of the Coven," she whispered. "I miss the constant touching and the openness of their love. I miss all the kisses, the licks, the caresses."

"You'll be home in a few months and experience all of it again. The Coven isn't the same while you're gone." Jeremy rolled her tight nipple. "These are hard all the time?"

She nodded.

"That's good. Is your clitoris larger? A bright crimson?"

"It's larger," Train said. "It's not a mature vampire crimson."

"Add ports to feed around it," Jeremy ordered. "Pull the blood through the area."

Train gazed at Jeremy and then carefully traced around her clit and jewels with his fangs. Warmth flooded her sex.

Pricks at her breast distracted her. She smiled down on Caleb and massaged circles on his back. "I love y'all."

Train lifted his head and smiled. "King, the ports are secure and connected to the others." He dipped and reengaged for a more complete feeding.

"Bend your knees and offer your body for him to gain nourishment. You're closing off your vampire side," Jeremy whispered. "Caleb and Train are here to guard and nourish you, and also to take nourishment from you. They can't do their jobs unless you open up to them and embrace your vampire nature. It's what you are."

"Move my body the way I should for them. I'm worried Dietrich or you will be upset if I enjoy the feedings."

"You should always enjoy the feedings." He lifted her leg and ran his hand along her inner thigh.

He stroked Train's back and neck. "Drink more. Don't hold back on the draw of blood. Get aggressive and tug at that clit. Demand it plump and grow to that of a mature vampire. Rock your chin against her pussy. She should be wet and juicy. Prepare her for me. She's been denied the attention she needs."

"Oh, God," she moaned as Train followed Jeremy's orders. Blood and heat rushed to her center like it had when they were inside the Heart of the Coven.

"That's my girl," Jeremy cooed. "Let them know it feels good. If you're not moaning from the rush of blood and heat flowing through the area, nourishing your body for regeneration, then they aren't doing it right."

Caleb rolled her breast and pulled at the ports.

She gripped his back and dug in her fingers. "That feels so good. So good."

Jeremy shifted her to the side and the men continued to feed on her. "Give me more room, Train."

Train licked her clit and lifted his mouth from between her thighs. "King, she will walk with the sashay of the Queen she is from this day forth."

He crawled behind Caleb and kissed the back of Caleb's head and then took her mouth in a deep, tongue-diving kiss. "I'll be back after I fuck my favorite bleeder. You make me so happy."

Train rolled off the bed and ran his hand over his hard rod. He thrust into his fist and wiggled his brows. He thrust again and dropped his hand. His cock bobbed up and down, hitting his abs. "I haven't been this hard or happy since we left Georgia."

"It is good to have your King and Queen together," Jeremy said.

Caleb dropped his mouth from her breast and moaned. He scooted up and offered his neck. She opened her mouth and bit into her favorite spot. She pressed against him and took a long, hard pull of blood into her mouth.

"My Queen," Caleb mumbled. "You're back."

She swallowed and reached behind her for Jeremy's hand.

Jeremy took her hand and placed it on Caleb's hip. He pulled Caleb flush against her. "He needs touch as much as you do. Rub against him. Activate your crest. It should glow all the time. You're not getting enough vampire-to-vampire body friction. You're the Queen. You must keep our Coven sensual, strong, and encourage procreation."

She rolled on top of Caleb and damn near dry humped him as she drank heavily. She gripped his ass and he thrust and thrust and thrust against her bare skin.

"My Queen," he groaned.

She licked his neck and kissed his mouth. "Thank you, Caleb." She grinned. "You are delicious in every way." She crawled off him and knelt between

Jeremy's legs. "My King." She bowed her head. "I offer my body and soul to you."

"Get on my cock," Jeremy ordered.

She crawled up, straddled his hips, and lowered herself onto his thick, pulsing cock. "Jeremy, my senses are heightened."

"Make small circles with your hips." He held her hips and guided her pelvis back over his balls. "Squeeze around the base of my shaft. Constrict your sex around my entire length. Tighten your abs and grind your clit forward."

Caleb sat up and caressed over her belly and down. "The golden glow on your skin has permeated into your muscles." He tapped his fingers on her clit. "Your juices sparkle with gold and soak into our King." Caleb kissed her belly and crawled off the bed. "You're both glowing where you're joined. The Heart of the Coven is carried inside you, my Queen." He exited the bedroom.

She gazed down and lifted her hips, gliding up his cock. *The Heart of the Coven is inside me?*

He smoothed his hands over the golden glow and made circles up to his navel as the color expanded over his lower torso.

Her gums tingled and her breasts swelled. Fangs descended as she lowered onto his hard cock. She ground her clit and glided backward toward his balls. Her center clutched his cock and elicited a delicious moan from him.

He curled forward and closed his mouth over her breast.

She arched her chest. "Yes."

He sucked over the crest, activating his connection to her pussy. He gripped her ass and thrust.

She squeezed and countered his movements. Fire rose within her. The energy of the Coven surrounded her, touched her, licked her, and kissed her as if her people joined them in the room, as if their people's survival depended on her.

Orgasms rippled at her pussy entrance and journeyed upward into her belly, through her chest, up her neck and into her head. Her body pulsed with a new pleasure as her mind wandered in peaceful bliss.

She lowered to his chest, relishing the buzzing of energy zipping through her.

He kissed the taut line of muscle along her neck. "I love you." Fangs sank into the spot of their old blood-bond. Sipping from her vein, he rolled to his side and took her with him. He pressed his wrist to her lips.

She closed her eyes and found the marks where she first drank from him as a vampire, and pricked the skin. *Sandalwood and sugar cane.* The ash she used to smell didn't come through his blood anymore.

He tugged at her vein, released her as she released him. They licked and kissed the wounds in sync.

"You and I, together, hold the life force of the Coven. You have to stay healthy and happy." He gently pushed her onto her back. "You won't always glow with a golden hue, but during your feedings and sex you should. When you are happy, our Coven will thrive. We want you happy. I want you happy."

She caressed her belly and over her mons. "Everything is better now that you're here."

Jeremy stood up and slipped into his slacks. "Dietrich, come in."

Dietrich entered the bedroom and stood beside Jeremy.

"Her belly and pussy should look like this after every feeding. If her pussy is not crimson and the energy surrounding her is not golden, send her into a private room with Train and Caleb. They know what to do. If a feeding is done correctly, Train and Caleb should go straight to the bleeder chambers." Jeremy opened her folds. "Her clit should look like this. If it doesn't, call me or bring her to me."

"Okay. Are the babies okay?"

"Yes, they're fine. They were in slight distress, but they're happy now. I'm glad you called. The feedings needed a little tweak."

"Are we done?" she asked. If she could have hidden under a rock, she would have. "I feel like a slab of meat you're inspecting, not a Queen or Alpha or a person."

Dietrich placed his hand on her belly. "Consider this a doctor visit."

Jeremy placed his hand over Dietrich's on her belly. "We're in this together. Two families united as one."

The room faded as a vision came forth.

The clouds hid the brilliance of the harvest moon, but the call to stand on Jeremy's balcony and feel the warm breeze against her bare skin shining silver with Dietrich's name under the golden glow of the Hunter Crest held her there.

Jeremy wrapped his arms around her and caressed over her ready-to-pop pregnant belly. "Come back to the bed where everything is prepared for their arrival."

Her belly contracted.

"The twins are ready to meet their baby sisters." He

guided her into the crimson bedroom and over to the bed covered in thick white sheets.

"Is Dietrich coming?"

"Yes, he'll be here," Jeremy said.

Caleb sat on the bed waiting as Train paced back and forth, feverishly tapping the screen of his phone.

She climbed onto the bed, joining Caleb. "I feel it coming."

"You can't control it," Jeremy said. "Dietrich will understand."

She gritted her teeth as the need to push took over. Caleb scooted behind her and supported her as the contractions hit. One after another after another. The stretching. The tearing.

She reached up and grabbed the bar Jeremy moved into their bedroom as a reminder of her rising and welcome into the Coven. She pulled at the bar as the pressure grew almost intolerable.

"Jeremy, I'm not doing this again," she shouted.

Caleb kissed her neck. "You are the Heart of the Coven." His sharp teeth delved deep into her neck.

"Push, Mere," Jeremy hissed. "The first one is crowning."

Caleb sucked and swallowed. The soothing sip and swallow of his mouth on her neck loosened her pelvic muscles, easing the tension and the need to fight against her body's natural process.

Jeremy's fingers dipped inside her. "I've got her. I've got her."

The tension ended as he held their child in his arms. She fell back against Caleb.

The loud cry of her baby filled the room.

Train massaged her belly and turned the baby inside her.

She met Jeremy's gaze. Black irises of a happy man.

She shifted forward with renewed purpose. "I love you."

He handed their baby to Nicholas and kissed her mouth. "Focus on keeping your body open and the pain and heaviness will vanish."

She barely pushed, but this time she welcomed the movement of her child leaving her body.

"That's it," Jeremy whispered. "She's here."

The wonderful cry of the baby flowed like a sweet song in her ears.

"They're gorgeous." Train massaged her belly and his eyes twinkled as he grinned. "We had a sleeper. There's one more. Stay open and she'll come right out."

Caleb drew long sips, pulling her entire world into the tranquility of his feeding.

"Here she comes," Jeremy cooed. "You're doing great, Mere."

"She's here," Train shouted. "The last one is here."

A loud cry couldn't drown out the sudden powerful contraction that shook her body like an earthquake.

She screamed as her body contracted and shifted into pre-pregnancy shape. Hormones surged and the heat of a werewolf and vampire ovulation cycle hit her like a hurricane. Her pussy throbbed with the need for new life to grow inside her.

"I need sex so badly," she moaned. "I need Dietrich. He was supposed to be here to quell the rush."

Train lifted her up and in seconds placed her on clean sheets. "The Coven has gathered."

Jeremy crawled over her. "He understands that

you can't control it." He thrust his glorious cock where she needed him most. "He would do the same, if I couldn't get to you in time."

Her people gathered around their bed. Magnificent hands drifted over her. Mouths pressed lovely kisses.

She succumbed to the need to procreate, to increase their population, to see and feel their approval and love.

He thrust and dots of energy filled the room. He withdrew and showed her his cock dripping with cum. He cupped his large balls and the Coven shouted for him to make love to her, to make more children, to show his eternal love for their Queen.

He guided his cock to her center. The emerald green in his eyes disappeared and midnight black filled them.

She purred as the wolf inside her rose, pleased with the King.

He thrust and their worlds collided. A small series of contractions rippled deep inside her like it had during their last conception.

It was done. Blood pulsed in her veins. Her pussy throbbed like the beating of a heart. Her flesh tingled and sparkled silver and gold.

Gentle, loving caresses and kisses blanketed her flesh. Fingers and tongues skimmed over her pussy and Jeremy's cock.

Jeremy kissed her, then rolled off the bed and helped her up. She stood in the center of her people. Translucent pink, red, and golden dots of energy appeared in the air and grew until the empty space sparkled with their life force.

The women of the Coven brought hot towels

and washcloths with water basins.

Jeremy let go of her hand and stayed beside her as the females joined together, washing her clean. The babies were passed from female to female until they joined her and Jeremy.

The tradition of the Queen's first feedings of the babies inside the Heart of the Coven started and Jeremy stepped in and fed her from his wrist.

With the babies satisfied and swaddled, they were passed from man to man until Nicholas placed them in their specially made crib near the bed.

The Coven filed out of the room and the lovely hues of crimson, silver, and gold energy returned to an invisible cloak she gathered around and drew inside her.

"How do they do everything without me noticing?" She stared at their bed with fresh, red silk linens and piles of new pillows just the way she liked it.

"We like our secrets." Jeremy stepped behind her. "They take pride in having you as their Queen. Unlike others in our past, you're low maintenance, so they go overboard for you."

Train ran to the door to the outer bedroom chambers and opened it. "The King and Queen have conceived. They are receiving visitors."

Dietrich strode into the bedroom clapping. "Congratulations, darling." He kissed her lips. "The triplets are beautiful." He placed his hand on her belly. "The Coven is having a baby boom."

"We have been blessed with many children recently," Jeremy said.

Dietrich nodded at Jeremy. "Our wolves have enjoyed the blessings of a rapidly growing population. My own crew is growing by literal leaps and bounds. The twins transformed to cute little cubs for the first time. They jumped all over the car and were quite thrilled with themselves. Quinn and Rebecca couldn't be shown up by their younger siblings, so they shifted into wolves and riled the twins up some more. I nearly had a wreck on the way here."

"*Were you wearing your glasses?*"

He kissed her nose. "Meredith, I don't need them." He swept her up into his arms. "I need you."

The vision ended.

She gazed at Dietrich. "Your claims are going to cover me again." *You seemed happy in the vision. Were you?*

He didn't answer her.

"We're going to have triplets," Jeremy cooed. "We are going to have a big family. More than five children." He dashed around the room. "We're going to have an enormous family."

"Slow down, big guy." She smiled. "It might be a while."

"Nope." Dietrich pushed his glasses up the bridge of his nose. *You sent your vision through our pack link. I'm getting crap about you harping on me about my glasses.* "Werewolves transform for the first time between nine and ten months of age." *Michael and Ethan are planning baby showers for you…oh, now they are including me.* He smiled and happiness twinkled in his eyes. *Thank you for warning me he's going to take two of your breeding cycles in succession. I might need the break. Baby werewolves are high maintenance. Vampires don't require much until they're teens.*

"Did you see my beautiful girls?" Jeremy slapped Dietrich on the back and took out his phone. "Picture time."

"I don't think so." Mere sat up and strode to the bathroom. She slipped into the black silk that she lived in and buttoned the side.

"Honey," Jeremy cooed. He moved so quickly and stood beside her with his arm around her back. "This is a monumental day." He guided her into the bedroom. "Dietrich and I found out we're going to finally have families. We've waited a long time. Him longer than me, but still."

Electricity surged into her hand at Dietrich's touch. *You're beautiful, Mere. Take the picture.* Dietrich stepped behind her and slid his hand to the center of her belly. *Mine.*

Jeremy held his phone and cuddled into her side. "Smile." He snapped several photos and put his phone into his pocket. "Mere, never doubt my love or Dietrich's love for you."

Dietrich lifted her into his arms and swung her around to face him. "We love you and always will. You are our home. And you're snuggling up to me." *I'm pretty sure I know how to make my mating marks on you glow silver again.* "I need some attention."

She waved to Jeremy. "You're staying for a few days, right?"

"A week." He winked. "We're having a staycation."

She laughed. "You do love me."

"I love you more," Dietrich growled.

"I love her more," Jeremy hissed.

"How about we leave it at you both love me, and I love both of you?"

Dietrich and Jeremy held their tongues.

"I'll take that as a yes from both of you." A gentle

vibrating bark, almost like a puppy's happy wel-come when it sees its master, filled the void in her chest.

Dietrich stopped inside the tunnels leading to his home. "Your wolf…" He chuckled. "Your wolf is happy." He spun around with her in his arms. "Your skin is sparkling silver with my mating claims."

She swung down out of his arms and stood in front of him, gazing into his eyes. "Is the heart on my cheek?"

He nodded. Tears formed in his eyes. "I love you. I love you so much and everyone will see how much I love you."

She gazed at her chest and his name rose from the hues of silver wolf bites covering every cen-timeter of her flesh. *Wow. You really marked the crap out of me.*

Yes, I did. I'm territorial and I am the World Alpha.

"And I am the Female World Alpha and Vampire Queen." She pressed her hand to the place where her heart had been. A soft rumbling…and move-ment. Pumping. But not her heart. She grabbed his hand and placed it over her heart. "What is this?"

He rubbed his lips together as teardrops cascaded down his cheeks. "Your wolf. She's—" His breath hitched as he tried to speak. "She's rising. Rising like a vampire. No heart. No lungs. She's strong."

He cupped the back of her head and squeezed her ass as he pulled her against him. "She's going to surface. She's probably going to feed like a vampire. We'll have to test you in your wolf form and check for compatibility within the Inner Power Pack. You're so unique."

His heartbeat called to her beast. His veins

bulged with the surging of his blood ready for her to drink. His life force expanded and joined hers.

She grazed her fangs over the flesh of his chest. She did what she was told never to do. She listened to the call of the pumping of blood through his healthy heart and sank her canines into his flesh.

He pulled her in closer, forced her wolf's fangs farther into his muscles. "Let go and let your wolf drink."

She trembled and her fangs thickened.

Thank you, her voice whispered into her mind, but the sound vibrated with need unlike her own.

Wolf? She asked. Her chest expanded and warmth spread all over her body.

The first sip bypassed Mere's normal system and spread through the layers of their mating links. Layers and layers, thousands of layers, of silver threads wove into mosaics of his life and vibrated like the strings of a guitar creating new music.

Our wolves are meeting for the first time, Dietrich said into her mind. *They're spinning their spirits into silver webs, marking each other. Finding another werewolf for your wolf to drink from might be difficult. My wolf is territorial.*

Another sip and it was over. Mere's fangs retracted and power filled her body. She licked his chest over the wounds.

He dipped her backward. "No one can know about this, not even Jeremy."

"He can hear you," she whispered. "We have incredible hearing, but we can't communicate through thoughts like werewolves."

"He can hear us whispering?" Dietrich said, his voice low.

She nodded. *He hears blood rushing through veins miles away. We all do.*

I did not know that. He is good with his secrets.

"Everything is going to be okay, isn't it?" she asked.

He closed his eyes. "Everything is going to be better than okay, darling. Jeremy and I believe that love triumphs over all evil. I never thought I'd say something like this, but joining forces with Jeremy has made all of us stronger and happier. Because of you, I'm a better man and leader."

"You are better," she whispered. "But if you get out of line, I'm going to throw your ass in jail." Jeremy's faint laughter echoed softly down the tunnel into her ears.

"That's my sassy mate." Dietrich kissed her and walked hand-in-hand farther down the passage-way. "I sound-proofed all the walls in our house. Will he still be able to hear us?"

"If he wants to he can," she said. "But I doubt he'll listen."

Dietrich chuckled. "You're kidding yourself if you don't think he'll listen. I listen to everything you do and think."

She hip bumped him. "That is not okay."

"I know," he grinned. "But you love me anyway."

She stopped and gazed into his eyes. She opened up the largest mental links that encompassed all werewolves.

I love you, Dietrich. I love all the werewolves across the world. She blinked as tears gathered in her eyes. *I didn't want to be a part of this world, but I can't thank you enough for loving me so much that you found a way to save me and show me that the past does not have to be my future. Because of your selflessness, you've given me two very different families—both strong and fierce. Both willing to fight for the world and continue to work to make our world and community stronger, better, and more powerful. Unified as one, we will follow love's path. With love guiding our hearts and souls into action, we will conquer all obstacles thrown in our way.*

"Mere," he whispered.

She lifted onto her tiptoes and whispered the way Jeremy taught her when she wanted to verbalize something no other vampire would hear. "Without you…" She let the tears she'd held back for far too long fall. "You broke Jeremy's blood-bond to save me. You transformed me so your power and love would form a barrier of protection around our children, around my wolf, around my soul, giving me the best chance at survival for what was to come. *You* didn't know if it would be enough, but y*ou* went to Jeremy anyway. You told him what he needed to do. And you did it all so I could live. You chose me over everyone else."

"I love you," he whispered. "Living without you—"

"Tell me you love me again."

"I love you, darling."

"The Coven needs me to visit." She kissed his cheek. "I need to visit. But I won't go without you. I need you with me. Can we go to Atlanta with Jeremy?" *Do you understand the importance of me being there more often?*

I understand that I don't know as much as I thought I did about vampires. We will go, but I must be allowed inside Jeremy's private chambers and into the Heart of the Coven.

You can enter Jeremy's chambers now. She took his hand and placed his palm up between her legs. *I give you permission to cum into the Heart of the Coven whenever you like.*

He shuddered and dipped his fingers into her center. *You're the Heart?*

She nodded. *Want to take me into your house and ravish my heart?*

He took her hand and ran to the vault door marking the entrance to his home. *Get your ass in my bed before Caleb and Train come running to feed you.* He opened the door.

She stepped over the threshold and slipped out of her dress. "Do we have to wait until we get into the bedroom?"

The End

Titles by Anna Lores

Paranormal Romance

One Night of Love
Cursed to Love

Contemporary Romance

Ella's Triple Pleasure
The Horse List
The Horse List Challenge
The Horse List Unveiled

For more steamy stories, visit Anna at
www.AnnaLoresAuthor.com

About Anna Lores

AN AVID ROMANCE READER, ANNA LORES STARTED writing steamy romance novels as a by-product of insomnia. One night, with a nudge from her husband to write a book, Anna borrowed her son's laptop and set about breathing life to her very own characters. After a month, she was surprised with a new laptop of her own to pursue her dreams of writing sensual happily ever afters.

The desire to fill her world with wonderful stories she and her close friends could not just talk about but gush over keeps Anna's fingers racing to keep up with her imagination. As the rest of the house is sleeping peacefully, Anna sheds her title as Supermom of Three to write sexy love stories

Sleeping might still be a battle Anna hasn't conquered, but armed with a B.A. in English Literature and all the hot men in her mind calling for their own story, she stays busy during those midnight hours writing her next international bestselling spicy romance.

Visit *www.AnnaLoresAuthor.com* for more information and to sign up for Anna's VIP Newsletter.